"My name is Rita. I'm not a teacher and I'm not a nurse and I don't have breast cancer. At least, not that I know of." She waited for them to laugh. They didn't.

She groped through her bag, then handed each of them a card with her phone number printed on it. "If you ever need me," she said, "well, feel free to call.

"I'm here because Doc Hastings asked me," Rita continued. "We have a chance to get funding for a full-blown Women's Wellness Center. Doc thought a support group would help convince our benefactor of the commitment and the need." She looked around the room and quickly added, "And help you, too, of course."

She did not say that her mother, Hazel, had said "poppycock" when Rita told her about it. "The world actually existed before support groups, Rita Mae," Hazel had said. "Now nobody pees without one." Hazel might have been right, but Rita had been startled because she couldn't recall her mother ever questioning something that Doc said.

The women looked at her.

"No offense," someone said, "but what makes you so qualified to lead a support group?"

Well, there it was—Rita's own self-doubt now smack out in the open. "Not many women here off-season," she replied. "I guess Doc had a lack of choice. And he knew I'd care . . ."

BEACH

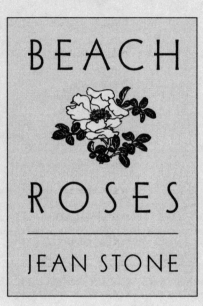

ROSES

JEAN STONE

BANTAM BOOKS

BEACH ROSES
A Bantam Book / April 2003

Published by
Bantam Dell
A Division of Random House, Inc.
New York, New York

ISBN 0-553-58412-X

Manufactured in the United States of America
Published simultaneously in Canada

OPM   10 9 8 7 6 5 4 3 2 1

To Linda, Nancy, and Cindy—
leaders by example,
inspiration to us all, with courage
they never thought they'd need or
dreamed that they possessed.

BEACH ROSES

PROLOGUE

Dexa-scans and mammo-scans and ultra-scans and everything. It was their chance to build a full-blown Women's Wellness Center on Martha's Vineyard, and Doc Hastings had parked all hope in Rita's reluctant hands.

Rita Blair Rollins. As if she were anybody special.

Doc had not told Rita who the benefactor was, the masked man or woman who would hand over a cool, few million if the islanders showed commitment to the cause.

Nonetheless, Rita stood outside the small hospital conference room, knowing that Doc hoped what she lacked for in qualification she might make up for in commitment because she was an islander and a woman, wasn't she? A forty-something woman whose red hair still was red, thanks not to God but science, and who, a few years back, had traded in her high-heeled sandals for a solid pair of sneakers, because Rita's life had changed and now she needed traction to get through her busy days.

She did not think, however, that she needed this.

Standing in the doorway, Rita peeked inside. It only took a moment before thoughts of Doc had vanished and she whispered, "Holy shit." Right there in the room, sitting on a plastic chair, was someone who looked an awful lot like Ms. Katie Gillette.

Katie Gillette?

The Katie Gillette?

Rita squinted to be sure she wasn't seeing things. But even without the sequins and the strobe lights, the glowing ankle bracelets and the rose tattoo that often graced the singer's left cheekbone, Rita knew that the raven-haired, big-breasted beauty was the Britney/JLo/Mariah Carey competition of the hour. She knew because of Mindy, Rita's foster daughter, whose bedroom walls were cluttered with glittering posters of rock stars.

Rita wondered how old the singer was and if she was in the wrong room.

Averting her eyes, Rita remembered that the women in the room would expect to remain anonymous. That would not be difficult: The Vineyard had long been known for keeping secrets—its own and everyone else's. But were traditions still respected by *Generation Katie?*

"If anyone can handle them, it's you," Doc had added while cajoling Rita into saying yes. "You're a formidable role model."

She knew that he'd been practicing his fine art of persuasion, but old Doc was a good guy who had always been there, who had seen Rita and many Vineyarders through sickness and through wellness, through joyous births and ugly deaths. When Doc Hastings talked, common sense told you to listen. And when he asked a favor, few did not oblige. This time, he'd asked Rita, perhaps because, living on an island, he'd had little choice. He'd asked, so she'd agreed. But Doc had failed to mention Katie Gillette.

Was she the benefactor?

If Rita screwed up her assignment, would she blow the deal?

She drew in an exasperated breath and moved her eyes to a second woman in the room, a plain but pretty blonde in a neatly ironed linen jumper that didn't quite conceal a well-defined pear shape. The woman also wore an uncertain, pink-lipstick smile and clutched a large cloth pocketbook appliquéd with tiny songbirds who were not singing now. Unlike Katie Gillette, she was an islander, a teacher of the seventh or eighth grade, though Rita didn't know her name.

What about her students? Did they know that she was there?

Rita blinked and turned toward the final woman, a svelte, silver-haired lady poised in fresh-pressed, pewter linen pants and a matching sleeveless top. Her lips and nails were polished a perfect powder pink and her silver brooch and earrings looked exquisitely handcrafted, not by someone on the Vineyard, but from somewhere more exotic such as Lisbon or Peru. She might have been in the VIP lounge at JFK, waiting to board the Concorde now that it was flying once again. A summer person, no doubt, from Chilmark or West Chop. Perhaps she, not Katie Gillette, was the mystery benefactor.

Three women—only three—who sat with empty chairs between them, as if not wanting to crowd one another's pain. Or have their own be crowded.

Then Rita realized she did not know where to look. It was so tempting to stare at the half-dozen breasts that crowned the plastic-molded chairs, to stare and wonder which might be foam rubber, saline, or the old-fashioned flesh kind.

She could stare or she could leave. But Rita had promised Doc. A *full-blown Women's Wellness Center*. This was their opportunity, and it was up to her. All Rita had to do was get up the nerve to go inside, and then the group of three would become four—three women with breast cancer and one formidable role model.

ONE

JANUARY—THREE MONTHS EARLIER

"Katie-Kate, we did it! We locked up Central Park!" Cliff Gillette tossed down the phone and whooped toward the tall, tinted window that overlooked the wide expanse of lawn where he'd been trying to book his daughter *for-fucking-ever*—his favorite made-up word, not hers. "July Fourth! Finally, we did it!"

Katie gulped. No. Not July Fourth. Not *this* July Fourth. Her heart began to race. "Oh, Daddy!" she cried as her thoughts scrambled for an excuse. Her father, of course, did not know the concert was impossible. He did not know because Katie had not, would not, could not have told him why.

"Oh, Daddy," she repeated, because she didn't know how to just say "no."

He turned to her and held out his arms. "Surprise," he said.

Surprise. An understatement.

She gulped again and smiled her best fake smile. Then she moved across the penthouse floor and wrapped herself around the gray-haired, gray-eyed man. Beneath her hands she felt the bony angles of the once-muscled, sturdy body that now was thin and gaunt. Too many nights spent on the road, too much stress of being both Katie's father and her manager, the man solely responsible for their fortune and her fame.

She'd need a good excuse, one that would sound plausible. She pulled back from her father and moved her eyes from him. "But what about *Katie, Live!?*" she asked. *Katie, Live!* was her next CD, scheduled for a fall release. The sound tracks would be cut from her six-week, fifteen-city tour, the tour that would begin next week, despite the tiny, nubby knots now forming in her stomach. She hated lying to her father who had sacrificed so much. "Let's put off Central Park until Labor Day. It will make CD sales stronger. Besides," she added as a hurried afterthought, "it's almost February. July's too soon to plan such an important concert."

He paused as if considering her suggestion. She turned and looked back at him. She hardly dared to breathe.

"*Central Park*, Daddy," she said, her words smothered with her guilt. "This is our dream!" She did not say that it was more his dream than hers. She pretended to remove a piece of lint from the shoulder of his black T-shirt. Black had been Cliff's uniform for as long as Katie could remember. Always black, from hat to boot, in summer and winter, day and night. At the Grammys' last year, his black suede sports coat made him look Hollywood as he crossed the stage with Katie to help accept her five awards.

Five Grammys.

Because of him.

Katie sighed. "You've waited a long time for this, Daddy."

There was no need to mention the other concert in the

park, when Katie's mother, the great Joleen, the undisputed rock-'n'-roll queen of the seventies and eighties, the first star Cliff had created, packaged, and sold to the public, had bailed out on her fans and simply not showed up.

He moved to the window and looked out at the Great Lawn where Joleen's concert should have been: the great, rolling stretch of land now reserved only for the philharmonic and the opera. Recent restoration to the grounds had cost a New York fortune, and park officials no longer allowed destructive rock-star fans. Katie would perform, instead, in the East Meadow at Ninety-seventh and Fifth. It was a few blocks farther north, but still in Central Park.

For several moments, Cliff said nothing. Katie stood silent, hating her deceit, yet unable to confess. She could not, would not, hurt him. It was a pledge she'd made on that late spring day when her mother had gone away, when Katie witnessed Cliff Gillette crumble from a tower of confidence to a heap of nothing that cried for weeks, then days, then not at all, which somehow had seemed worse.

She could not, would not hurt him. Yet now . . .

"Labor Day?" he asked.

"It's perfect for the park," she whispered. "So many people are back in the city; kids are getting ready for school . . ."

"It can get cold," he said.

"Or warm. Summer's last hurrah." She flinched. It was what they used to say about September, the weeks they'd loved to spend out on Martha's Vineyard, the welcome gap between Joleen's summer concerts and the holiday shows, the time they'd be together, just the three of them.

If Cliff made the connection, he didn't say. Instead, he stuffed his hands into the pockets of his jeans and turned back to Katie. "It's taken years to get the park again. If I start asking favors . . . well, it's not a good idea. We can mix the CD off the first few roadshows. Then I'll push the studio for a July Fourth release. You're a star, Katie-Kate. But even stars have to know when to push and when to compromise for the sake of the big picture."

He walked away from the window and toward the closet in the foyer, where he took out his heavy black wool jacket. Then he left the apartment for a place unknown to her. He often did that without explanation, and Katie did not ask because she was his daughter not his keeper.

She touched her stomach and gently rubbed the knots, dreading what he'd say when he learned about the baby that would ruin all his plans.

Even in baggy sweats, a parka, and a blonde ponytail wig that stuck out from the back of a New York Mets baseball cap, Katie felt exposed to the public and the media when she left the apartment. But she needed to see Miguel, and outdoors seemed oddly more private.

Brady, naturally, followed closely behind, because Brady was well-paid to keep his six-foot-six-inch, bodyguard-body behind her at all times. His sharp eyesight and quick instincts compensated for the fact that he'd lost most of his hearing from too many venues where the decibels exceeded those allowed under the law. Loyal, quiet, and kind, he tailed her like a bad but dependable detective whom time had proved would not run back to her father and report the where-she-went's and what-was-said's when she was with Miguel.

"I have to tell my father," Katie said now to Miguel. Her words danced on little clouds of crisp, cold, winter breath. "I must tell him today." They strolled along museum mile, past the Met and into the park, a seemingly ordinary couple on an ordinary day.

"You can't," Miguel replied. They rounded the curve and headed toward the reservoir. "Not yet."

They had talked about it countless times: about their baby that was due at the end of June, about how Katie would be nearly six months pregnant once the tour was over, and, by that time, the world would see the situation for itself. The world, including Cliff.

Then it would be too late to make "other arrangements."

"He booked Central Park for July Fourth," she said. "How can I do Central Park if the baby's just been born?"

Miguel stopped. Brady almost slammed into his back. "*O Dios mío*," Miguel said, then his voice dropped. "I didn't think he'd get the Fourth."

Katie blinked. "You knew that he was trying?"

"Well, yes."

"And you didn't stop him?"

"What could I have said? Should I have told the truth?"

Brady stepped away, as if wanting no involvement in a quarrel.

"Maybe the baby will come early," Miguel said, then added, "can't they make that happen?"

"Miguel, this is a baby. Our baby."

"And this," he said, with a flourish of his hand, "is Central Park. A million singers would give anything for this."

Heat rose in her cheeks. "I'm not a million singers!" she shrieked, then turned from him and ran up the incline toward the fence.

"Kate!" he shouted after her.

She reached the fence and clung to the wrought iron. Brady silently appeared on her right side. A bowl of tears threatened to spill out of her eyes. She stared across the water at the pristine lake that always seemed so out of place, as if it should be on the Vineyard and not here, not uptown.

From her left side, Miguel reached out. "I'm sorry," he said.

This time Brady did not move, and Katie did not care. For two years Miguel had been her video producer and her road manager. All that time, she'd slept with him. She thought he would have understood her needs by now.

"Forget about the concert. Let's get married, Katie." It was not the first time he'd suggested it.

She moved away from Brady. Miguel was at her heels.

How could she tell him she was not convinced he loved her the way that she loved him? Were her doubts because his dark eyes sometimes flicked away when she was talking to him, as if something or someone more interesting had captured his attention? As if she were not the center of his life?

Her father hadn't said Miguel was only using her for her money and her connections, that secretly Miguel wanted to be a singer, too. He'd said that about the others, the few men who had come and gone, in and out of Katie's life. He'd said that about them, but not about Miguel.

Perhaps Miguel was fooling both of them.

Or perhaps Katie didn't want another man putting more restrictions on her.

The dry, winter air chilled her nose, her ears, her eyes. She held her breath, tried to be strong. "I'll tell my father now," she said. "We'll do the six-week tour. He'll change the date for Central Park."

Miguel did not reply.

"No matter what," she added, "this baby will be born. My father will not force me to have an abortion. Not this time, he won't."

Miguel nodded slowly, then he jogged away. And Katie was left alone to wonder why life had to be so complicated, and why it was always up to her to make up for the wrong done to her father by Joleen.

Sequins: pink for the first set, to rev the audience; purple for the second set, to build their passion; black for the last set, to lure them into thinking of nothing but pure sex, because that was what live performance was totally about.

All of which Katie eagerly had complied with before she had been pregnant, before those unfamiliar hormones invaded her body and silently removed her lust. It had not been this way the other times. Then again, she reasoned, as she stood in the dressing room of the apartment awaiting Ina's arrival with the pincushion and scissors, Katie's prior pregnancies had lasted only a few weeks.

She ran her hand lightly over the slight round of her stomach. She wondered if she should change her image, if Ina should alter the costumes to a Stevie Nicks' mien, draped and flowing and sensuously ethereal, loose enough to hide a myriad of sins, even pregnancy, perhaps.

She wondered if changing her attire might also elevate her songs to the notch where Stevie reigned, and transform Katie from a silly, sequined, teen idol into a legendary diva as Stevie was and Joleen once had been. Or perhaps Katie simply should be grateful that she could do the one thing that she loved: perform onstage before a crowd and fill their hearts with joy.

"Oy," Ina groaned, interrupting Katie's thoughts as the woman's mouselike figure hastened into the room with the swift agility of someone half her age. "Oy" was Ina's favorite word, as if she were of Jewish, not Hispanic, origin. "You'd think it was nine o'clock in the morning for all the traffic outside. I thought the bus would never get here." Despite the fact that Katie often offered to have a driver pick Ina up, the woman did things her way. Apparently it was okay for Ina to be Katie's costume designer, schedule-keeper, and all-around assistant, but there was a line between cultures that she simply would not cross. Ina would not leave the declining Washington Heights neighborhood where she still lived. Nor would she pretend to be the elitist she was not.

Ina dumped her bulging bag onto the floor and parked her bony, hardworking hands on her tiny hips. "I did my best," she said, "but the pink sequins were tough to match."

Though Katie's weight hadn't yet budged, her waist had grown almost two inches. And two inches in her costumes was expansion toward disaster.

"You're telling him today?" Ina asked, opening the bag and extracting a brown cardboard box that was crisscrossed with string the way bakeries tied bundles of cakes and pastries and all sorts of yummy things. The box was part of Ina's shield from others on the bus, so they would not suspect that she worked for Ms. Mega-Star, the girl who once again was pregnant, thanks to Ina's son, Miguel.

"He booked us for Central Park," she told the seamstress now, then ignored the look Ina shot at her whenever Katie referred to Cliff as booking *us*, as if he would be in the spotlight next to her, performing his heart and sweat and guts out, as if he wouldn't be stage right, waiting, watching in the wings while she did all the work.

Katie reached for the box and untied the string. She lifted the lid and pulled out a small, pink-sequin minidress, a dress originally designed to cling to a nonpregnant form.

"July Fourth," Ina said, "Miguel told me." She waited until Katie pulled off her bodysuit, then helped her put on the dress. "If the baby's late, will you give birth onstage?"

Without replying, Katie shook her long hair free and pulled the strapless dress on. She studied her image in the mirror. There was no way this dress would make it past the first two weeks of the tour.

"He'll have to cancel Central Park," she said, her voice less convincing now, even to her. The knots in her stomach knitted together again. *It's the baby*, she realized without knowing how she knew. *It's not because I'm nervous or upset. It's the baby moving!* She stood in place a moment, then sank onto the pink overstuffed sofa. Without warning, she burst into the tears she'd held back for too long. "Ina," she cried, "what should I do?"

On any other day, for any other reason, Ina would have sat beside her. She would have put her arm around Katie and tried to comfort her. Instead, Ina stood in the middle of the room. "You are asking about my grandbaby," she replied. "The question is not fair."

If not Ina, who could Katie ask? If she had a mother who'd acted like a mother, she supposed she'd have asked her. But Joleen was . . . well, Joleen had become a stranger, a distant woman whom Katie thought of mostly as "Joleen," not "Mom" or "Mother," a sad, reclusive woman to whom Katie once was close but now was not. "He can't make me, can he?" Katie said quietly. "He can't make me have another abortion?"

Ina hesitated, then handed her a tissue. "Your father's decisions are usually best for you."

"What decisions?" a voice resounded from the doorway. Katie did not move. She stared down at the floor. She realized that what had seemed so possible suddenly did not.

"Katie-Kate?" her father asked as he stepped into the room. "Why are you crying?"

She could not look at him. She could not look at the person who'd been mother and father, boss and friend. Despite that she was twenty-one, she could not look because she could not stand to see the disappointment on his face. Fat drops of Katie's tears plunked onto the floor.

She stood and walked into his arms. "Oh, Daddy," Katie said, "I'm afraid I've done it once again."

The doctor was the husband of a friend of Ina's and had a small clinic that specialized in family planning. He had once been affiliated with a much larger center, but bombings and threats of bombings had coerced him into moving to a nondescript section of town.

Katie sat on a cold, paper-covered table in the examination room. She'd eluded Brady by slipping out at eight A.M. It was not the first time that she'd been there, but it was the first time she'd been there so late, past her first trimester, past the safe point for an abortion.

It was the first time she thought she'd been determined not to be there.

Katie looked around the room in search of a distraction. Twice before she'd sat right there: once with another baby fathered by Miguel, once with one by Jean-Luis, the struggling Canadian actor she'd loved before she'd loved Miguel, before her father had sent Katie with Ina to Puerto Rico for a post-abortion rest, before Katie saw Miguel standing on the beach, his copper skin aglow, his white, white teeth set in a wide smile just for her. He was older, already close to thirty. And so, so handsome. After two weeks with Miguel, she'd forgotten Jean-Luis, which perhaps had been her father's plan.

She shifted on the table now; the paper cover crinkled. She moved her eyes to a poster on the wall.

¿EMBARAZADA? The poster's headline read.

¿SOLO?

And then: ¿ESTA LISTA PARA SER MADRE?

Katie bit her lip. Yes, she was pregnant and felt very much alone. But was she ready to be a mother? Would her father ever let her?

Joleen had not been ready.

"Your mother's had a nervous breakdown," Cliff told Katie shortly after she turned nine. They were in New York; Katie was sitting on the floor watching Mr. Rogers, though, according to her father, she was "too old" for it. "She's gone off to a hospital," her father said. "I don't know when she's coming back."

The scent of lilacs was thick in the apartment air, because Ina was their housekeeper back then and she said fresh flowers made for a happy life.

Katie's father had left the room and Katie turned back to the television neighborhood that wasn't anything like hers. Her mother never did come back, and each time Katie smelled the sweet scent of purple lilacs, she felt the hurt return.

And now Joleen was sequestered on the Vineyard, painting watercolors that weren't exactly good, but brought a good price from the tourists because she'd painted them.

Katie hadn't seen her for a year, or maybe two. It had become easier to simply be too busy.

"Ms. Clifford?" The doctor had entered quietly. It took a second for Katie to remember that Clifford was the fake name she used for such occasions. "I understand you're pregnant." He did not say "again," though it had been less than a year since Katie had been there.

"I need an abortion. I should have come sooner."

Doctor Ramos told her to lie back on the table. And then the uncomfortably familiar ritual began. For several minutes the doctor pressed and prodded, pushed and poked, below Katie's waist, along her hips, between her legs. Katie did not attempt small talk; there was nothing to say.

The doctor asked her to raise her arm. He then held Katie's right breast and slowly, firmly, massaged it. The room was cool; Katie's nipple stiffened. She hoped the doctor didn't think the caress excited her.

Then, with a small frown, the doctor said, "Raise your other arm." He repeated the massage, this time on Katie's left breast, then back on the right.

"I don't want to alarm you, Katie," Doctor Ramos said, "but before we schedule an abortion, we need to check out something else."

TWO

FEBRUARY

"If you ask me, it's a big, fat waste of time, but Doc Hastings wants a biopsy done on my breast." Hannah made her announcement at the dinner table after everyone had savored their share of homemade peach cobbler, except, of course, fourteen-year-old Riley, who barely ate anything, let alone dessert. And except for Hannah, because it had been a long, comfortable winter and even though the five-mile road race was still ten weeks away, she didn't know if last year's shorts would stretch from hip to hip. It was time to pay the fat-and-calories piper.

"What's a bi . . . pop . . . sie?" seven-year-old Denise asked. Hannah did not correct her youngest child's pronunciation; it was difficult enough as an adult to relate to the word.

"It means she has cancer," eleven-year-old Casey piped up. "Are you going to die? Gerald Payne's mother died right after Christmas."

Hannah sighed, wishing her husband, Evan, would help the kids understand. Instead, he sat, staring at her, as if she'd just said that the world as they knew it would end tomorrow, on an unimportant day at the end of February. "Gerald Payne's mother had a brain aneurysm," Hannah said to her son. "I'm not going to die. It's just a precautionary measure." That had been Doc Hastings' term—*a precautionary measure*—when he'd received the results of Hannah's mammogram, her first. Though Hannah was only thirty-eight, Doc had suggested baseline films before her fortieth birthday.

Riley stood up, her navel poking out between a short-cropped sweater and low-rider jeans. "Grandma Jackson had cancer. She died."

Across the table, Hannah's husband winced. "Grandma Jackson had a different kind of cancer," Hannah replied.

"You won't get breast cancer," Casey chided his older sister. "You don't have any breasts." With his thumbs and forefingers, he pulled at the front of his Patriots shirt, forming two small cones of fabric. He crossed his eyes. Denise giggled.

"*Mother*," Riley whined, tossing back her shining mane of jet-black hair, "make him shut up."

Hannah pushed back her chair and stood. In the small eat-in kitchen of their expanded Cape Cod-style house, she was nearly eye level with the five gold hoops pierced through Riley's left ear.

"Stop it!" Hannah cried. "The only reason I mentioned it is because the biopsy is tomorrow and that's basketball day. Denise, you and Casey need to find a ride home from school." She picked up the cobbler bowl and went to the sink.

Evan pushed back his chair. "I'll be in the shed," he said.

When they'd all left the kitchen, Hannah picked up the serving spoon, scraped the edges of the leftover dessert, and finished it in three bites. She'd run an extra mile tomorrow, after the test was done.

. . .

It wasn't really a shed, but a large greenhouse filled with new flats of pansy and geranium and impatiens seeds ready to sprout.

After cleaning up the kitchen, Hannah stood in the doorway of the shed and deeply inhaled the rich aroma of damp soil. She felt only a smidgen of guilt that she was, in fact, sniffing not for the scent of dirt, but for a telltale sign of pot. As far as she knew, Evan had kept his promise and had not smoked a joint in nearly five years. Hannah did not ask about it in case the answer was not the one she wanted. It had been painful enough when he'd told her that he'd been addicted since Vietnam. Twenty-seven years, he'd said. By then they'd been married ten of them, and she'd never had a clue—or had not wanted to have a clue—that his greenhouse solitude was spent in a haze of thick, sweet smoke.

He was in the back, scooping peat moss into cardboard egg cartons. He was not smoking pot.

"Evan," she said, "I'm sorry. I'll be fine. You know that, don't you?"

He hoisted the egg carton on top of another, then began scooping peat moss into a third. "Cancel your appointment," he said without looking up.

Cancel her appointment? "I can't," she said. "Doc is insisting."

Evan nodded and pressed his thumbs into the peat moss, creating half-egg shapes that were rich and brown and soon would flower and end up either planted in the landscape of his many Vineyard clients or in one of Hannah's decorative pots. Tourists paid three dollars more for her flowerpots, which she'd wrapped in fine burlap, then appliquéd a lighthouse, and tied with a cheerful bow.

"Then you'll go to Boston," he said. "I don't want Doc Hastings to do it." He bent his head more closely to his work. Hannah could see the round bald spot that had appeared over the last three years since his mother had been gone.

Didn't Evan remember that Hannah couldn't go to Boston? Hadn't she once told him that she'd never go back?

She'd almost gone last year to watch the Boston Marathon. At the last minute, however, she'd regained her senses.

She looked down at the front of her long bib dress, at the bouquet of tiny wildflowers she'd embroidered on the front. No, Hannah did not belong in Boston. She was an islander now, a dedicated teacher, a Vineyarder at heart, who made simple crafts more for the fun than for the profit, who ran two miles every day to keep her endorphins charged and happy and her thighs under some semblance of control. The last place she wanted to go was Boston. "No, Evan," she said, "I want to have it done here."

Evan stopped his work. "Why? So Doc and his cronies can kill you, too?"

She felt her cheeks turn pink. "Doc didn't kill your mother, cancer did. I don't even *have* cancer."

He did not respond.

"Besides," she continued, "it no longer has to be a death sentence." She hated melodrama, hated that she heard it in her words.

He wiped his hands on his jeans, then dragged another twenty pound sack of peat moss onto the floor. He leaned against it. Despite his thinning hair, Evan was still lean and strong and good-looking in an outdoorsy, Vineyard-sort-of-way. It was easy to forget that he was twelve years older than she was. She never, however, forgot that, of all the women on the island, he had married her. They had met at the theater group, where Evan's mother dragged him to so he might meet a "nice girl" and finally settle down. Hannah was a volunteer and she was nice enough. She had been wide-hipped even then, though Evan said it didn't matter, that he loved what she was inside.

Would he still love her if her insides had cancer?

"I won't argue about this," he said.

Except to ask for patience when he first stopped smoking pot, Evan hadn't asked for anything in the fifteen years that they'd been married. He hadn't even asked her to take care of Mother Jackson in the two years of sickness-before-death; Hannah had done it willingly, dashing back and forth from their house to hers, then staying there at night because Mother Jackson lived by the water and wanted to die in peace in her own home, not in a sterile hospital room with IVs in her hands and plastic bags above her head.

Hannah closed her eyes and thought about the hospitals in Boston: the long white corridors, the scent of clean soap and disinfectant, the low, deliberate sounds of voices saving lives, the innocent optimism of a first-year medical student—her.

"I can't," she said. When they'd first met she'd told Evan she'd dropped out of medical school. She said she'd not been smart enough to be a doctor after all. It was a lie but Evan had no way of knowing that.

He stayed motionless for a moment, then slowly went back to work.

Hannah stood there and watched him briefly. Then she left the greenhouse and prayed he wouldn't light a joint now that her back was turned.

.

Donna Langforth was in her kitchen when Hannah returned from the greenhouse. Donna was their neighbor and a carpooling mom, too, and Donna didn't work, so she was always around.

"Casey called and asked if I can bring the kids home tomorrow," she said, a pained expression fixed on her winter-pale face. "You're having a biopsy?"

There was that word again: biopsy. *B comes before C,* Hannah thought. *Biopsy before cancer.* "Want some coffee?" She filled two mugs from the ever-present, brewed pot, then ushered Donna down the hall to her workroom. It was a small, boxy place that contained a folding table covered with felt and burlap squares and rolls of calico ribbon, and a small desk heaped with Hannah's lesson plans and books. One wall displayed a panoramic poster of the Boston Marathon and a THANK YOU MS. JACKSON sign from last year's second-period class whom she'd taken on a field trip to Woods Hole. Across from that, flowerpot designs were thumbtacked floor to ceiling, interspersed with a colorful clutter of photos of her kids, laughing, smiling, sticking out their tongues.

Donna sat down at Hannah's worktable. "I can't believe it," Donna said. "Did you feel a lump?" She touched her own breast as if a tumor might be waiting there as well.

Hannah shook her head and picked up a new pattern she'd designed of a woven Nantucket basket. She'd been meaning to search Mother Jackson's antique trunk; Hannah remembered several pieces of imitation schrimshaw that might be packed inside, accents that would turn the flowerpots into lovely Vineyard souvenirs. She traced a strip of tan felt; she answered, "Mammogram."

"God," Donna said, "nobody's safe. Just yesterday I heard that Lena Payson out in Tisbury— Remember her? She has a son Riley's age that they sent to military school?"

Hannah nodded, but she was thinking about Evan. Would he feel better if they made love tonight? How long had it been? They'd stopped when Evan's mother died and he'd lost interest in most things, including Hannah. She tried to be understanding; she tried to be patient. But when John Arthur—the junior high vice principal— moved to town, he paid attention to Hannah. He smiled and encouraged her to take up running. And he stirred up feelings that reminded her she was a woman—and that she was human. Still, Hannah was a faithful wife and hadn't acted on her feelings, well, not yet, anyway.

She eyed the felt strip. She clipped out one and then another. Maybe she and Evan could make love tomorrow. After the biopsy. After her two- , no, three-mile run.

"So I said to her," Donna continued, " 'Lena, what did you expect? The stress that you've been under . . .' "

Hannah began to weave the felt strips together and realized she could sleep late tomorrow, which meant she could stay up late tonight, maybe finish a dozen or more flower-pots that would be in demand once the season started.

"Donna," she interrupted, "could you do me a favor? Evan is tied up in the morning. Would you take me to the hospital?" No sense asking Evan; he'd only get more upset.

Donna shrugged. "Sure. What time?"

Hannah smiled. "Nine-thirty?"

She was lying on her stomach on a way-too-hard table. Her breast had been stuck through a hole and now it dangled from her like an unwanted growth. On top of feeling humiliated, Hannah was freezing.

She tried to block out the murmur of voices—the radiologist, the technologist, the whoever-else-ologists who were there in the room, touching and tapping and taking pictures of her breast as if it had nothing to do with her.

She refused to be scared. Instead she pictured herself running the five-miler, in pace beside John Arthur, gliding along the shady, tree-lined road toward Chilmark, the early-morning sun warming her insides. She tried to sense her legs and the muscles of her butt and feel a stride that would be steady, forward, strong, almost sensuous.

"Don't move."

Hannah winced. Of course she wasn't going to move. As if she hadn't been lying there half an hour already, hardly blinking. She knew what came next. The radiologist would insert the needle and begin sucking samples. *Sucking samples*—cores, they called them—telltale buggers that would be sent out and tested and returned with the label of malignant or not.

She tried to focus on positive thinking, walking—running—through the fear. It had brought her this far in life. Besides, the percentage of biopsies that came back malignant was only . . . ?

She couldn't remember.

Was it thirty percent? More? Less?

Why couldn't she remember?

"Almost there," the radiologist noted, as if they were at mile-marker four and their destination was in sight.

Hannah squeezed her eyes shut.

She thought about mid-term exams; about the race this year and if the weather would be nice; about Donna Langforth, who was sitting in the waiting room, perhaps flipping with benign indifference through a tattered *Family Circle*.

She tried not to think about Evan, or that somewhere on the island, he no doubt would be thinking of her now, and that he'd have a knot inside his stomach just like the one lumped up in hers.

It would take three days for the results. Hannah refused to think about it. Instead, she used the time to catch up on cooking, cleaning, laundry; shopping for more flowerpots and creating lesson plans that would take her classes through to June. She supposed her busy-ness was some sort of denial, but what the heck, she thought, at least she was productive.

The third day at last arrived. Hannah stayed home so she could take Doc's phone call privately without an audience that might include the junior high vice principal.

After the kids had left for school, she decided to look for scrimshaw in Mother Jackson's trunk. She climbed the pull-down stairs up to the attic. With a small twinge of reluctance, she left the trapdoor open in case the telephone rang.

For a brief moment Hannah indulged the fantasy that the call would never come, that she wouldn't have to hear a voice say, "Hannah? Doc Hastings here."

Shaking off her thoughts, she plunked into an old rocking chair that sat beside the trunk. It had been a long time since she'd been up there: she'd forgotten the quiet and the comfort of being near Mother Jackson's things.

With a small smile, Hannah lifted the trunk lid. She sorted out the neatly piled contents, parts of Mother Jackson's life: program guides from the Vineyard theater she'd established, scripts that she'd adapted, clippings from the island newspapers that praised productions of *Death of a Salesman* and *The Cherry Orchard*.

And then she found the overalls, the child's costume Hannah had made for Scout—played by the aspiring Riley Jackson—in *To Kill a Mockingbird*. Riley had been eight and Mother Jackson had passed her love of drama on to her. When Mother Jackson died, Riley said it didn't matter that the theater was abandoned. She said she was "too old" now for pretend.

Beneath the overalls Hannah found scraps of yarn and fabric and a cigar box filled with several bits of plastic scrimshaw, small round and oval shapes with black ink sketches of tall ships. They'd used them once as buttons on a sea captain's navy coat; the play was about old whaling days and had been written by an islander.

"Thank you, Mother Jackson!" Hannah said happily.

She removed the box and scraps of fabric, careful not to disturb the false bottom of the trunk, the place where Hannah had once tucked some memories of her own—memories that had no need to be remembered.

As she began to close the lid, Hannah noticed something else—an unfamiliar velvet purse, another prop, perhaps, whose plump sides were as bulging as her curiosity. She unsnapped the catch and reached inside. The purse was filled with several thick rolls of paper—no, of dollar bills! *Silver Certificate*, the top one read; valuable, Hannah surmised. Four rolls were there, each banded neatly.

"Surprise!" read a note inscribed on the band that encircled one. Hannah recognized the penmanship as Mother Jackson's.

Hannah laughed aloud. It had been that way with Evan's mother: so much spontaneity, so much unexpected fun. Hannah stared down at the money and felt her smile fade. Mother Jackson had loved Hannah and Hannah had loved her. She'd welcomed Hannah into the island community and never questioned Hannah's past.

They'd made a good family; they'd made a good life with the kids and the neighbors and the safety of it all.

And then Mother Jackson died.

And Evan withdrew.

And Hannah began to think about another man.

And now, downstairs, the phone rang.

Cold air rushed up at her from nowhere. She dropped the purse into the trunk and sucked in a short breath.

The telephone rang again.

THREE

MARCH

If she could possibly be objective, Faye Randolph might have wondered why, of the two Randolph sisters, she was the one who always ended up with the short end of life's stick, while Claire seamlessly moved from one European trip to another health spa vacation, from one cocktail party to another round of golf.

It wasn't that Faye wasn't capable of being objective. Standing in the walnut-lined conference room of her Boston marketing firm, Faye only had to glance around at the shelves of awards and acknowledgements to know that objectivity was a huge part of her success. She had learned how to dissect the corporate bellies of her clients; how to unearth their flaws, redirect their strengths, and create programs that launched their new products into a global marketplace.

She pressed her forehead against the glass of the floor-to-ceiling windows that overlooked Beacon Hill, the Boston Commons, and the notorious Big Dig. From her perch seventeen stories above Back Bay, she knew it was easy to be objective when it came to business.

It was not as easy when it came to herself or her life or the breast cancer that she'd thought she'd put behind her eight years ago. It was not as easy when it came to "recurrence," that dreaded, three-syllable word.

She had looked it up. *To happen, come up, or show up again*, Mr. Merriam-Webster had proclaimed. She looked down at her small breasts that were covered by the gray silk suit weskit and wondered why the bad things tended to *recur*.

Technically, it wasn't a recurrence, because this time it was her other breast. But the way Faye saw it, cancer had recurred inside her body, so who cared which location it had picked?

She had searched for a bright side: at least this time her treatment had been only a lumpectomy and radiation, so her discomfort had been less. At least this time no one had known—not her employees, not her sister. Faye had lied to keep her privacy; she'd said that she was here or there on business, never that she was stretched out on a table in a lead-lined room.

"You should be fine," the doctor said, because what else would he say to a fifty-something woman who'd now had cancer twice? Would he admit what her battered heart believed, that her body and her spirit were finally breaking down?

The first time, Faye had studied everything she could— she read every breast cancer book and digested what few related Web sites were around eight years ago. Stages One, Two, Three, and Four; invasive, noninvasive; low-grade, high-grade. She exhausted and confused herself with knowledge. Finally, she found solace in her work. Solace, courage, and a false will to go on. This time, though, it was different; this time she was simply tired.

"I've been looking for you," the voice of Gwen, her buttoned-up, right-hand assistant called as she strode into the room. Faye squared her tired shoulders and tried to get back to work.

"The results for *Summer Lace* are in," Gwen said as she set a stack of color-coded file folders and an armload of ivory-and-pale-blue boxes on the conference table.

"How do they look?" Faye asked. With twelve years in the business, Gwen was the most capable of Faye's dozen employees. She knew how to analyze focus groups, including those for *Summer Lace*, a new line of toiletries that appeared to come from a cozy cottage industry on Cape Cod in New England. In reality, the cottage was owned by RGA, a Chicago conglomerate, and its products were manufactured in Taiwan. Faye had been hired to determine if the products would sell. From San Diego to Boston, her network of consultants had quizzed groups of female consumers about the fragrance, the lotions, the packaging, and the proposed ads.

"It should be a winner," Gwen replied, "except on the West Coast, where it's considered too homespun and quaint."

Faye nodded; it didn't matter. RGA already had the West Coast saturated with other collections. She sat down on a deep burgundy leather chair. Two decades ago she'd insisted on a masculine-looking office, because those things had still mattered, especially in business, especially in Boston. Now, like *Summer Lace*, it all seemed trivial.

Gwen leaned against the table. "By the way, did you forget lunch with your sister?"

Claire. Damn. "I forgot," she said.

"She called four times."

"I was needed at the hospital. The new brochures arrived." She turned from Gwen as if her assistant might see through her deception.

It was true that the brochures for the children's center fund-raiser had been delivered. And Faye *had* dashed to the hospital. But the real reason she'd gone was for her last radiation treatment, her souped-up, power boost.

"See you in two weeks," the perky receptionist had said. Faye was scheduled for a mammogram in two weeks, final proof—or not—that the cancer was really gone. She did not plan to go. She did not want or need to hear what she already thought she knew: that cancer liked her body and was not going to leave for good. She did not need three strikes to know when she was out.

"Gwen," she asked her assistant now, "can we review RGA later?" The results needed to be compiled into a detailed, yet concise narrative; a formal presentation needed to be arranged in Chicago.

Gwen shrugged. "Sure."

Faye removed the large, Bailey Banks & Biddle pearl clip-on from her right earlobe as if she were going to answer the phone. Instead, she rolled the earring between her fingers—a worry stone that had been in her family for three generations and was passed on to Faye not because she was the older sister, but because Claire preferred pink diamonds to classic pearls. "I'm going home early," she said. "I might be coming down with the flu."

Before she left the office, she supposed she should call Claire.

·   ·   ·

"It's rude, Faye. You should be grateful, but instead you're rude."

Well, Faye supposed she'd asked for it. Claire, after all, led the tribe of family and friends and acquaintances on this side of the Charles River, and some on the other side, who'd been trying to set Faye up with one man after another since the belated demise of her marriage. That day's missed lunch had been with a widower named Adam Dexter from Nashua, New Hampshire, whom Faye had left sitting in a Newbury Street café with, of all people, her sister. Faye often wondered how it happened that she was such a sharp-shooter in business and such a screwup with men. She looked out at the skyline and wished she hadn't made the call.

"I'd suggest you reschedule," Claire continued, "but I'm sure Adam wouldn't bother. You're not the only woman over fifty searching for a rich man."

Was that what Faye was doing?

She ran her hand through her silver hair—"the color of polished pewter," her stylist boasted, as if he, not Mother Nature, were solely responsible. She'd once thought of dyeing it, but Gwen said it looked regal. Claire did not look regal: at forty-seven, she looked a little foolish with platinum-blond highlights and her hair pulled into a pony-tail as if she were still seventeen. Faye closed her eyes. "I said I was sorry, Claire."

Claire's sigh resonated from her Brookline mansion to the seventeenth floor in Back Bay.

Faye studied the floor and wondered why she and her sister bothered staying in touch. The only time they'd really gotten along was when they'd spent summers as kids on the Vineyard. With their parents both gone now, what on earth was the point?

Then, while Claire prattled on, Faye's eyes landed on the package comps for *Summer Lace*. She thought about summer, the beach, the Vineyard. Was it time to get away? She could go down to the island for a week or maybe two. Maybe then she'd have a chance to piece together what was left of her life.

"Claire," Faye interrupted. "I'm sorry, but I have to go. A client has just arrived." She rang off abruptly, without mentioning the Vineyard. Perhaps the less she and Claire were involved in each other's lives, the easier it would be to tolerate each other.

She did not care that it was only March and the Vineyard house was not open. After leaving the office, Faye drove her new Mercedes to her Park Square condo, her post-divorce, downtown Boston condo that she supposed she should be used to since she'd been living there for four years. She said hello to the doorman, whose name still escaped her, rode the elevator to the large, sunny domicile she'd paid someone to decorate, and, upon entering, tried to ignore the ever-present feeling that someone else lived there and she was just a guest.

The Vineyard house was not like that. For all the good and bad times it had weathered and not weathered, it was familiar and friendly and, God help her, it was home.

She smiled at the thought of going, and at the notion that she, Faye Randolph, was being irresponsible, especially in the middle of the week.

"Mouser," she called out, not that she expected her ancient Persian cat to respond or reveal his whereabouts. "We're going to the beach house."

She went into the bedroom and there was the cat, lying

in the center of the thick down comforter, looking at Faye as if to ask why she was intruding. She wondered what would happen to Mouser if something happened to her. Claire would probably not take him. Claire and her husband, Jeffrey, had been too self-centered to have children, let alone pets.

Shaking off her thoughts, Faye began to pack. Surely the sea air would recharge her soul and make her feel as "fine" as the doctor said she'd be. But as she zipped the suitcase and began to change her clothes, Faye made one mistake: slipping off the recommended soft, cotton bra, she looked down at her breast. Her tattoo stared back at her, the inky cluster of purple dots that were not a fashion statement, but had been etched into her flesh in case more radiation was to come, so the technologist would know exactly where she had been zapped.

Zapped.

Branded for life.

Radiation was here.

She dared not look at the other breast or its deep underwire scar.

She closed her eyes; she sucked in air. "Goddamnit," she said, because no one was listening except maybe the ghosts of her parents, who would be appalled because they hadn't raised their daughter to "swear like a trooper," as Father often remarked. He'd never clarified if he meant a state trooper, a paratrooper, or some other kind of trooper, and how he, a Harvard archaeology professor, would have known anyway.

Thinking of her father, the kindest man she'd ever known, comforted Faye, and helped smooth the edges off the ache.

She finished changing into a fleece-lined jogging suit.

Though the calendar said it was now spring, Faye had a hard time staying warm. She reapplied her makeup and quickly brushed her hair. Then, with Mouser's carry-on in one hand and a suitcase in the other, Faye headed from the room. Halfway out the door, she caught sight of the photo that sat atop the bureau. She did not mean to look, but she could not help herself.

Dana.

Greg.

Faye's daughter and son. Smiling from the sailboat that skimmed across Vineyard Sound. Young and eager, with eyes that were bright and hearts that were hopeful, and why wouldn't they have been?

The ache grabbed her again. She set down the carry-on and the suitcase and tried to remind herself how much she'd been through and how far she'd come. But even in her sickness, even through all her troubles and, yes, her success, too, one thing in her life was as yet unresolved.

Faye stood in the doorway of the apartment that she hated and wondered if she should make peace with the past now that her future was uncertain.

It was an easy drive across the bridge to Cambridge, to the old Tudor that belonged to R.J. Browne, the investigative agency Faye had retained prior to her divorce. It was not surprising that she knew the way.

Mouser would not like being alone in the car, so Faye took him out of the carry-on and brought him in with her.

The receptionist in half-glasses, whom Faye remembered as Suzanne, did a quick double take. "Ms. Randolph," she said. "My goodness, it's been a long time."

Faye wondered if Suzanne recalled the eight-by-ten black-and-white photos that R.J. had taken of a naked woman who had sat with legs secured around Faye's simi-larly naked husband. Faye had seen one photo, but had not looked at the rest. One was all the ammunition needed to finally rid herself of him, the man who'd cheated on her for years as if she hadn't known.

"How have you been?" Faye asked, slow-petting Mouser.

Suzanne stood up and eyed the cat. "Fine," she said. "He's gorgeous."

"I'd have left him in the car, but . . ."

With a wave of her hand, Suzanne said, "No problem. Is R.J. expecting you?"

"No. I took a chance."

Suzanne smiled. "He's here. He's available." She leaned over her desk and whispered with a wink, "And he's not drinking."

Faye laughed to think Suzanne remembered the joke they'd shared the first day Faye had gone to R.J. Browne. She'd expected a pulp fiction private detective: a man who swigged whiskey in the morning, ate beef jerky and greasy donuts, and paid the rent by taking divorce cases between chasing ambulances.

The clichéd joke had been on her. When Suzanne had opened the door to R.J.'s private office, he was helping him-self to a glass of freshly-made carrot juice, having just fin-ished pumping God-knew-how-much iron. He had biceps and triceps the size of Mount Rushmore, and if Faye had been ten years younger and not so, well, not so *Boston*, she might have made a play for him right then and there. Then he mentioned that he was a private eye now and a former Congregationalist minister.

A minister? Not an active alcoholic? She'd hoped her embarrassment had not been as obvious as his muscles.

That had been five years ago. She wondered if, in that time, R.J. had changed as much as she had.

"As long as he's not drinking," she replied to Suzanne and smiled another smile, then wondered why she kept smiling when what she really wanted was a good, healthy cry.

He kissed her cheek as if she were a long-lost friend. Faye kissed him back, grateful for the gesture of attention.

"You look wonderful," R.J. exclaimed. He did not say that the divorce must have agreed with her. He would never be so crass; he was not her former husband. He led her to a damask sofa, then sat in the chair placed cozily beside it. "What brings you to my side of town?"

She glanced down at Mouser, who peered at R.J. over the crook of her arm. She was glad the cat couldn't speak; he might reveal that Faye's heartbeat thumped a little faster since they'd walked into the room. "I need you to find someone," she stated. As an afterthought, she smiled again. "In California, I think. Could you handle that?"

The muscled ex-minister tented his fingers. "The state doesn't matter. What does matter is whether or not the person wants to be found."

Faye frowned. "I don't know the answer to that."

"Is he or she in hiding?"

"From what?"

He shrugged. "The law? An old lover?" He grinned. "You?"

She glanced back at Mouser. His fur swallowed her palm. "No, I don't think he's hiding."

R.J. waited for her to continue. She remembered his technique of listening patiently.

"Greg left a decade ago," she said. "We had one postcard from San Francisco saying he was all right. We had none after that." She was surprised at the tears that clogged her throat. Hadn't she come to terms with his departure, years ago? Hadn't she moved on with her life, hopeful, always hopeful, that someday he'd return, that someday he'd come home?

But it had been ten years and he hadn't come home.

"Greg is your son?" R.J. asked.

Faye blinked. Hadn't she mentioned that?

"Yes," she said.

"How old was he when he left?"

"Nineteen." Nineteen years old and three days, she could have added, but she did not. There had been no birthday party for her son that year.

"Did he go alone?"

Faye shrugged. "I think so." She was suddenly too tired to continue, too weary to recall the anger and the shouts between Greg and his father, or the way that she'd retreated to her room with her overflowing briefcase, as if she planned to work late, as if nothing had happened to forever change their lives.

By the time morning had arrived, Greg had left the house.

R.J. leaned toward her. "If you have his Social Security number, I can start looking."

For years Faye had wanted this. She had stayed awake many long nights, but had not searched for him. At first she could not; she was too angry, too hurt. Then weeks turned into months and work conveniently took over, and then there was the breast cancer, and then the divorce, but, oh, God, he was her son. Why had anything else ever mattered?

She drew in a breath. Her lower lip began to quiver. "Please find him," she said. "Once I know where he is, I'll decide what to do next."

He nodded and she gave him Greg's Social Security number. Then she stood up and held Mouser more tightly. "It's time for Greg and me to work on some forgiveness."

R.J. stood up quickly. "Forgiveness," he replied, "was once my specialty."

FOUR

APRIL

"My name is Rita. I'm not a teacher and I'm not a nurse and I don't have breast cancer. At least, not that I know of." She waited for them to laugh. They didn't.

She groped through her bag, then handed each of them a card with her phone number printed on it. "If you ever need me," she said, "well, feel free to call."

She sat on one of the remaining plastic chairs and tried to keep her thoughts off Katie Gillette. Wouldn't Mindy love to know that Rita had been in the same room, breathed the same air, as her idol?

"I'm here because Doc Hastings asked me," Rita said. "We have a chance to get funding for a full-blown Women's Wellness Center. Doc thought a support group would help convince our benefactor of the commitment and the need." She looked around the room and quickly added, "And help you, too, of course."

She did not say that her mother, Hazel, had said "poppycock" when Rita told her about it. "The world actually existed before support groups, Rita Mae," Hazel had said.

"Now nobody pees without one." Hazel might have been right, but Rita had been startled because she couldn't recall her mother ever questioning something that Doc said.

"We have a need." The voice came from the teacher with the songbirds on her purse. "Personally, I think we're fine, but a women's center would improve perceptions."

It was music to Rita's ears, not Katie's flashy music, but something deep and soothing, like Joleen's "Goin' Home," the song that had been number one for more weeks than most people could count. Rita sat up straight and waited for other comments that did not come. She tapped her toes, she chewed an annoying hangnail on her little finger. Then she reached into her bag and held up a small notebook. "I've read that it helps to write a daily journal. Put down your thoughts. Stuff that you feel: good stuff, bad stuff, not just about breast cancer, but about your 'other' life."

They looked at her.

"No offense," the singer said, "but what makes you so qualified to lead a support group?"

Well, there it was: Rita's own self-doubt now smack out in the open. "Not many women live here off-season," she replied. "I guess Doc had a lack of choice. And he knew I'd care."

The teacher smiled. "How about if we go around the room and introduce ourselves?" she asked. "Tell one another who we are. Whatever else we want to share."

Rita was grateful for the change of subject. Besides, she knew the exercise. They did it each September at the Parent–Teachers group. Of course, most everyone at school knew everyone else, and Rita ordinarily would have balked at such, well, "poppycock," but after becoming an instant, fifth-grade parent two years ago, she'd found it oddly reassuring. She hoped Katie Gillette wouldn't think it, too, reeked of small-town, unsophisticated ways.

"I'll go first," Katie quickly announced. "Everyone probably knows who I am anyway."

The teacher folded her hands and waited patiently. The silver lady stared at Rita and did not seem to blink. Rita tried to pay attention and not obsess about what time it was and how much longer it would be until she had fulfilled her obligation and could, in good conscience, go home.

"I'm Katie Gillette and I'm a singer." The girl's speech was flat and toneless. She fixed her gaze onto the scrubbed, white tile floor. "I have Stage One breast cancer, which is pretty weird for someone as young as me. One in two thousand five hundred chances, or so I'm told." She blinked and looked up at the others, as if surprised she hadn't beaten those odds. "Anyway," she continued, "I had a lumpectomy. I'm putting off radiation until my baby's born."

Rita's eyes fell to Katie's belly. Yes, it was apparent that a BABY was ON BOARD. Rita didn't know how breast cancer mixed with babies, but doubted if being rich and famous would give Katie an extra edge.

"I haven't made any of this public," Katie added. "I hope you will respect my privacy the way people on the island have always respected my mother's." She raised her head and tossed back her hair. A few strands fell across her face. "Speaking of my mother, she doesn't know I'm here. I'm staying at an inn in Edgartown."

For a moment no one spoke. Then Rita said, "Thanks, Katie. And, yes, everything is confidential; I hope you all know that."

The silver lady crossed her legs and swung her foot. She continued to stare at Rita, but did not say a word. Rita had to make an effort not to squirm.

"Concentrate on getting well and having a healthy

baby," the teacher said, her pink cheeks lifting in a cheer-ful grin. "Do you know if it's a boy or a girl?"

Katie shook her head. "I want to be surprised."

The teacher nodded, and Rita asked her to go next.

"Well," she said, clasping her hands around her purse, "I'm Hannah Jackson. I'm married to Evan, the nurseryman in Vineyard Haven. We have three kids and I'm a seventh grade science teacher. I used to run every day, but lately I've been too tired." She paused. "I have Stage Three, which isn't real good, but it's not terminal. The good news is it isn't in my lymph nodes."

"That's great news," Rita said. Wasn't that what she was supposed to say?

"Unfortunately, my husband is one who thinks the med-icine gods are up in Boston, even though he's known Doc Hastings all his life. Heck, Doc taught Evan how to fish." Rita didn't know what that had to do with doctoring, but she did not interrupt. "I need a mastectomy," Hannah con-tinued. "Doc said not until the tumor shrinks, so I'm having chemo first. I've had two treatments already." She reached up to her head. "I used to have such pretty hair. May I show you what's happened?"

When the others nodded, Hannah pulled off her wig.

Her head was nearly bald, except for little tufts of light-colored fuzz. Rita's stomach turned inside, then out. "The chemo's not too bad," Hannah continued, "but this is what I'm left with. I get up every morning and I look into the mirror . . . And I just don't look like me."

"I've heard it grows back more beautiful," Rita said. She tried not to look too relieved when Hannah put the wig back on.

"I read about one lady whose hair was black but grew back red," Katie interjected. "If I end up needing chemo, will my fans still love me if my hair turns red?" She wrung her hands and Rita noticed her fingernails were not long and painted metallic green or blue or black like in the pictures on Mindy's wall. Instead, they were unpolished and bitten raggedly.

"There are worse things in the world than red hair," Rita, the natural redhead, said, and Katie giggled embarrassedly and Hannah laughed out loud.

The silver lady neither giggled nor laughed, but scraped her chair against the floor as she stood up. "Ladies," she said, her voice low and in control, "I wish you all the best, but I do not belong here." Then, with one fluid, graceful gesture, her long legs carried her across the room and out the door.

Rita looked back at Hannah and at Katie and wondered if she had just kissed the Women's Wellness Center one very firm good-bye.

Outside in the parking lot, Faye's head ached so badly she thought that it might burst. As she fumbled, trying to fit the key to her Mercedes into the door lock, she realized she was trembling. Through eyes glazed thick with tears, she checked the car to make sure it was hers, that it did not belong to someone else. Someone like Rita Blair, for instance, who might think she could fool the others with her wit and with her charm, but Faye didn't need a calling card to recognize that rag mop of red, unruly hair. It hadn't been that many years since their lives had crashed together and Faye had paid the price.

"We hardly talked about the journals," Rita lamented to her mother when she at last arrived home. "A woman walked out on me. I warned Doc I couldn't handle this. I warned him I'd be no good."

She wished her husband, Charlie, had not gone to Nantucket with Ben Niles for God-knew-how-long, to build a subdivision that year-round residents would be able to afford. Charlie could be counted on to agree with her in silence, to make her feel as if she wasn't insane.

She wished her best friend, Jill, Ben's wife, was not in England visiting her son and her new granddaughter. Jill would have offered Rita sound advice.

Hazel, on the other hand . . . well, Hazel had already made it clear what she thought about support groups.

"What kind of journals?" Hazel asked as she poured a cup of coffee and set it on the kitchen table in front of Rita, who pouted, plunked down, and shook her head.

"Diaries. It's a form of therapy. I read about them in a pamphlet that Doc gave me."

Hazel cocked a gray-white eyebrow.

Exasperated, Rita stood. "Never mind, Mother. Maybe you were right. Maybe this is a waste of time."

"If Doc gets the Center, he'll probably be able to afford a real instructor," Hazel said. "Until then, it seems like you're the only one he's got."

Rita spun around. "Careful, Mother. I might think you've changed your mind about the group."

Hazel shook her head and padded over to the stove, placing the old-fashioned coffeepot squarely on the back burner. Her awkward movement revealed the slight hump of her spine—a touch of osteoporosis. Would her affliction have been prevented with a benefactor's funds? "I learned long ago," Hazel said, "that what's right for one, isn't always right for another."

Folding her arms, Rita studied her mother. Was Rita going to be such a pain when she was eighty-and-a-half?

"Are the twins asleep?" Rita asked, because she didn't want to talk about the women anymore.

Hazel nodded.

"Mindy?"

"She has a geography test tomorrow."

"I should have helped her study." Geography was not one of Mindy's favorite classes, maybe because the girl's real mother was tramping around the globe, having put her wanderlust before her flesh and blood, having agreed with social services that Mindy should be raised in a more stable environment, such as Rita and Charlie's home.

"Don't change the subject, Rita Mae," Hazel said more sharply. "I wasn't finished talking about the support group."

"I was."

The eyebrow shot up again. "You're not too old to get a thrashing." As if she ever had or would.

"Mother, thanks for your concern, but I sucked tonight. That woman who left might have held the purse strings for the Center, in which case I've wrecked that, too."

Hazel muttered something, the way she'd taken to muttering in the last two or three years or so. Then she sat down. "When I was studying to be a nurse, they taught us that we can't save everyone."

Rita did not mention that times and attitudes and expectations had changed since then.

"Besides," her mother added, "you weren't so bad. Before you took your sweet time coming home, you had a call from Doc. He saw one of the women after your meeting. She said the group was great and she can't wait to go next week."

Katie cocooned herself in a warm blanket and sat in a rocking chair in front of the window that overlooked the strip of sand that led out to the lighthouse, which marked the harbor's mouth and its afterthought of Chappaquiddick.

She thought about the meeting earlier that night. They were nice, Rita and Hannah, despite the fact they all had first-night jitters, much like performing in a new town with no familiar faces sitting in the front row.

"Oh, good," Rita had said when the older woman left, "all the more stuff for us." She'd dug into her bag and pulled out hats and scarves and wigs to try on, all of which were old and awful: hand-knit beanies and red bandanas and silky black tresses blunt-cut like Cleopatra's. Hannah pretended to like a lime-colored turban that was rimmed with synthetic golden curls, then she tossed it in the air and laughed and said she'd hold out for something more grotesque, something, perhaps, in purple.

Rita suggested that once they had the new Center, hopefully the choice of "heads" would improve. She returned to her bag and produced an armload of cosmetics and lotions and all things "good and girlie," donated, she said, by those "wonderful folks who bring you chemotherapy."

The ice at last had melted and they tried out the makeup and were starting to have fun, when Hannah asked if Katie planned to see her mother. She said that real support systems started in the home. She had no doubt meant well.

But how could Katie explain that she needed a break? After two months with her father, who wouldn't talk about her illness, who said neither Miguel nor Ina could be told because no one could be trusted . . . after all that, Katie had needed air.

Her father had canceled the six-week tour, saying Katie had been stricken with fatigue. He postponed the CD, *Katie Live!* He would not cancel Central Park; he said there was no need. Surely it would fall between the baby's birth and her six weeks of radiation.

He was, as usual, so one-track-mind determined, it was hard not to believe him.

"You'll be fine," he said after the lumpectomy. "If you'd had the abortion, we'd know that even sooner."

Why did it always come down to an abortion?

Still, she had refused. She sometimes thought God punished her with cancer because of the abortions that she'd already had.

Yes, she'd needed air.

She'd gone to the Vineyard because she couldn't stand her father hovering; she couldn't stand Miguel's pleas to get married; she couldn't stand to know that Ina didn't know the rest; she couldn't even stand loyal, caring Brady—she did not want his 24/7 allegiance right now.

She'd gone to the Vineyard because, from a distance, being with Joleen seemed the sane thing to do, the lesser of two dysfunctional evils.

But when Katie had arrived, a new feeling greeted her: for the first time in her life, Katie was free.

Free to think.

Free to do.

Free.

Instead of going to her mother's, she had the taxi take her to Edgartown, to the Harbor View. That had been two weeks ago, and she'd gained respect for solitude. She almost understood why her mother preferred it to the bother of other people.

For fourteen blissful days Katie had been alone. She had only yielded to responsibility when she'd called Doc Hastings, a name she remembered from long ago when Joleen had a miscarriage.

Doc examined Katie. He told her about the support group. He hadn't pressured her to call her mother.

The baby kicked inside her now.

Katie held her arms around it. "Sssh," she whispered. "Sssh, my sweet one." Then, softly, Katie sang to her baby the lullaby her mother had sung to her at night, the lullaby Joleen had written for her little girl.

The night is yours and mine alone
For magic in all things
While other boys and girls sleep tight
We'll fly on butterfly wings.

You and me we'll float on high
We'll visit queens and kings
We'll travel off to sweet, sweet dreams
On lovely butterfly wings.

We'll live a life of fairy tales
Of silver crowns and golden rings
Just Mommy and her baby
We'll fly on butterfly wings.
On lovely butterfly wings.

The baby rested. Katie put her head against the chair back and thought of Joleen, the gifted poet. In recent years there had been tension between mother and daughter, but now that Katie was pregnant, couldn't that somehow change? Didn't babies bring out maternal instincts in women?

She closed her eyes and felt a small smile curve up at the corners of her mouth. And Katie decided it might be okay to try and go home after all.

It was one of those rare mornings when Oliver and Olivia sat together on their playmat in a Norman Rockwell tableau, studiously arranging foam rubber blocks together

as if the two-year-olds always got along and never screamed
or cried: Olivia, the screamer; Oliver, the crier. The morning, indeed, was rare, and Rita savored the quiet. Hazel was
at the Senior Center and Mindy was at school and Rita
was on the floor next to the twins, looking through the
brochures and articles Doc had given her, wondering if anyone had written anything about what to do when a patient
got up and walked out.

The phone rang.

"Shit," Rita said softly.

"Shit," Oliver repeated.

"Shit," Olivia said.

Rita sighed and heaved herself up from the floor. Sometimes she simply wasn't used to being a mother again, never
mind one who, at forty-nine, had spent too many years as a
single woman without a care of what she said to whom.

She grabbed the phone on the fourth ring. "Yeah?"

Silence.

"Hello?" Rita asked.

No reply.

"If this is some kind of crank call, I'd appreciate it if
you'd call back another time. Like when my husband's
home."

She was about to slam down the receiver, when a soft
voice asked, "Is this Rita Rollins?"

Well, apparently it wasn't the wrong number. "Who's
this?"

Silence again.

"I said, who is this?" Her voice was tight. Just then,
Olivia toddled to her mother and pulled the phone off the
end table. Across the room, Oliver jettisoned to the pile
of breast cancer brochures and quickly scattered them.
"Sorry," she said quickly, "but I have to go."

"Wait." The voice grew louder. "Rita, it's me. Katie. From last night."

Rita covered the receiver with her hand. "Oliver, stop that!" She turned back to the phone.

"Katie Gillette," the caller said.

Rita's jaw went slack. Katie? Katie was calling her? She looked quickly around the room to be certain Mindy wasn't there, even though she knew the girl had gone to school.

Olivia punched at the number buttons on the telephone. A shrill *beep-beep* sounded in Rita's ear. She grasped Olivia's hand and moved it from the phone. "Hello?" she said again. "Are you still there?"

"I'm here," Katie replied. "I'm at the Harbor View. Could you drive me to my mother's?"

FIVE

Hannah woke up in the morning to a familiar soft, white stillness that told her it was going to snow, despite the fact that it was April and the crocuses had already peeked their purple heads out. The weather station said it could be a nor'easter.

Evan said he didn't care if there was ten feet of the white stuff.

Gazing out the window of the pickup truck now, Hannah could not believe they were headed up Route 28 toward the Bourne Bridge, toward Boston, toward the ultrasound appointment that she'd allowed Evan to make.

Doc could have arranged for her to have it on the Vineyard, but Evan had gone silent and Hannah had decided to relent. The test, after all, was at a satellite office on the South Shore. She would not have to go into the city; she would not have to face her past. Besides, she and Evan still had not made love. Perhaps she could at least do this for him.

At the meeting last night, she wanted to ask about how to help her husband deal with the breast cancer. But when the older woman left, the mood had lightened, and

Hannah hadn't wanted to darken it again. It would have been easier, however, to ask the detached strangers than any of her friends.

She wondered if John Arthur would have handled things better if he'd been her husband.

They'd only spoken of the cancer once, when he approached her at her locker in the teachers' lounge.

"Hannah," he'd said. "Oh, God, I am so sorry." He had, of course, been told. The school grapevine had been at work. "I've missed our morning runs."

They'd never had a structured schedule, but often met on Beach Road in Oak Bluffs and run together in the silence and the solitude of the morning mist.

"I've missed running, too," she'd said and forced a smile. She did not say that maybe it was for the best because he was as married as she was and had three kids as well. She did not say it because she would not acknowledge that she had lust-filled feelings for a man who was not her husband.

He'd started to speak again, but then the French teacher entered the lounge, dropped onto a faded sofa, and began to chatter about the inconvenience of teachers' meetings being held on Friday afternoons.

Hannah had averted her eyes from John and had not looked into them again.

And now she turned her eyes from the window of the truck, where a different kind of storm was building. She noticed Evan check his watch. "I'm sure we can reschedule," Hannah said as he steered around the rotary, past the family restaurant and the sign that asked if you were "desperate," and prominently displayed the phone number for the Samaritans.

"No chance," Evan said. At least he wasn't angry today. "It's April, Hannah. If a storm comes now, it won't be bad." He said the word storm as if it didn't have an "r." She shifted on the seat and sensed that if an earthquake were predicted, her stubborn Yankee husband still would have made the trek.

The truck climbed the hump of the bridge. Looking down upon the steely waters of Cape Cod Canal, Hannah saw no vessels bunched along the narrow waterway, slugging their way from New Bedford to Provincetown or back again. The weather, she supposed. "I called Sally Dotson. She'll bring the kids home and stay with them until we get back."

Evan nodded and did not mention that she'd already told him that at breakfast. He checked his watch again; he punched his foot on the accelerator. "I hope the state police are in the barracks, resting for the storm."

"We don't have to speed, Evan. The ultrasound isn't until one o'clock." It was only nine-thirty; Boston was ninety minutes away.

They glided from the bridge and landed on Route 3. "Actually, we have to be there at eleven-thirty," he said.

Hannah was puzzled. "Why?"

A trace of a smile curled around Evan's mouth. He leaned his left elbow against the bottom of the window on the driver's door. "Honey," he said, "I don't want to upset you. I've done something you might not like, but you'll be grateful later on."

Hannah was too stunned to speak.

"The appointment at eleven-thirty isn't at the clinic. It's at Brigham and Women's in the city. With an oncologist."

A state law prohibited minors from being in a place where alcohol was served, not because of the booze, but because of secondhand smoke or the possibility thereof. But Rita didn't have time to worry about that now. The only one who'd be available to watch the twins would be Jill's daughter, Amy, who was at the 1802 Tavern getting ready for the lunch crowd, which wouldn't really be a crowd because it still was the off-season and which also meant that law enforcers might not be around, or, if they were, they might look the other way. Hopefully they would not be in West Chop, where Rita would be driving Katie because that's where Joleen lived.

After a quick shower, Rita packed two pastel quilted bags, as if the twins were going on vacation for a month or maybe more. She loaded twins and bags into the minivan and drove to the tavern a few blocks down the road.

With beef stew already simmering and chowder on the stove, Amy was sitting on a bar stool, studying for her MBA. A catch came into Rita's throat, as it so often did when she saw the girl: Kyle would have loved her right, if only there'd been time, if only he hadn't died in that awful fire so many years ago.

She said she'd be glad to baby-sit, emergency or not. "Anytime, Rita," the fresh-scrubbed blonde with her mother's built-in elegance and easy smile said without hesitation. She slid off the bar stool and bent to hug the twins, wrapping one up in each arm. Rita blinked away her sorrow, said thanks, and quickly blew out the door.

Back behind the steering wheel, she wondered how many more emergencies would be linked to the support group before they had the funding and Doc found them a real leader.

Then again, who would have ever thought that Rita Rollins would have the chance to meet, of all people, Joleen?

She drove past the swollen surf and barely paid attention to the heavy layer of clouds suspended from above, poised to dump their cache of snow.

Joleen.

How many hours had Rita spent listening to Joleen's music, the music of the seventies that had taken her through those long, long hours after she had left the island and had hidden out in Worcester at her aunt's, first with a pregnant belly and no husband, then hiding with the baby that Rita refused to give up? Kyle. The child she brought back to the Vineyard along with a sad, made-up story about a GI that she'd married who'd gone off to war and not returned.

Joleen's low, throaty ballads had helped Rita through the loneliness and given her the strength to face each day, as if she, too, would one day be "Goin' Home," like in Joleen's greatest song. There still were days and nights since Kyle died when Rita dusted off the old LPs and turned on the stereo.

And now, there she was, headed to pick up Joleen's daughter and bring her to Joleen's house, because now Katie was the one who was "Goin' Home."

As Rita pulled into the Harbor View and the snow began to fall, she realized that the worst part was that she was sworn to secrecy and couldn't share the news. Not with Mindy or with Charlie or with her best friend, Jill. Not even with Hazel. But wouldn't they just shit?

It had seemed like a good idea at the time. But as the bellman set Katie's bags inside the minivan, Katie had second thoughts. Nostalgia, after all, was one thing; reality was another. She handed him a ten, then climbed into the front seat. She closed the door and looked over at her driver. "Thank you, Rita."

"No problem," Rita answered and backed out onto the street.

Katie did not know what else to say. She stuffed her hands into her pockets. "Hard to believe it's snowing."

"A nor 'easter, they're saying."

"But it's April."

"I know."

They wound around the curve and wove through the white-housed, gray-shingled maze of Edgartown until they reached the main road. Inside Katie, the baby did not kick, but seemed to twist.

"I guess I'm really nervous," she said.

"About going to your mother's?"

"My mother's not exactly a regular kind of mother."

Rita paused a moment, then said, "Well, of course she's not." She did not say that Katie should not be nervous.

Katie looked down at the console of the van. A tiny baby doll rested in the cup holder; a small cloth book had fallen beside the seat; what looked to be a few crumpled Cheerios were sprinkled here and there.

"I was a mother long ago," Rita continued. "And now I am again. If ever there was an unlikely mother, it would be me. Be patient with her, Katie. My bet is that she loves you very much." She took her eyes off the road and glanced at Katie's stomach. "You'll see," she said, and smiled.

Katie turned her head out toward the hemline of the road that curved along the beach. Tears came to her eyes. "The doctor said I should have had an abortion. Then a mastectomy. That it would be quicker, safer."

Rita didn't say anything at first, then, "Why didn't you?"

"I would never look the same. You know. In certain costumes." She shrugged.

Rita nodded. She did not say she didn't think that was true today, that reconstructive surgery had come a long, long way.

"It's okay, though," Katie added. "I had already started

my second trimester, so it's not like radiation is that far away. I'll be fine. I know I will." She laughed. "God, I'm only Stage One! That poor woman, Hannah. Stage Three. Yikes."

Snow began to frost the windshield; Rita turned on the wipers. "Are you seeing Doc Hastings while you're here?"

"Yes."

"Well, you can trust he'll give you good advice."

The baby twisted again. Katie grabbed her stomach.

"Are you okay?" Rita asked.

She closed her eyes. "Some days I'm not sure I can go through with this."

"Which might be one more reason to be with your mother."

Katie opened her eyes and used her hand to wipe away the fog inside the window on her side. She looked out at the snow that was sprinkled on the water. She wondered what Rita would think if she knew the truth: that Katie had called Rita because she'd been afraid to call a cab, afraid she'd be dropped off at the end of the long driveway only to have Joleen turn her away.

And then what would she have done?

The ultrasound had been simply that. Hannah barely paid attention to the routine procedure; she was too busy trying to stuff down a load of anger at her deceitful husband, who was now sitting in a chair beside her in the doctor's office, awaiting the results.

"Mrs. Jackson," said the white-coated man who entered the room. He was young, not old and kindly like Doc Hastings, and he was foreign, Indian perhaps. Evan quickly stood up; the doctor waved him to sit down.

"Your ultrasound looks good."

Hannah let her breath relax.

"But I've been on the phone with your doctor on Martha's Vineyard."

But. Hannah did not like that word. Evan shifted in his chair.

"According to your records, your tumor has only shrunk a small percent. By now, we would have hoped for more."

She stared at the doctor. She did not know what to say. Then she realized Evan's hand was on her arm. When had he put it there?

The doctor riffled through a file, then held a paper up. "Doctor Hastings also gave me a list of the chemo you've been taking. You've had two rounds so far?"

Hannah nodded, mute.

"He was planning one more round. We agree that it should be two. The treatment you've been getting is right on target, though. I would have administered the same dosages. We simply can't control how the body will respond. The trick is not to get discouraged."

Hannah nodded once again.

The doctor set the paper down. "Keep on your current course of treatment. If you want to come here for your mastectomy, certainly that's up to you."

She should have felt some satisfaction in what he said; that it had been unnecessary for Evan to deceive her and drag her into Boston, that this doctor would have handled her treatment the same as Doc. But as they left the office and went down the elevator and walked the long, long corridor, all Hannah could think of was what the doctor said: *Your tumor has only shrunk a small percent. By now, we would have hoped for more.*

And then his other words: *The trick is not to get discouraged.*

She hadn't been discouraged, until right now, when suddenly she realized her anger had dissipated; in its place was left a space that was empty and afraid. With an involuntary motion, Hannah steadied herself against her husband's arm.

They walked some more in silence, and when they reached the front door of the hospital, she saw the falling snow: it swirled and whirled around the windows, and a dangerous accumulation was already on the ground.

At the end of the driveway, Katie said, "Right here."

Rita turned onto the rutty, dirt-packed path. She wondered if Katie was clenching her jaw as tightly as Rita was clenching hers.

"My mother doesn't go out much," Katie said.

Rita nodded because it seemed impolite to say, "Yes, I know. The whole island knows she's pretty much a recluse." She maneuvered the van within ten or twelve feet from the door. She wondered how many people had ever come that close to the place where Joleen lived.

Rita parked the car. They sat a moment.

"Would you like me to go in with you?" Rita asked, because, though she was positively dying to, she knew she shouldn't interfere. Still, to have a glimpse inside . . .

Before Katie replied, the back door opened. Rita clenched again.

It was Joleen.

The great Joleen.

She was older. Well, of course she was. Her hair was long and tied back from her face. It was no longer shining auburn, that polished, bronzy color that had graced so many album covers. It was now rather dull, a tapestry of gray and brown. From where Rita sat, she could see the slight sag of eyelids and of jowls, the unkempt wrinkle of the long cotton skirt and the thick black sweater that the woman hugged around her waist.

But still she was a star.

She stood with self-assuredness; she was steady; she was serene.

And then, she strode toward the minivan.

Rita did not move, but her eyes followed every step the woman made. When Joleen reached the passenger door, Katie touched the handle, then she stopped.

"Kathryn," Joleen said from the other side of the closed glass.

For another moment in which Rita and the world came to a speechless halt, Katie paused. Then, at last, she opened up the door.

"Kathryn," Joleen repeated, and then Rita clearly heard the throaty, legendary voice that she recalled so well, "I've been hoping you would come."

SIX

The house was modest, much like Rita and Charlie's house, which had been left to Hazel long ago by a dead but appreciative lover; the same house where Rita had been raised, then Kyle, and now the rest of them. Katie had not been raised in Joleen's cozy cottage, but only spent sporadic weeks there as a young child, in between private schooling in Manhattan and her mother's tours. Katie hadn't said as much, but Rita had always paid attention to the news, especially news about Joleen. There hadn't been much news for several years, except mentions of Joleen's watercolors and how they looked a lot like other people's.

Joleen invited her inside.

"Oh . . ." Rita said, fumbling with her words. After all, this was *Joleen*. How lucky could Rita get? "I won't intrude. I'll run along."

"Please come in, Rita," Katie said, and Rita recognized a plea for some support, which was what she'd promised Doc, wasn't it?

"How about some hot chocolate?" Joleen asked after they were situated inside the house.

Katie paused as if to survey her surroundings. "Sure," she said at last.

"Sure," Rita echoed quickly. She nudged Katie farther into the kitchen, then did not stop her eyes from making their rounds around the room that was beige and blue like sand and water. A huge vase of colorful spring flowers stood on a small, white table in a corner.

"Hard to believe it's snowing," Joleen said, taking three pottery mugs from the cabinet. Using a paper towel, she wiped them out as if they'd not been used in quite a while.

"A nor'easter, they're saying," Rita said. There were no dishes piled in the sink, no stacks of old newspapers collecting Vineyard dust. Rita felt oddly comforted that the recluse kept her house neat and pretty despite, word had it, that she never entertained.

"Snow in April. Can you imagine?" Joleen replied, and Katie simply stood motionless, more like the guest that Rita was.

Rita moved to the cozy dining area that had been converted to a sunroom. It overlooked the water. Another large pot of flowers sat by a window seat. Perhaps tulips and daffodils were Joleen's friends. "What a great view," Rita said. "I used to be in real estate. I could have easily sold this house."

Just then, Katie walked in front of Rita and leaned against the window seat. "I used to love to sit here and watch the boats go by," she said. "Especially the big ferries. Back and forth. Bringing all those people, then taking them back home."

Behind them, Rita heard the filling of a teakettle, the rattle as it was set upon the stove, the *pouf* of the gas jet as it ignited.

"And so one finally brought you home," Joleen said from across the room.

Rita did not mention that Katie had most likely come by plane. She angled to one side so she would not be standing directly between mother and daughter, in the line of friendly fire, so to speak. She wished she could tell if the tension in the room was real or her imagination.

Katie kept her eyes fixed on the sea, her back toward Joleen. "I have breast cancer," she said.

Rita cringed.

"I know. Your father told me."

"He called you?"

"Yes."

"I thought you never answer your phone."

"I have a machine now. He left a message; I called him back."

Rita fixed her gaze on the red tulips and tried to forget what she'd just heard: Joleen never answered her telephone? She was that much of a recluse? And what difference did it, should it, could it make to Rita?

"Then you knew I left New York."

Oh, God, Rita thought, no longer feeling lucky that she'd been invited in, but more like the antagonist in the ancient adage "three's a crowd."

"Your father said you came here. I made some calls; I learned you were at the Harbor View. Not many inns are open year-round."

If only Rita could shrink like Lily Tomlin in that old movie, then she could slide beneath the door. She silently cursed Doc for putting her in this position.

"I'm pregnant."

"Yes."

Not that it wasn't obvious.

"After the baby's born I need to have radiation."

"Your father's worried about you."

"He's worried about my career. He's worried about his future."

Outside the window, snow fell heavily. And Rita felt her angst turn into sadness for Katie, for Joleen. No matter what Doc thought, Rita was not cut out for this.

"He loves you, Kathryn. You are his world."

Katie folded her arms over the rounded top of her tummy. She turned to Rita and said, "Thanks for the ride, Rita. But I think I need to rest." She disappeared out of the room and her footsteps padded up the stairs.

Rita looked over at Joleen just as the teakettle's whistle blew.

Forty-five minutes later, Rita walked into her house with Olivia on her hip, Oliver holding on to her hand, and snow over all of them. She stumbled over See 'n Say and stopped herself from saying "Damn." Instead, she unzipped and unbundled and called out "Nap time!" The twins miraculously agreed and scurried upstairs to their room, followed closely by Rita, who wished that she were younger. Thank God for Amy, who'd spent half an hour with them in the potty and layered them in clean diapers just in case she'd done it wrong.

Once they were content—as content as two-year-olds could get—Rita glanced up at the clock: plenty of time to call Doc before Mindy came home from school. Plenty of time to call and ask if there would be any more surprises and what he really expected out of her for the few million they might or might not get. She picked up the phone in the upstairs hall. She quickly placed the call.

He was in his office.

"Thanks for the kind words to my mother about the

group last night, but it's bullshit, Doc. I feel like I've been duped."

"Duped?" he asked, as if he didn't know.

Rita stretched the phone cord down the hall. "Katie Gillette. For godssake, Doc, you didn't tell me she'd be there." She walked a few more steps, then stopped outside Mindy's room. Even from there, with the door partially ajar, Rita could see two of Mindy's favorite posters, both of Katie—healthy, smiling, glittering from head to toe. Rita leaned against the doorjamb and felt the sadness return.

"The women in the group have breast cancer, Rita. They need your support, not your admiration."

She sighed. "The older woman left," she said. "I thought you ought to know." Of course, Rita would love to ask if the woman was the one behind the bucks, but Doc might say that she was too damn nosy, which she supposed she was. A genetic flaw from Hazel, one of the not-so-charming ones.

"Just do the best you can, Rita," Doc was saying now. "That's all anyone can ask."

She closed her eyes but still could see the glitter in her mind, Katie's glitter, that hung on Mindy's wall. "Doc?" she asked, because he'd sworn her to damn secrecy and she couldn't even ask Hazel, if Hazel ever made it across town from the Senior Center in the storm. "Is Katie going to be okay? She's pregnant, Doc. And with the breast cancer . . ."

"Just do the best you can, Rita," Doc repeated. "It's not up to you to make her well."

He said good-bye and Rita hung up. She rubbed her forehead, then opened up her eyes. And when she did, she noticed that the door had been opened all the way. Just inside stood Mindy, her jaw slackened, her mouth agape.

Rita blinked.

"They let us out early because of the snow," Mindy said,

and stood there without moving, waiting for Rita to explain what she obviously had just overheard.

They checked into a room at the luxurious Ritz-Carlton that had a view of the Public Gardens. Evan said as long as they were snowed in, they might as well enjoy the city. Hannah didn't want to stay, but even if they made it to the Cape, she knew the ferries never ran in a nor'easter. Still, she felt a little foolish when the doorman said that he'd valet-park the truck. She hoped he wouldn't comment on the peat moss in the back.

"The swan boats must be frozen on the pond," Evan said after they'd picked up toothbrushes and deodorant at the sundry shop.

Hannah didn't tell him that the swans themselves were safely harbored on the South Shore for the winter, that they'd be brought back in May on a day of celebration. She didn't want to tell him because she didn't want to share things she'd learned while she'd lived in Boston; she wanted no reminders of what might have been.

"Honey," Evan said. He had moved from the window and stood beside her now at the foot of the bed. He put his arms around her.

She stepped away from him. She folded her arms and stared at the Ethan Allen furniture and the matching fabric draperies. "Maybe you were right," she said. "Maybe I should have come here first." He did not disagree. She went to the window because though the room was large, there was nowhere else to go.

He was next to her again. He put his arm around her, then dropped his head onto her shoulder. "I will not lose you, Hannah. I will not lose you, too."

She knew her husband was thinking of himself, thinking of his own pain. He'd hidden it so long, the way that she had hidden hers. "I still miss her, Evan."

"Me, too," he said. "She was my mother."

Mother.

Oh, she thought, and could not fight the instinct to think about her own.

It was the perfect time to tell Evan about her mother, the woman folks said Hannah looked like her despite the fact that Hannah was fair like her father instead of black-haired like her mother. Black-haired like Riley. It was the perfect time to tell him her mother's name and where she was and why, so if Hannah died he would know to notify her other next of kin.

She drew in a breath for courage, just as Evan began to cry. "She was so full of life," he said. "She always seemed so healthy. The way she ran the theater . . ."

The perfect time had come and gone: Evan had slid into his memories and his sorrow; he would not have room for hers. So Hannah simply moved more closely up against him. He rubbed her arm and she rubbed his. Together they stood in silence at the window and watched the city turn to white.

How did one tell a twelve-year-old girl she'd be grounded for her life if she breathed one iota of what she'd heard?

Rita and Mindy stood speechless for a moment, neither one apparently knowing what to say. Then Rita remembered she was the adult, just as she was the facilitator of the support group and was supposed to be in charge. She fought off another wave of anger at Doc Hastings and simply said, "Well, I guess it's pretty obvious I didn't know that you were here."

Mindy looked at her with disbelieving eyes. "Rita? Is it true?"

Rita walked past her and went into the room, ignoring the rhinestone rose tattoo that Mindy had glued to her left cheek sometime between when the school bus had picked her up that morning and when it had dropped her off. "We need to talk," she said, and sat down on the pink blanket on Mindy's bed that faced a trio of Katie Gillette photos in successive, onstage poses.

Grabbing the chair from the small desk in the room, Mindy sat and leaned toward Rita, her mouth still slightly open, her eyes awaiting more.

"I know you know how important it is sometimes to keep a secret," Rita said. *Love her like a kid; treat her like an adult*, she'd decided long ago. "This is one of those times." She did not say, "The last thing Katie needs is the media on her doorstep," because the word "media" alone might tempt a twelve-year-old.

"Is she going to die? What about her baby? Is it Miguel's?" She barely took a breath before adding, "Oh, no! What about Brady, her bodyguard? He must be devastated. Some people think he's secretly in love with her."

So now there was Rita, plopped in the middle of a gripping daytime soap.

Mindy spoke, of course, as if she were an intimate friend of Katie's: The tabloids and TV and magazines had no doubt exploited the rock star for attention.

Then Rita had a thought. "It's none of our business, Mindy. Just as it's no one else's business why you live with us. Like Mr. Mason at the hardware store—it's not his business—or Jenny at the ice cream shop or Hap at the dry cleaners. Can you understand that?"

Mindy seemed to consider it.

"Katie is going through a rough time right now," Rita

continued. "We need to respect her privacy the way yours should be respected."

Mindy fiddled with the rhinestone rose. "But Rita, it's so awful."

Rita nodded. "Yes. Which is why I promised Katie and Doc Hastings that I wouldn't tell anyone. A promise is a promise, Mindy. I'm sorry you overheard me, because that means you have to keep that promise, too. Can you?"

Mindy shrugged.

"Mindy?"

"I guess," the girl replied.

"No guessing allowed. We don't want to hurt her, do we?"

Mindy blinked. "No."

"It's a big responsibility."

"Yes." One of the rhinestones peeled off in Mindy's hand.

Rita stood up and kissed the top of Mindy's head. "Please," she said. "I'm counting on you." Then she left Mindy's room, hoping that a half-baked promise would not succumb to the pressures of being twelve.

"Mommy! Mommy!"

It was Dana's voice, crying out from somewhere beyond the blurred horizon, caught upon a wave, trapped in its fierce wake.

Faye's eyes shot open. The first thing she realized was that she was in a pool of sweat and her heart was racing quickly and her breath was short and shallow.

She let out a mournful wail. Mouser jumped onto the bed and placed his paws beside her and stared at her. She pulled the covers over her face and waited for the pain to go away.

When it did not, Faye crawled from the bed and stepped into her slippers. With the big comforter around her, she went to the huge staircase where she had once descended, lady of the manor, mother of the children, wife of the husband, keeper of the fortune.

She thought that she might kill herself, but she didn't own a gun.

She made her way into the living room and slowly built a fire. Mouser did not leave her side.

"She's dead," Faye said, maybe to the cat, or maybe to hear the words out loud, as if repeating them would make them somehow more real. But it had been ten years, and Faye had said the words hundreds of times, and still they did not ring true.

She stoked the fire, then made a nest out of the comforter and curled up in it on the floor.

It had not been Greg's fault, though he had wound up with the blame. Older brother, wiser. Should have taken better care.

The fire snapped and cracked and Faye listened to its sounds and let herself remember what was easy to forget when she was immersed in work, *drowned* in being busy, for lack of a better word.

Dana had been drinking. Though she was only seventeen, it hadn't been the first time. Too much money, Faye surmised. Too many spoiled friends like she was; too few rules from a mother who was too busy with her career and a father who was too busy chasing other women when the mother was at work.

They had sailed to Chatham and halfway back, Greg and his college friend. Dana had gone with them and brought her boyfriend-of-the-week. The two had stayed on deck once the sun went down, to neck and drink and God-knew-what. It was several minutes before the boy pulled himself together to alert Greg that his sister had gone overboard back a few hundred feet.

It had been too late. And the pain they'd all endured had been too steep a price to pay, especially for Greg.

When Faye's breast cancer came along two years later, its punch of trauma and disbelief was weak and insignificant by comparison.

She rolled onto her stomach, aware of the saline pouch that had been implanted after that, aware of her remaining breast, now tattooed for what was left of her shattered life. And then Faye listened to the fire and wondered if there was a God and if there was a heaven and if she would see Dana when she finally died.

SEVEN

It could have been a day since Faye had curled up on the floor. It could have been a day, or maybe it was two, that she had only moved to stir the fire or to add another log, only rose two or three times to pee. Even Mouser seemed to sense the need to just stay put, to lounge in and out of napping without noticing the world.

She did not know how long she'd been there when the pounding sounded at the door.

"Faye! Let me in!"

It was her sister, Claire, who had no business being on the island at this time of year, let alone at Faye's house when she'd not been invited.

"Faye! Goddamnit!" *Pound, pound, pound.*

Faye ran her hand through her hair and considered not answering the door. But the Mercedes was in the driveway and the noise had suddenly alerted Mouser, who rubbed against her back and who, no doubt, wanted food.

A loud *thud* followed by another suggested that in another heartbeat her perfect sister would break down the goddamn door.

"Just a minute," Faye shouted at what turned out to be

the top of her lungs. The volume was surprising because she'd not heard her voice for hours, maybe days.

She hauled herself up off the floor and knew she must look ridiculous, with matted hair and mottled, unwashed skin. Clutching the comforter around her, she made her way to the back door.

Claire was not amused. "Let me in, you ungrateful, lying bitch." She did not wait for an invitation, but bullied her way through the door, her fur coat leaving the scent of a slightly damp, slightly gamy animal in its wake. In the living room, she yanked off the coat and threw it on a sofa.

"I drove through two feet of leftover snow to get here," she announced.

Faye blinked and took another look outside. Though the sun was shining now, indeed, a thick shelf of snow carpeted the yard. She doubted it was two feet, though.

"I would have driven through seven feet, but that's how I am." She rubbed her arms as she stood in front of the dying fire. "You didn't tell me," she said. "I can't believe you didn't tell me."

So Claire had learned about the cancer. After all these weeks, just when Faye thought she was off the hook, somehow her sister had found out.

"How do you think that made me feel? I kept calling you at home and at your office. Finally Gwen said maybe I should call your doctor. I said, 'I can't just call her doctor.' She said, 'Yes, you can if you pretend you're her.' So I called and said I needed the date of my next appointment. The woman laughed and said it was in two weeks for the mammogram, how had I forgotten that? She didn't think forgetfulness was a side effect of radiation."

Gwen? Faye had called the office when she'd arrived on the Vineyard. She'd asked Gwen to finalize the RGA study. She'd asked if she would mind presenting the results in

Chicago. She had told her she was on the island, but she had not mentioned breast cancer. Then again, Faye paid Gwen well because she was so smart.

"What did you think?" Claire went on, her voice trembling now, shaky from anger, Faye knew, because she knew her sister and her sister's moods and her reactions as well as she knew her own. "Did you think I wouldn't stand by you? Did you think I would make matters worse?"

She marched around the room while Faye remained standing in one place. Claire waved her hands around; Faye caught a glimpse of the tiny ring of wampum on Claire's little finger. She turned her head away.

"And what about poor Adam?" Claire went on. "The reason I was trying to find you was that, believe it or not, he said he'd like to try again to meet you. I know it was just a lunch date, Faye, but wouldn't it have been kinder to simply say 'Sorry, I'm not dating right now because I have breast cancer again'?"

Faye briefly wondered if Claire had any idea how absurd her last comment had sounded.

Suddenly Claire whipped around and flailed her arms at Faye. "I'm just goddamn mad, that's what I am! I'm just goddamn mad that I drove all the way down here and caught an impossibly rocky ferry and nearly heaved my breakfast just so I could come and tell you that I'm sorry and—*Look at you!*"

Faye bent her head to look at herself.

"You are a mess! When was the last time you had a shower?"

Leaning down, Faye picked up Mouser and held him against the comforter and against her breast, the one that was maimed but not yet gone. She kissed his head. She turned and went into the kitchen to get the cat something to eat. She left Claire standing by the fire. By the time she found the cat food, opened the can, and dumped the contents on a plate, Claire had put her fur back on and stormed out the door with the same explosive force with which she had arrived.

And then Faye realized that she hadn't said a word to her younger sister because Claire had not asked how she was feeling and if there was anything that she could do to help.

"So far I've completely alienated one woman and leaked the secrets of another. Can they still call it a support group if the membership is only one?"

"Rita, calm down," Charlie said into the phone. He said that lots of times to her, because it was his job as the kindly, understanding husband. It was, however, easier to take when he was sitting next to her and not over on Nantucket, building other people's houses.

"This wouldn't happen if you were here," she said, and knew it made no sense and was glad he didn't point that out.

"Think about the Women's Center," he said. "Remember, it's for the island."

"Yeah, yeah, yeah." She looked out the kitchen window and wondered if the damn snow would ever melt or if she'd have to pay a kid to shovel, after all. God, she hated feeling like a single parent, head-of-household once again.

"Besides," he added, "it will keep me home, if you can stand it."

"What?"

The line crackled a little; calls between the islands sometimes did that.

"Ben and I reviewed Doc's plans today," Charlie said above the crackle. "When we're finished on Nantucket, we're coming home to build the Center."

Rita smiled. Her husband was coming home. "Yeah?"

"Only if you want me there," he said with a Charlie-chuckle, which he did because he knew there was nowhere else Rita wanted him except in their home and in their bed. "As long as you don't screw up the funding for the place."

If he meant that to be funny, Rita was not amused.

She did not take a shower, but she took a bath. The water helped to warm her; Faye could not remember it ever being so cold in the big, old house, except for the night that Dana died.

She brewed some tea and tossed a wedge of cheese and a ragged piece of a baguette onto a plate. She vaguely remembered stopping at the store; she must have gone out just before the storm, because the bread was fairly fresh.

Taking her food into the living room, she sat on the sofa in a more civilized manner. She glanced at the phone and wondered why Gwen had not called to warn her about the coming of perfect Claire. But seeing the phone only reminded Faye that she had not heard from R.J. Browne.

What if Greg could not be found?

The bread was not as fresh as she had thought. She washed it down with a long drink of tea, then started to tap her foot, her senses slowly reviving as her life kicked in again.

Glancing around, Faye wondered what had possessed her to keep this old place after the divorce. Was it because Claire had a cottage down the road? Was it so Greg would always be able to find his mother? She thought about Rita Blair. Had Faye simply kept the house as some form of revenge?

No commission for you, my pretty.

Ha!

Faye pictured Rita as if it were yesterday. She was dressed like a hooker in a sleeveless white tank dress that barely covered her crotch and did little to obscure anything about her breasts except her nipples. She had that mass of red, red hair and wore ridiculous stiletto heels.

"My name is Rita Blair," the woman had said. "I'm the owner of SurfSide Realty."

She was, of course, there to get laid. Faye knew that, because she knew her husband, Joe Geissel, better, even, than she knew her sister. Rita Blair was there to get laid and she had not expected to see Faye because Faye usually spent summer weekdays in the city—it was what she had been doing since Dana died, because she could not stand to sit still, especially on the Vineyard.

It was not the first time Faye had been faced with the reality of Joe's indiscretions, but it was the first time one had stood on her back stairs, claiming she had a buyer for her house that was not for sale.

It had made her sick, though Rita Blair would not know that. It was not until the woman had rattled her old car down the driveway that Faye allowed herself to calmly go into the bathroom, remove her beige linen shorts and sleeveless silk shirt, step into her robe, neatly tie the long sash, then move to the toilet bowl and vomit her last meal.

They met again, that time on the ferry when Rita had followed her. She'd said she had an offer of two million for the house.

Faye had tried to change seats.

"You do know that while you're in the city each week, your husband is conducting his own business, don't you? His own very personal business?" Rita stuffed a business card into the book that Faye had been reading. "Call me by Tuesday or the offer is gone."

It had been several years and a long divorce ago. And

though Faye had never called her, she hardly could forget that woman or her red hair. It was apparent, however, that Rita did not remember Faye, whose hair had not been silver then. Perhaps Faye had merely been one of a string of summer people Rita had tried to screw. Literally. Figuratively.

Faye sipped her tea again and realized it was now cold. Cold like the house. But she still sat there, holding on to the cup, when an hour or so later, another knock sounded at her door.

It wasn't Claire this time; it was Doc Hastings.

The first time Katie had seen Joleen after Joleen's nervous breakdown was at a sprawling house somewhere in the Berkshires. Katie was thirteen and her father had just finished her first music video. The song had been an old one of Joleen's.

She cried when she saw Katie. "My Kathryn," she had said, but seemed afraid to hug her daughter who was, by then, nearly as tall as she was. Joleen was still beautiful, in her earthy sort of way.

They'd walked through a cemetery down the street from the sprawling house. Across from the cemetery was a bell tower.

"An old man plays the chimes every day at twelve o'clock," Joleen told Katie and her father. "There's a woman on my floor who goes insane when he does." Then she laughed. "That's some joke, isn't it? That she goes insane?"

Katie had laughed because she loved her mother and had spent four years without her.

On the drive back to the city, Cliff told Katie he had filed for divorce. Katie just stared out the car window at the

Hudson River, which snaked alongside the road. "You understand, don't you, Katie-Kate?" he asked. "Our lives are going to change now. Your mother will be better off without us."

The next time Katie saw Joleen was at her high school graduation. Although she had three hit records by then (all remakes of Joleen's), Cliff had insisted that Katie finish high school. She did not notice Joleen until the ceremony was over, when she caught sight of a woman at the back of the auditorium. The woman had long hair and wore a long black dress and shawl. She disappeared among the crowd.

When Katie was nineteen, she went to the Vineyard, because that was where Joleen had gone after she was cured. The visit had been tentative. Katie talked and Joleen answered and they went to a bean supper at the church, because it was off-season and nosey tourists would not bother them. They had not really bonded, because Katie's father—not his presence, but his existence—seemed to get in the way.

Katie sat in the middle of her bed now and tried to pull her knees up to her chest—they did not come close. Nearly seven pregnant months had eliminated both pink sequins and flexibility from her life.

Stretching out, she lay her hand on top of her growing baby-mound. "Are you okay in there?" she asked, but did not get a response.

With a small sigh, Katie wondered what to do that day and the next. Joleen, no doubt, was painting, sequestered in her studio. They ate their meals together and spoke cordially, but the wall of years stood fast between them: there were few words; there were no hugs.

She supposed that she could write a song. But Katie's biggest hits were Joleen's songs, not hers. "Joleen with a nineties twist," Cliff promoted Katie early on. It no longer was the nineties, but Katie still sang her mother's songs.

She rolled onto her side. She could call Miguel. "Come and get me and our baby," she could say. "I will marry you."

They would not need to tell Cliff until it had been done.

But would Miguel still want to marry her if he knew that she had cancer? Would Ina want him to?

She pressed her fingers to her temples. If she'd had the mastectomy, her fans might or might not still love her. But what about Miguel? Would he still love her if they had a baby but she had no breast and no career?

She could not call him. The baby was his, but the cancer was hers alone. Whatever was she thinking? "Cabin fever," the old salts of the island called it.

She thought about Jack Nicholson in Stephen King's *The Shining*. If she didn't get out soon, would Katie lose her mind?

"Damn," she said and sat up. Before she turned into Jack Nicholson, she supposed she could start a journal the way Rita had suggested. It's not as if anyone would see it, out there on the Vineyard.

First, she needed paper and a pen. Maybe she could find something across the hall in Joleen's bedroom.

"I'd offer you a drink, but I'm not sure what's here." Faye had let Doc into the house and directed him to the living room, where the fire's embers barely glowed.

"Nothing, thanks," the old man said as he sat down.

Faye turned to the fireplace and began to layer on more logs. Despite the fact that wood was a welcome mat for field mice, she was grateful she'd stockpiled it last fall; it was almost as if she'd known she'd be back before the summer and would need a cozy fire. It was almost as if she'd known about cancer-number-two.

"How are you feeling?" Though Doc was not her physician, he had seen her through much pain: the summer Dana died; the other summer after her first diagnosis. He had talked her through the rough spots; more than a doctor, he had been a friend. When she'd arrived on the Vineyard ten days or more ago, he'd been the only one she'd called.

"I'm okay," she lied, "most of the time." She stoked the fire; they talked about the storm. Then she turned around and sat down. "Rita told you I walked out on the group." Her eyes moved to his kindly face. "I don't need a support group, Doc. It's foolish at my age."

Rubbing his hands, he leaned forward on his knees. "I'm sorry you feel that way."

At least he didn't scream at her the way Claire had done.

She would not, of course, tell him the real reason she could not go back. "Rita wants us to keep a journal," Faye said, then added with a snicker, "I haven't done that since I was a kid. My sister found my diary and read every word. 'Faye loves Jimmy O'Brien.' She taunted me with that for a year. I swore I'd never write."

Doc sort of smiled again.

They sat in the silence. The fire hissed and popped.

"They're scared," Doc said. He folded his hands and seemed to study his fingers, his age-thickened knuckles, his brown-spotted skin. "I brought Hannah's husband into the world. And her three kids. Buried her mother-in-law just three years ago. Ovarian cancer."

Faye's eyes moved to the fire.

"Katie's only twenty-one," he added. "I had hoped you might help them."

She glanced at him, then turned her head away. "I

thought you suggested the support group to lift me from my depression." His words had not been exactly that, but close enough.

"And I thought you might help them," he repeated. "You've been through it, Faye. They haven't."

She'd been through it, all right. As if cancer was not bad enough, she'd been through a confrontation with a woman with red hair who'd been fucking her husband as if she'd been entitled. She'd been through two more years of veiled denial until she'd had the courage to hire R.J. and start the steps to the divorce. Faye's eyes filled with tears. "I'm scared, too, Doc," she said quietly. "Would anybody believe that I might be scared, too?"

Her tears fell in big drops; Doc did not try to stop them. "Like it or not, Faye, you're a strong woman. Not every woman has been through the things you have. Not every woman has built a load of fortitude from which to draw."

"Is that what I've been doing? Building a load of fortitude?"

He laughed. "Would that be so horrible?"

No, she supposed, it would not.

"All I ask is that you think about it again, Faye," he said, then stood up. "We don't always get to pick the people who need us."

If he was talking about her, he had the grace to keep it to himself.

EIGHT

Katie hadn't been in her mother's room since her father had slept there, too, when they'd huddle on the big bed, just the three of them, singing silly songs or reading from great books or making stories up about the kings and queens in her mother's bedtime song.

She'd never gone inside if the door was closed. She'd known it was their "private" time together, her father's and her mother's. But he was gone and she was nowhere to be seen and there was nothing private between them anymore, anyway.

Katie held her breath a little, then opened the door.

The room still looked the same. The flower-print wallpaper had darkened, the small braided rug had faded, but the four-poster bed remained tucked under the slanted roof, its covers rumpled and inviting, as if none of them had ever left. She felt an ache of longing, a familiar ache that had been dulled by time and life, but was not completely gone.

Pausing in the doorway, she could almost hear their laughter.

"Katie-Kate," her father said, tickling her rib cage.

"Don't call me that!" the five- or six- or seven-year-old giggled.

"Katie-Kate, Katie-Kate." It was his favorite game.

She hated it, but still she could not stop giggling. She burrowed under the covers until her mother rescued her. "He's a goofy old man," Joleen had laughed. "Come on, let's get him!"

And the two would scurry to the head of the bed and attack Cliff Gillette from either side until the three of them laughed so hard that one of them peed their pants, usually Joleen.

Katie listened at the doorway, but did not hear the laughter now.

She stepped inside. She recalled the reason she was there. *Paper*. A notebook perhaps. A pen.

She moved to the small secretary that stood beside the window. The *Secretariat*, her father called the desk in jest, giving it the name of the horse that won the Kentucky Derby the year Joleen's first album went platinum.

Katie did not know when the laughter stopped; it might have been that last summer when her mother had the miscarriage.

Pulling down the desktop, Katie peered into the cubbyholes lined up along the back rim of the green-blottered wood surface. The compartments were jammed with papers: wrinkled, folded papers, littered like old bills someone forgot to pay.

Her eyes drifted to the bookcase that sat atop the desk. Behind its glass doors, the books did not stand up like normal books. This was Joleen's house, where the books lay on their sides as if they'd just been read and the reader set them down in stacks, the last-read on the top.

She did not see any notebooks.

Poking through the pigeonholes, Katie unearthed more

clutter. Her forehead tightened in a frown. Was Joleen in debt? Was the money Katie earned for her not enough?

"The remakes of your mother's music help keep her alive," Cliff said several years ago. "Without the royalties, she might break down again; she might lose her Vineyard house."

"What about her own royalties?" Katie had asked. "Lots of stations still play her songs." She might have been a little jealous: Each time Katie recorded one of her own compositions, the stations seemed to limit airtime. They loved Joleen; they only liked her daughter, Katie.

"Joleen's own royalties are not enough," Cliff said. So Katie kept rescoring and recutting her mother's biggest hits so that Joleen would not break down again. The ploy had worked: The world had loved Joleen's music with the nineties twist. And Katie had put away her own songs and quietly didn't mind, because she'd rather be onstage than writing anyway.

Pulling out a fistful of papers, Katie shuffled through them. But something wasn't right. Since when did bills arrive scrawled on yellow, lined sheets? She looked more carefully. Then she realized she did not hold a batch of unpaid bills, but pages of poetry.

It was a bright, blue morning
when the smile of the sunshine
sparkled off the water
and glinted off the land.

And then a host of anger
crashed into the smile
and the suffering began
and the suffering will not stop
over a bright blue land.

Above the words were tiny, hand-pencilled letters. A. B-flat. D. Not letters. Chords. And this was not a poem; it was a song.

Katie turned the paper over. Nothing indicated when Joleen had written it, if it had been penned yesterday or thirty years ago and was as old as the flowered-paper on the walls.

And then she saw a small notation in the corner. September 11, 2001. Not decades ago.

Quickly, Katie scanned the other papers in the secretary. More poems. Songs. Verses of creation from her mother's silent soul. Verses so much more magnificent than Katie's had ever been.

"My God," she softly said.

"Your God, what?" came Joleen's voice from the doorway.

Katie dropped the papers. She did not turn around.

"How dare you enter my bedroom without asking," Joleen said in a voice that had fallen to a husky whisper. "How dare you go through my things."

Katie inhaled a small breath. "I didn't mean to . . ." Slowly Katie turned and faced her mother. Anger was not common to Joleen: It showed its mark now in deep parentheses at the corners of her mouth.

"I was looking for some paper," Katie said. "Rita wants us to keep a journal." Why was her heart racing? Why did she feel so . . . awkward? "Mother," Katie said, "these are beautiful. I didn't know you were still writing."

With eyes set on the mismatched scraps scattered on the floor, Joleen undid the elastic around her long thick ponytail. She toyed with it a moment, then snapped it back in place. She left the doorway and withdrew down the hall.

· · ·

They had made love, if not like teenagers, then the best they could for a fifty-year-old man and a thirty-eight-year-old woman with breast cancer and no hair. Evan told her she was beautiful. In his arms she actually believed it.

Back home now, Hannah pulled herself from their bed and adjusted the scarf around her head. Beautiful or not, she wore the silk-and-polyester square. She did not want the children to see her head uncovered.

Evan. Hannah was convinced that the Lord had made the spring blizzard just so she and Evan would be stuck in Boston and end up staying not one but two nights because it was so good to be together, alone again like before the kids, alone with nothing or no one but each other to be with and to love.

She was silently ashamed for her attraction to John Arthur; she said a prayer of thanks that she had not acted on it.

Hannah wondered if the kids had noticed any difference between their mother and their father when they'd finally returned home, if they'd seen that Evan put his arm around her while she stood at the kitchen sink, or that they'd gone to bed the same time as the kids—except, of course, for Riley, who'd insisted on watching Letterman.

"Pink is on," she'd said, but Hannah suspected it was another test grown out of her daughter's new defiance. She tried to remember when Riley had metamorphosed from a sweet, loving child into a sometimes-angry, always-unhappy girl.

Hannah went into the bathroom, slid from her robe, and stood unclothed before the tall, oval mirror. She inhaled a long breath and began her checklist of the day:

Bleeding. None.

Bruising. None. Well, there was that little purple mark

under her elbow where she banged her arm against the bed-post when Evan . . . well . . .

She smiled.

Other bruising. None.

Fever. None.

Rashes. Nada, nada, nada.

She'd escaped the perils of the toxic chemo monster once again.

She put her robe back on and sat down at the counter. The small stool creaked beneath her.

"I keep hoping chemo will make me skinny," she'd said to Evan when he'd traced his fingers across her stretch-marked belly.

"I just want you well again," he'd whispered.

She wondered how it had happened that she'd become this lucky.

The oval glass sent back her smile. She noticed that her skin was not yet gray; maybe she'd avoid the ghastly pallor; maybe Evan's love had given her a new glow.

Evan, her husband.

It was nice to feel in love with him again.

She removed the scarf around her head and studied the tufts of hair. Touching one, it fell out in her hand.

"Well, so much for my smiling self," she said aloud. She sat there, staring at the puff of blonde that insisted she was sick, not well. It did not care that her husband thought she was beautiful; it did not care that today she was not bleed-ing or did not have a rash. Hannah still had breast cancer—Stage Three—one stage from the grave.

Two tears dropped onto the puff of hair. She blinked an-other tear away, then looked up just in time to see Riley re-flected in the mirror, staring at her. Their eyes met for an instant, then Riley turned and quickly walked away.

. . . .

"My mother caught me going through her things," Katie said when the group convened again. "I was only looking for some paper for my journal. But I found some songs she'd written. I wish I could put them in my journal. Maybe we should do that—instead of just our thoughts and feelings, maybe we should include pictures, ticket stubs . . . things. Souvenirs of our lives." She paused, then added, "Anyway, I feel bad that my mother caught me. Like I'd been doing something wrong."

They were silent for a moment.

"My daughter caught me without my wig on," Hannah said. "She hasn't spoken to me since."

Rita gripped the edges of the plastic chair. She did not mention that Mindy had caught her talking about Katie, about her baby and her cancer. Instead, she turned to the silver-haired woman who, for an unknown reason, had returned. Did that mean the Women's Center was not a dead deal after all?

The woman did not meet Rita's eyes. "Doc Hastings caught me feeling sorry for myself," she said, her voice not as regal as before, yet still well-bred and well-spoken, like any of many summer people educated in private schools because their families had the means. "I don't know how well any of you know him, but trust me, that's not what you want to have happen."

Yes, Rita silently agreed, Doc had little patience for self-pity. Much, Rita supposed, like her. Was that the real reason he'd asked Rita to run the group?

"Years ago, before my cancer or my divorce, I had tragedy in my life," the woman continued. "It happened right here on the island and Doc helped see me through it. He could have told me to go home to my own physician.

Instead, he encouraged me to talk with others who'd gone through something similar. He forced me to find a reason to go on."

A quiet filled the room, a gentle pause that waited to learn what the reason was.

"As frightening as it is to be told you have breast cancer," the woman said, "it can't compare with the horror of losing your child."

There was no motion in the room. No words, no sound, no breath. Then Rita realized that her mouth was open. She thought of Kyle—of course she thought of Kyle—and knew the woman was correct. Nothing could be worse than losing a child. Doc had suggested that Rita go to a support group, too. But Rita had not gone. Another flaw inherited from Hazel.

"So," the woman went on, "that's why I'm here. Because Doc was right. I've been feeling sorry for myself. And because those other people who had been through something similar helped me to survive back then." She folded her hands with practiced poise. "This is my second time with breast cancer," she said matter-of-factly. "It's not exactly a 'recurrence,' but, to me, it doesn't matter what they call it." She told them about her diagnosis, then and now. She asked if they had questions.

"If you already needed one mastectomy," Katie asked, "why didn't they do another?"

"This was a different type. And it was caught early."

"I have a question," Hannah interjected. "What's your name?" she asked. "We don't know your name."

The woman hesitated, then gave a small, slow smile. "Faye," she said. "My name is Faye."

Rita looked at the woman who had breast cancer for the second time around and who had lost a child and who had gone through a divorce, as if the rest wasn't bad enough.

The weird part was, the woman now seemed familiar. Was it because she'd lost a child? Her name was Faye. Did Rita ever know a summer person with that name?

"She has to be the benefactor," Rita said to Hazel later that night, because what the hell, Mindy already knew about Katie Gillette and Rita had to talk to someone about the mystery woman. Sometimes being curious by nature could be exasperating.

Rita shook off her thoughts and poured them both more coffee. "Whatever happened to Faye's child must have been more than eight years ago," Rita went on. "That's when she had cancer for the first time."

Hazel shook her head. "Tragedy happens, Rita Mae. Even on the island."

Her mother was no help at all. "But think, Mother! Can't you remember a tragic time when a child died?" She did not mention Kyle, the worst accident most folks knew of because he'd been twenty-six and he was one of theirs and he had burned to death. She did not mention Kyle because, though it had been nearly seven years and a lifetime ago, some days Rita still did not think she could cope.

Hazel shrugged. "I never cared much about the summer people. We were too busy looking out for one another, trying to survive."

We, of course, meant all the islanders—the ones who truly did belong.

"And don't forget that I was gone for years." A faint smile crossed over Hazel's face. She must have been remembering her unexpected marriage spent down in Coral Gables, Florida, in a mobile home, with a man rumored to have had a ton of money, though Hazel claimed he never showed it to her. "If they were famous people," Hazel added, "it would have made a difference."

Was Faye someone famous? Was that why she seemed familiar?

"Of course, if the death wasn't 'natural,' it surely would have made the papers."

Rita set down her coffee mug with a bang. Shit. The newspapers. Why hadn't she thought of that? It would be so simple. She could go to *The Gazette*. She could dig through the archives.

She jumped up from the table and wondered when Amy could watch the twins again and if they'd be ruined for life by spending too much time inside a tavern, all because their mother was too damn nosy and could not stop herself.

It can't compare with the horror of losing your child.

Katie sat on the edge of the bed in the room that once had been her home. She cupped her hands around her belly and thought about Faye's words. She thought about Miguel. How could she not?

With one eye on the telephone, Katie rocked back and forth. Was the real unfairness that she hadn't told him what was really going on? That she hadn't given him a choice to go on loving her . . . or not?

Then she saw his smile as clearly as if he were beside her. His wide and wonderful smile, the one he said he saved for her.

I have to tell him, she thought so suddenly and so clearly that it came as a surprise. *No matter what my father says, I have to tell Miguel about the cancer.*

She wondered if she could make a call without waking up Joleen.

The baby kicked. Katie smiled. She slid onto the floor

and brought the phone down beside her. Then she placed the call.

He answered quickly, as if he'd known that it would ring and that it would be her.

"I'm on the Vineyard," she said softly, "with my mother."

He was silent a moment, then asked, "Are you all right?"

She cried. "I'm fine, Miguel. Our baby's fine." She cupped her hands beneath her stomach again and laughed. "He is moving, Miguel! I can feel him moving, kicking his feet."

He hesitated; she did not know why. "It might be a girl," he said at last. "The baby might be beautiful like you."

"Or handsome like you."

He did not reply to that.

"Miguel," she asked, "will you come and see me?" She gripped the phone cord, afraid he would say no. Why would he say no?

"You want me to come out to that island?"

"Well, yes. I don't think it's a good idea for me to be seen in the city." She closed her eyes and pictured him in the small apartment he'd taken in the basement of her building; the studio that he'd rented to be close to her—his love, his star who lived so many flights up. She'd tried not to think of the symbolism there.

He laughed. Why did he laugh? "You know how I hate small planes, Cara Katie."

Didn't he want to see her? "Take the ferry," she replied. "It's really much more fun." He did not answer right away and she heard herself give him directions from the train to the bus to Woods Hole to the boat that would bring him across Vineyard Sound to her.

"Katie, I don't know." The tone of his voice was level, steady. "I thought we agreed to wait."

She closed her eyes. "Miguel . . ."

"No, Katie. I'm trying to adjust to this. You have no idea how hard it's been on me . . . that you left New York. That you took away my baby . . ."

How hard it's been on him?

What about Katie's father? Poor Cliff had taken her to the hospital for the lumpectomy. He'd waited in the lobby, claiming hospitals made him dizzy, while she'd been sent upstairs with a stranger who wheeled her into the operating room and asked if there was someone in the waiting room they could notify when the procedure was complete, and she'd said, No, no one would be there.

How hard it's been for him?

But, of course, Miguel knew none of that. Because she had not trusted him. Because her father had told her not to.

"Friday," she said quickly. She would need tomorrow to think about this, to plan what she would say and do. And Hannah had offered to go with Katie on Saturday, to pick out a layette for the baby. Besides, Saturday might be too late; she might change her mind by then. "Friday," she repeated. "Please?"

She rang off without saying that she loved him, or giving him the chance to say—or not say—it back.

NINE

"How did you know?" Faye tried not to sound angry when she phoned Gwen.

"It was warm in the office one day," Gwen said. She seemed unruffled that it was late at night and that Faye must have awakened her. "You took off your suit jacket. You had on a sleeveless sweater: I saw black marker lines under your arm. My Dad had radiation. I knew it was a sign."

It must have been the day she'd had the CT scan, when they'd pinpointed the area that needed to be *zapped*.

"Plus," Gwen added, "after that, you left the office every day at the same time for six weeks."

Faye laughed at herself, because she thought she'd been so secretive, so clever. "Actually it was six and a half weeks," she replied. "But didn't you think it might be something else? Maybe I was getting fitted for a new implant?" Gwen had been so supportive during Faye's first diagnosis. She'd kept the office running smoothly and earned her boss's trust.

"I knew it was the other side. Forgive me if I crossed any boundaries, Faye, but I was worried about you. I remembered your doctor's name from the last time. I called the hospital and said I was you and that I'd been there that morning and misplaced my scarf and wondered if anyone had turned it in."

"And no one had, right?"

"No, but the receptionist was very nice. She said she didn't recall that I'd been wearing one when I'd walked in that morning."

Faye laughed again. "So you told my sister to pretend to be me, too. I guess that's why I hired you. Because you are so brilliant."

Gwen grew silent. "Faye," she said, "I am so sorry. And I'm sorry you didn't feel you could tell me this time."

"Nothing personal. I just didn't want to talk about it."

"And now? How are you now?"

"I'm okay. I've had my last treatment. Now I'm catching up on a few things. Sleep. Life." Faye did not mention business.

"I'm sorry about Claire," Gwen said. "She cornered me, not that that's an excuse."

"No matter. I can handle my sister."

"You handle her and I'll take care of things here. I'm catching an early morning flight to Chicago to meet with RGA."

Faye's eyes darted to the sideboard in the dining room where her laptop sat, unopened. She knew she should feel guilty, but she did not.

"Thank you," she said. "I'm sure it will go great."

"I'll call after the meeting."

Faye wished her luck, then hung up and wondered for the first time if she should get out, if she should sell Gwen the business and stop pretending she still cared.

On Thursday, Donna Langforth hadn't been available to take Hannah for chemo, nor had Sally Dotson or Melanie

Galloway or anyone else who had spent so many hours in Hannah and Evan's small kitchen. At first they'd been supportive—chokingly supportive—bringing casseroles for dinner and offering to watch the kids. But as the weeks had passed, the offers dwindled, and Hannah's friends returned to their own busy lives. She supposed the same would happen if she were to die.

Evan could bring her to the hospital, but he could not stay: The storm had delayed the work for spring, and now he was expected to be in three places at once. But because he didn't want Hannah to have to be alone in a dreary closet-of-a-room, propped in a high-backed chair with her feet on a footrest, her arm hooked to an IV that was hooked to a pole for two and a half hours, Evan had made other arrangements. She liked that he seemed to want to be protective; she was not as sure his methods had been the most appropriate, but she had not interfered.

They pulled into the parking lot: Evan, Hannah, and the princess-of-pouting, Riley. Last night Hannah had heard Evan's orders through the thin walls of their house.

"You will go with your mother tomorrow."

"Why?"

"Because she is your mother."

"I didn't ask to be born."

"And I'm not asking anything either. I am telling. You will go with your mother."

"You can't make me."

"No, but I can ground you for a month."

"I haven't done anything."

"I can ground you for being selfish."

"No you can't."

"Yes I can. I am your father. I make the rules."

So Riley was with them now, alighting from the truck as soon as Evan stopped.

"She'll get over it," Evan said.

"Sometimes being the oldest must be difficult," Hannah replied. They watched her stalk across the lot and disappear inside the doors to the Emergency Room. "Well," Hannah said, "I guess I'd better go."

Evan touched her arm. His eyes glistened, but he had no more words.

Hannah picked up her purse. "I'll see you tonight." She tried to sound upbeat. She kissed him on the cheek. Just then a *rap-rap* sounded on the window on the driver's side.

Turning to the window, Evan hesitated, then rolled it down. "Morning, Doc," he said quietly.

Oh, Hannah thought, she could have done without a confrontation between her husband and her doctor, the former fishing buddies whose friendship Evan had abandoned after Mother Jackson died.

"How're you doing, Evan?" Doc asked.

Evan nodded but did not say, "Fine, and you?"

"He's real busy on account of the storm," Hannah interjected. "Riley's going to sit with me this morning. She's already gone inside."

It was Doc's turn to nod. "Well, if either of you need anything, you know where to find me," he said, and reached inside and patted Evan on the shoulder. Then he headed off toward the building, and Hannah and Evan watched him go, the way that they'd watched Riley.

The nurse took Hannah's blood pressure and her blood as well. She guided Hannah into the lounge, sat her in the big chair, then wrapped a heating pad around her arm, to warm the veins and ease the IV insertion.

After the nurse left, Riley spoke. "This is bogus," she said, as she flipped through an issue of *Seventeen.*

"What's bogus?"

"Breast cancer. I saw an article on the Internet that said doctors are treating women who don't even have it. That it's a fad now, like the way they did hysterectomies back in the fifties. It's all done for the money, because doctors are losing so much since managed health care took over."

She sounded so adult, so authoritative, Hannah had to remind herself that this was her daughter, her fourteen-year-old daughter. "You don't believe that, do you, honey?"

"Why not? Could you prove otherwise?"

The nurse came back and removed the heating pad. She searched for a decent vein.

Hannah did not blink when the needle went in.

"The only way to prove otherwise is to stop treating people," the nurse said. "Are you willing to risk your mother for some tabloid garbage?"

Riley looked up from her magazine. Her eyes moved to the IV, then up to the nurse.

"Besides," the nurse added as she adjusted the drip-drip, "if your mother had been a doctor like she almost was, I'm sure she wouldn't want her patients thinking all her hard work was 'bogus.'" After one last look at Riley, she left them alone again.

Hannah sighed. She'd never told her children the truth about her life before Evan, before Martha's Vineyard. She hadn't told the kids that she'd once planned to be a doctor: She hadn't wanted them to think that she wasn't "smart enough," that she was a quitter.

She kicked herself for the nervous admission she'd made to the nurse during her first round.

Riley shot a sharp look at her mother. "You? A doctor?" She laughed. "Now *that's* bogus."

"No," Hannah said quietly. "It's true."

"Oh, right. And I'm sure you decided that being a junior high science teacher would be more exciting." Riley stood up. "Think I'll go sit in the waiting room. This is boring."

Moments after Riley left, Hannah felt the rush of the chemicals swoosh into her, especially the one that went coursing from the back of her hand straight to her vagina. She repositioned herself in the chair to quell the orgasm that the Dechadron created. The nurses called it the "hootchie-cootchie" drug, the one reward of pleasure amid the anguish of the rest . . . anguish that had now surfaced with one of her many secrets.

"He's coming here?" Joleen asked Katie as Katie stood at the bathroom mirror, putting on makeup, trying to look like the star Miguel expected. He'd left the message last night: "I'll be there in the morning on the eleven-fifteen boat."

Katie knew she should be pleased that her mother was interested. It was the most communication that they'd had since Joleen had found her in the bedroom.

"He's coming because he loves me, Mother."

"And the baby?"

Katie shifted on one foot and leaned into the mirror with her mascara wand. If she'd had permanent makeup done like her father always suggested, she wouldn't have to worry about being beautiful for Miguel. Then again, she'd avoided it because at least this way she could choose when to look like Katie the star or just Katie the kid.

"He wants the baby. I told you he wants to marry me."

"And what about the cancer?"

She swept up her lashes—top, then bottom. "I'm going to tell him today."

Joleen remained standing, watching her daughter.

"It will be fine, Mom," Katie said. "Miguel loves me. I am carrying his child. I want him to know the truth."

"And what if it's not fine? Men start acting strangely when there are complications."

Katie sighed an exasperated sigh. "Miguel and I would have been married by now except Daddy wouldn't let me. He didn't think it would be good for my career." Blaming Cliff was easier than saying she hadn't married Miguel yet because she wasn't sure that it was right.

"I got married," Joleen replied.

"You married Daddy. That was different."

She studied Katie in the glass. "Are you going to tell Miguel about my songs? The new ones that you found?"

It was the first time Joleen made reference to those bits of yellow paper that Katie had returned to the pigeonholes in the desk. "No," Katie replied, "I won't tell Miguel."

"Well, with or without the cancer, if he thinks there is new music . . . if he thinks you'll still be a star . . ."

Gripping the mascara wand, Katie stared into the mirror. "Is that what you think? That I need your songs to be a star?" At least Cliff had never come right out and said it.

Joleen chuckled. "Oh, no. Oh, no. You're much better at that than I ever was, Kathryn. Much better. Since you've been singing my songs, we make more money than I ever could have imagined."

Katie frowned. "Mother," she asked, "are you okay? Financially, I mean."

Her laugh was off-center, but it was definitely a laugh. "Honey, I have more money than I know what the hell to do with." Shaking her head, Joleen toddled down the hall, leaving Katie to wonder if that were true, and why Cliff thought otherwise.

•   •   •

Rita didn't have a chance to get to *The Gazette* until Friday because Olivia had an ear infection and Hazel was wrapped up in plans for the Senior Center's Spring Bazaar, and Amy was off-island registering for courses at Northeastern. Even for a bunch of islanders, life could get complicated.

But on Friday Rita had been determined to get to the newspaper office, which was why she now stood in the archives room, which wasn't a room at all, but a long row of filing cabinets that held clippings cross-referenced with a database by event and date. Hopefully the room was not in the part of the building where the resident ghost hung out.

Then again, maybe a ghost had seen a thing or two and could help Rita on her quest.

She stared at the file drawers without a clue where to begin. She did not know either an event or a date. *A woman named Faye lost a child on the Vineyard,* was hardly a definitive lead.

At least eight years ago, she remembered. And most likely in the summer. Faye was somewhat older than Rita, which meant she could have had a child over thirty years ago, probably no more than thirty-five. Rita couldn't base her research on how long Doc had been on the Vineyard because he'd been there forever, or at least as long as Rita had been alive, and some days that seemed pretty much the same.

A maximum of thirty-five years, a minimum of eight. 1968 through 1995. June through August.

She plunked down on a folding chair and opened up a drawer, wondering how long this would take and why it seemed so damn important.

When Faye had been a child, they'd come to the Vineyard: her mother, her father, and Claire. Few summer people owned property on the island back then: most rented for a week or two or for the whole month of August if they were privileged. Because Faye's father, however, taught archaeology at Harvard, they spent entire summer vacations on the island. Because his brother, her Uncle Patrick, was linked to what was called the "Irish Mafia," they used a cottage right on the water at no charge. Her mother used to say Uncle Patrick was despicable, but they went to the Vineyard every summer nonetheless. If her parents knew who actually owned the place, they never mentioned a name in the presence of the kids.

Faye loved the Vineyard. She loved it for its beaches and its sand dunes and the comforting cries of its seagulls. Mostly, she loved it for the freedom that it wrought, for chasing the tide line and digging up clams, for searching for Indian treasures like wampum and clay, and for making good things to eat like chutney and chowder and feel-good Irish scones. They were riches she'd tried to pass on to her kids, memories of simpler days, neatly packaged with the odd belief that life had once been perfect.

Because of that, and on the off-chance Claire had stayed, Faye steered her Mercedes toward her sister's cottage down the road.

She owed Claire an apology. As much as she could say Claire was self-centered and shallow, Faye supposed she had contributed to her sister's societal demise. Faye Alice Randolph was the smarter of the two, the apple of their father's eye, the honor-roll student, the student council president, the leadership club leader. Claire sought nothing except their father's acceptance, and tried to achieve it by surrounding herself with other males, which only further distanced the one man she adored, because Father did not know how to handle his boy-crazy daughter, except to admonish his wife to "Talk to her. Please."

In the end, of course, Claire perhaps had fared better, because her wealth had come from marriage, while Faye's had come from hard work.

"You're so jealous," Claire had said on the night of the prom, when Faye said her dress was ugly and that the flower corsage from Claire's date—the football and track star—was a *gardenia*, for godssake, how tacky could you get.

Claire was right, however; Faye was jealous. She had also been jealous when Claire married Jeffrey Scott—of the Lexington Scotts—and had seven attendants and received wedding gifts that mostly came from Tiffany's or Shreve, Crump & Low's. Faye stopped being jealous when she had her babies and Claire had none.

Faye turned onto the dirt road now and remembered that she had been the first to buy a house on the Vineyard, though Claire followed suit within a year. It didn't seem to matter that she and Jeffrey only used it a few weekends a year.

Claire was not there. Faye stopped the car at the foot of the driveway and looked beyond the thorny, leafless bushes that lined the way to the house. A couple of inches of leftover snow remained layered on the ground: no car had driven on the driveway, no footsteps had trod its earth. Clearly, Claire had returned to Boston as quickly as she'd arrived, perhaps only touching down at Faye's to yell and then be gone.

Faye rested her forehead on the steering wheel and wondered why it was that she was the one who needed to apologize. She sat there a minute, and thought of the others in the support group: Katie seemed to feel a need to apologize to the world; Hannah, the need to apologize to her family, at least.

Was that a common denominator of all breast-cancer

patients? A need to say, "I'm sorry," as if the disease had been their fault?

And was that the real reason Faye had commissioned R.J. Browne to find her son, so she could say she was sorry for the past and the present and her abbreviated future?

Greg. She saw him in her mind. He was riding on a sailfish; he was smiling into the sun, his hair wet and salty, his yellow baggy shorts clinging to his frail frame. He had been so young and so filled with life.

She wondered what Greg, the man, looked like now. If he still resembled her sister Claire.

"Food!" he'd shouted every day of that last summer when they'd all been there together, every time he raced inside the back door after hours playing in the sun.

Faye had laughed and produced her latest baked delight: cookies or cakes or, his favorite, those Irish scones made from the secret recipe handed down on her father's side, the side that was despicable.

Raising her head a little now, Faye felt a small, sad smile. Instead of feeling sorry for herself, she knew what she could do. She'd go to the store and buy ingredients. Then she'd go home and make some feel-good scones. She'd bring a few to Hannah. And she'd drop some off to Katie while they were still warm. She knew where Katie's mother lived; every islander did. But what about Hannah? Could Faye track her down?

Moving the car into reverse, Faye backed out onto the road, feeling less lonely now, feeling less alone, and knowing that she'd make an extra batch, in case her Greg came home.

Nineteen sixty-eight on the Vineyard had been a fairly calm year compared with the rest of the world: the assassinations of a King and a Kennedy, riots at Kent State and at a national presidential convention. The island made up for its quiet in the year that followed, with the incident at Chappaquiddick, when the nation's eyes were on them. The next year Rita got pregnant and left the Vineyard to hide her shame; by some miracle, that item had not been newsworthy, at least not in *The Gazette*.

She clenched her jaw and forced herself to turn over another clipping, to not be lured by reading the local news that she had missed while she was on the mainland in seclusion, having Kyle.

A new development allowed on the west side of the island.

The July Fourth regatta race won by a pair of college boys from Boston University.

A record crowd at Illumination Night in Oak Bluffs.

No reports of children kidnapped, missing, or killed.

Rita rubbed the back of her neck and wondered if her mission was a waste of time.

TEN

Because it was still April, Katie did not hesitate going to the pier to meet Miguel's boat. It was too early for tourists, and others might not recognize her because they would not expect to see her there in public, without her rhinestones and her makeup, or with her very pregnant belly.

She was nervous. More nervous than the first time when she went up onstage, when she was ten and Cliff had introduced her as "The Great Joleen's Only Child"; more nervous than when Katie found out she was pregnant for the third time, silly, unthinking Katie who had not used birth control, but who had held a secret dream that a baby would make her life complete. There had not been time for nervousness when she learned that she had cancer; it had happened way too fast.

The boat bumped against the pier. She clenched her hands inside her jacket pockets as the giant flap came down and the cars and trucks of another world waddled onto land. Her fingernails dug uneven crescent moons into her palms.

And then she saw Miguel. He walked down the ramp and she took one look at his handsome, Latin skin, and she longed to feel him hold her, to be protected by his love.

She pushed past those around her and went straight into his arms. She folded herself into him, into his warmth, into his lightly musky scent that was so wonderfully familiar. He kissed her hair and her face and her mouth; she felt him grow hard against her thigh.

She quickly reminded herself that they stood on the pier, that other people were close by including . . . Miguel's mother?

Katie did not need a double take to know the elfin woman in the large sunglasses was Ina, Miguel's mother, Katie's right hand and her left.

"Ina," Katie said weakly, because Miguel's embrace had, indeed, made her weak, and because she could not feign excitement that he had not come alone. Oh, God, did Ina know about the cancer?

Her eyes flashed to Miguel. Did he know, too?

Ina said, "How are you, dear," and Miguel pulled away his warmth and his erection.

Katie tucked a loose tendril under the floppy hat she wore. "Fine," she said, "I'm fine." But she was not fine, not any longer.

"I'm not going to intrude," the woman said, giving her a quick hug. She looked down at Katie's middle and she smiled. "But I had to see for myself that you are okay."

Had Katie's father told her? Had Doctor Ramos? Wasn't it illegal for a doctor to betray a confidence? Katie's thoughts raced as quickly as sandpipers on the beach.

"I'm fine," she repeated, then added as she rubbed her belly, "we're both fine."

Miguel smiled that electric smile and touched his hand to the baby. He cocked his head a bit as if expecting to hear something, a cry perhaps, or soft baby words.

She tried to smile and pretend that she was happy to see

them, both of them. But how could she be happy when her plans had just unraveled?

They could not walk along the beach now. They could not share a hamburger at The Black Dog or be alone at the house, even though Joleen had gone up-island painting for the day. They could not do those things; they could not make love, because Ina was there.

"I'm not going to get in your way," the woman said as if reading Katie's mind. "Point me to a beach. It's been years since I spent a whole day at the beach."

"You're not going to sit anywhere alone," Katie said. "You'll come out to the house. My mother's not home, but you'll be comfortable. And if you want a beach, there's one right there."

"No," Ina said, "you two don't need me. I'll enjoy being alone, honestly I will." She patted her bag. "I even brought my lunch. A Cuban sandwich from home."

Katie laughed. Of course Ina would have brought her own lunch, just the way she took the bus across town instead of a cab. A lifetime of self-sufficiency had not changed simply because she now had the means to do otherwise.

"Point her toward the beach," Miguel reinforced. "She'll be much happier, and, cara mia, so will we."

He slid his hands from her belly around her thickened waist and looked deeply, so deeply, into her eyes. Then he hugged her again. This time Katie closed her eyes and did not care that the world might be watching or that his mother stood there. She only knew that, for the first time in weeks, she was not scared, because she was back in Miguel's arms.

The scones were no longer warm, but Faye's intentions still were good. She had finished her baking, taken several long, rejuvenating breaths, then bravely picked up the phone to call Rita for Hannah's address. Though Faye had tossed out the card Rita had distributed at the first support group meeting, the red-haired woman's name was listed in *The Island Book*. Perhaps Rita had never felt she'd had anything to hide.

Rita was not home.

How could a woman with twin toddlers, a twelve-year-old, an elderly mother, and a husband be out in the middle of the day? Somehow, Rita had not struck Faye as one who had "help." Who did the laundry and cleaning and cooking for that brood, and why did Faye care?

Because Rita had not been home, Faye had called Doc.

"I can't give you Hannah's address," Doc had said. "The group is anonymous, remember?"

"Oh, for godssake, Doc," Faye had replied. "I baked some damn scones. I thought you wanted me to be nice."

She told him she did not need Katie's address.

Faye went there first, down the winding drive that had enough overgrowth to suggest no one lived there, that this was just another summer home closed up until June. The Mercedes bumped over the ruts in the hard-packed sand, then finally arrived at a clearing. She stopped the car in front of a house not much more than a cottage, more befitting of a lobsterman than a rock star who'd been famous once upon a time. The house was not closed up, but it sat in seclusion, staring toward the sea.

With her clutch purse in one hand and a tinfoil pack in the other, Faye left the car and went to the front stairs, which simply were flat rocks, the kind of place a black snake or two had been known to live. There was no doorbell, so she knocked.

No response.

No sounds from within of footsteps or of talking; no indicators of life, which did not mean no one was home. With a small sigh, Faye tucked one of her business cards under the flap of the foil, then set the package between the screen door and the wooden one, with hopes that snakes did not feed on fresh-baked Irish scones.

Back in the car, she headed for Tisbury, following the directions Doc had given her. It was a side street, a lane, really, like so many lanes on the Vineyard, not much more than a path, where people somehow managed to live year in, year out.

Her eyes fell to the remaining foil package that sat on the seat. "Neighborly" was the word that came to her mind, a word that worked on the Vineyard but no longer did in Boston, because neighbors there now kept eyes straight ahead, intimidated by the constant clash of cultures that had consumed the once old-Yankee city.

Suddenly the driveway appeared. It was marked with a mailbox in the shape of a Canada goose, which bore a sign on the top that read JACKSON GARDENS, and one that hung from shiny chrome S hooks on the bottom: OPEN 7 DAYS.

Unlike Joleen's driveway, Hannah's was paved. Unlike Joleen's house, Hannah's seemed to say "Welcome."

Faye parked between a blue pickup truck and a gray-shingled Cape Cod-style house that could have been any of thousands, maybe tens of thousands, of lookalikes from there out to Provincetown—P' town—and up to the North Shore. She breathed deeply and remembered her mission: to be neighborly, to be nice. She'd do it for Doc. She'd do it because she really had nothing else in her life except a business that no longer interested her and a cat that barely bothered with her and a sister who would not, in a million years, understand. She'd do it because somewhere out there in the world, she still had a son who might one day come home.

•   •   •

She lay in the bedroom with the shades pulled and drapes drawn.

It had been Hannah's third treatment. The other times she'd been invigorated afterward, cleaning the house and doing laundry and sweeping through the rooms with drug-enhanced, domestic bliss. She'd decorated dozens of flowerpots. Once she'd even run, not two miles, but one.

She had not retreated to her bedroom and pulled the drapes closed.

She could not stop thinking about Riley. Her daughter hadn't spoken on the cab ride home.

What did Hannah expect? She had lied to Riley; now Riley was angry. But there were so many lies . . . so many secrets that not even Evan knew . . . Hannah pushed down the nausea that swelled inside her stomach. What would they all think of her if the whole truth ever emerged?

"Mom?" Riley's voice called from downstairs.

Hannah rolled onto her side and slowly opened her eyes.

"Someone's here to see you."

She did not want to see Donna or Sally or Melanie. She turned onto her back. "I'm not feeling well," she wanted to reply. "Please say thanks for coming and I'm sorry." But she couldn't very well shout it down the stairs.

And then another voice came from the hall outside her room. "It's me, Hannah. It's Faye. From the support group. I've brought Irish scones to brighten up your day."

Faye? From the support group?

Hannah propped herself on one elbow and stared back at the door. "Faye?"

The silver-haired woman stepped into the room. "Are you okay?" she asked. "Sometimes after chemo, all I really needed was someone's hand to hold." She sat on the edge of the bed and wrapped her long, dry fingers around Hannah's soft, moist hand.

Hannah didn't say a word. The comforting felt nice, the kindness of a stranger.

And then, "Mom?" Riley's voice called again, not from downstairs but from the doorway where she stood, looking quizzical. "Mom, you have a phone call. It's Mr. Arthur. From the school."

Katie picked up a foil package from between the front doors. She looked at the business card and frowned. BOSTON MARCOM. MARKETING SOLUTIONS FOR BUSINESS AND INDUSTRY. FAYE RANDOLPH, PRESIDENT.

"What is it?" Miguel asked.

Katie only knew one person named Faye. She quickly slipped the package under her jacket, as if Miguel might know that Faye was from the breast-cancer group, as if he might figure out that she was one of them. "Just something from a neighbor," she said, unlocking the door and going inside.

She dropped the foil package on the kitchen counter, then hung their jackets on the pegs by the back door. She moved in slow motion, as if they had forever, and not only this day, this one day together.

Suddenly Miguel was behind her, his arms encircling her, his hands resting once again on their baby. "Cara Katie," he whispered. "We must get married. I want to marry you, Katie. Please."

She closed her eyes and savored his nearness, the warmth of his body moved against hers. How could she doubt his love for her? "Maybe soon," she answered. "Maybe soon, but not right now."

He burrowed his mouth into her hair, then lifted it gently. He kissed the back of her neck. "Now," he said. "I want to marry you now, before our baby's born."

His hardness was there again, touching her back. He moved his hands down toward the moistness that tingled beneath her stretch jeans, between her thighs. With a kind of primal instinct that she could not control, Katie arched her back and pressed herself against his need.

He slid his hand between her legs. He pushed the thick denim against her flesh. He rubbed the seam firmly. She moaned. She arched back again and felt the bulge of his hardness move back and forth, straining against fabric, want against want.

Then his hands moved up from her crotch, over her belly to her breasts. His fingers groped her shirt, he quickly found her flesh.

He didn't know.

He couldn't know about the breast cancer or he wouldn't touch her . . . there.

Katie grabbed his wrists and pushed his hands away. She forced herself from him and crossed the kitchen to the counter. She tried to bring her breathing back to normal; she did not dare look at Miguel.

"What?" he asked. "What's going on?"

"I can't," she said. "The baby."

She sensed him move toward her. "We won't hurt the baby," he said. "Please, Katie, I love you."

She shook her head. She cried. She couldn't help it, but she cried. She clutched her stomach as if that were the problem, as if it was the baby and not breast cancer between them.

"No," she replied. "I can't. That's all."

· · ·

Hannah told her daughter to tell Mr. Arthur that she would call him back if he would leave his number. She couldn't, after all, talk to John Arthur with Faye sitting there, not to mention Riley. They might notice a slight blush in her cheeks and guess why it was there.

Once she finally was alone, Hannah made the call.

"Would you like," John asked, "to activate a leave of absence?"

He had not called to simply ask how she was doing. It was school business, of course it was.

"Oh," she lied, "I hadn't thought of that. I'm feeling fine most of the time." She sat in the kitchen and twirled a lock of false hair as if it were her own. "Must I?"

"It's up to you. I thought it might be easier."

"Well," she answered, "let me think about it. Let me talk it over with my husband." She supposed she'd said *my husband* for a reason: to keep him at a distance, to keep things in perspective.

"You won't be running," he said.

The race, she remembered. It was just two weeks from now. Hannah knew her energy must be saved for healing.

"No," she said.

"I'll miss you."

Her eyes traveled the kitchen in case anyone had heard. "Yes," she said, then gritted her teeth because she knew that sounded stupid. "I'll miss it, too." She did not add, "And you."

In the brief moment between them, she pictured him on the porch at Alley's General Store, taking a break, swigging green Gatorade, sweat-soaked and smiling.

"Yes," she said again.

"You could clock," he said suddenly.

She opened her eyes. She hadn't realized she had closed them. "What?"

"If you can't run, you could clock time. Help out. You know."

"Be there," she said.

"Well. Yes. If you feel up to it."

She twirled the silky strands again. "Well," she replied. "Yes. Maybe." She rang off and wondered why she'd said that when everything between Evan and her had become so good again.

Faye had to admit that she felt better. She'd never been the type who rushed to help out others; she'd never thought much about it, she'd been so caught up in her own world. But her brief visit with Hannah had helped to raise Faye's spirits, helped put into perspective the drudge her own life had become.

A *drudge?* she thought, letting herself into her house. Was that what she now thought of life?

The light on the answering machine was flashing. *Gwen,* she thought. Back from the RGA presentation, no doubt, filled with the chatter of the business high, the then-I-said, then-he-said discourse of the meeting that most likely had gone well because Gwen knew her stuff.

Faye sighed. She turned from the machine and went to the kitchen to make tea, half-wondering if she'd ever regain her lust for her work or if the last bout of treatment had irradiated that as well.

Setting the kettle on the stove, she lit the gas jet just as the phone rang.

Gwen again? Did persistence mean it had not gone well, and if not, why didn't Faye have the energy to offer some support? Baking scones was one thing; conducting business required thought and reasoning.

She stared at the phone across the room. The answering machine clicked on: a voice came on.

"Faye?" It was not Gwen. It was a man's voice. "I'm leaving the city to chase down a lead."

She scowled a little.

"It's R.J. Browne. Sorry I missed you. I'll try again."

She leapt across the room, into the dining room. She bumped her hip on the edge of the table and skidded on the hardwood floor. She fought to regain her balance. She finally grabbed the receiver.

"R.J.?" Faye shouted into the phone, but an insistent dial tone told her he'd hung up.

In 1971 a restaurant opened at the five corners in Vineyard Haven. It was called The Black Dog Tavern and planned to specialize in family fare. Patrons, of course, would have to bring their own bottles because no liquor was served in Vineyard Haven, because serving booze was illegal in any restaurant in any town without an "o" in the spelling of its name.

Rita rubbed the back of her neck again. She'd been at *The Gazette* all morning and had only reached 1971.

"Can I help you with something, Rita?" Nettie Drake asked her now. Nettie had been a few years ahead of Rita in school, but they knew each other as most Vineyarders did. She was straight-laced and proper, the kind of old Yankee that had made Rita decide to have Kyle in secret so he would not be shunned, a bastard of the island, an illegitimate child.

Rita sat up straight. If anyone would know about Faye's child, it might be Nettie Drake, whose phone line had been known to work faster than a gossip column and was attached to every household from Edgartown to Gay Head, long before Gay Head was called Aquinnah. Rita looked at Nettie. "A child died on the island somewhere between 1968 and 1995. It was during the summer. The kid's mother was called Faye. Does that ring any bells?"

Nettie took off her glasses as if that would help her think.

"Boy or girl?"

Rita shrugged.

"How did it die?"

"I have no idea. I suppose it was tragic." Well, of course it was tragic if a child died. "I mean, I don't know if it was an accident or an illness, but my guess would be an accident."

"Last name?"

"Don't know that, either."

"Why not ask Doc?"

"What?" Rita asked.

"Doc Hastings. If there was some kind of tragedy, I'll bet that he would know."

Rita would have kicked herself if she'd had half a brain. Why didn't she think of that? Of course Doc would remember. The only question was: Could Rita convince him that, as the support group leader, she had a need to know?

ELEVEN

"He didn't leave his number," Faye said frantically into the phone. "He said 'Sorry I missed you.' How could he not leave a goddamn number?" Faye twirled the phone cord every which way. If she had bought a cordless, she would be pacing now. But this was the Vineyard, where she'd tried to keep life simple. The same. Of all people, Faye should have known that sameness couldn't last forever.

Suzanne, R.J.'s receptionist, was caring and polite. "Men," she groaned. "Even the smartest ones can be so stupid." She then recited R.J.'s cell phone number to Faye. "Good luck, Faye," she added. "Maybe he has some good news."

Good news, indeed, Faye thought. She quickly said goodbye and dialed his cell phone number.

A loud, wavy tone assaulted her ear. She had dialed too fast.

She pushed down the button on the receiver, held her breath, counted to three. She hissed with exasperation and dialed again.

A pause.

Another pause.

A ring.

She squeezed the receiver.

Another ring.

And another.

"Answer, goddamnit," she seethed.

Another ring, then a click. "The Bell-Cell customer you are trying to reach is not available at this time. Please leave a message." *Beep*.

She suppressed a scream.

"R.J.," she said, trying to keep her voice steady, "it's Faye Randolph. I'm at the house now. On the Vineyard. Please call me. I'll be waiting."

She repeated her phone number in case he was on the moon. Then she hung up the phone and looked at her watch. It was just after noon. Nine A.M. on the West Coast, if that's where R.J. was headed, if that's where Greg still was.

One would think that at noon Doc Hastings would be at the hospital, if not in his office, then in the cafeteria eating a bachelor's lunch of meatloaf and green beans. He was not.

Rita sighed and checked her watch. It was Friday, the day the twins went to play group while she volunteered at the school, making photocopies and correcting papers and anything to help out because she was a mother and the school needed her.

She'd skipped out to try and find Doc.

"I was in the neighborhood," she lied to Doc's assistant, Margie, whose office was across the hall from Doc's and whose door was open. "I wanted to ask him about the journals for my support group." It was a lame excuse, but better than nothing, and better than saying, "I'm trying to find out about someone who had a kid that somehow died."

Margie rumpled the wax paper in which a half-eaten sandwich remained, then tossed it into the basket. She brushed a few crumbs from the front of her polyester smock that was imprinted with pink teddy bears dressed in stethoscopes and old-fashioned nurses' caps. "Doc's off-island," Margie said. "Dentist appointment."

While there were plenty of good dentists right there on the island, some folks still preferred to travel to the mainland. Rita wondered if it had more to do with a day's vacation than with crown and bridgework. What if a benefactor came up with a few million dollars to open a comprehensive dental center with every service from orthodontics to implants to plastic take-out teeth? Would Doc still catch a boat?

"Someone in the group suggested that they not only write in their journals, but that they paste things in them, too."

Margie's eyebrows rose over the top of her full-framed, round glasses.

"Pictures," Rita said, because she couldn't very well mention that Katie had wanted to paste in her mother's songs. "Photos of their families and friends. Favorite recipes. Memorabilia. To help create a better sense of who they are. A visual record, not just a bunch of words." Well, at least Rita had not forgotten the fine art of Vineyard bullshit. If Hazel were there right now, she'd be rolling on the floor.

Margie nodded and took a banana from a small brown bag. "Good idea," she said, peeling back four perfect yellow strips.

"Yeah, well, I just thought I'd mention it to Doc. In case he knows of some psychological reason why they shouldn't."

Margie shrugged and bit into her banana.

"Well, you never know," Rita continued, because she was off and running now, so what the heck. "It might be too hurtful to some of them. I know it would be hard for me to paste a picture of my Kyle into a journal. God, sometimes just saying his name is enough to bring me to tears." Her voice cracked on that part, and it was not made-up. Seven years later, Kyle's name could still do that. She said a quick prayer that he'd forgive her for exploiting his name and tragedy as a quick means to her end.

"I suppose there's no reason not to try," Margie said.

"Well, I didn't know if, for instance, someone else in the group lost a child. Maybe had a child who died tragically, the way that Kyle did?" It seemed pretty transparent, her request for information as to whether one of her three "patients" had a child who'd died. But though Margie was pleasant enough, she'd never been known for her intuition or her brains. "Do you know if any of them have?"

Margie shrugged again. "Doc says the group is anonymous. I was in charge of giving you the materials, but I don't even know who goes."

Rita would have said "Shit," but did not want to offend Margie, because you never knew when you might need someone later on. She glanced at her watch again. She should get back to school.

"I'll tell him you stopped by," Margie said.

Rita shook her head. "Don't bother. I'll catch up with him later." The last thing she wanted was for Margie to hint that Rita was prying into the life of the woman who might be their benefactor.

Hannah liked Katie's idea. She decided to decorate her journal with programs from her favorite plays: *To Kill a Mockingbird* which had starred Riley, and *The Belle of*

Amherst, the one-woman show about Emily Dickinson that Mother Jackson had starred in, and which had captivated every audience for each standing-room-only show.

But when Hannah opened the trapdoor and let down the attic stairs, a rustle from above abruptly stopped her.

Bats? Oh, no. Did they have bats again?

Gingerly, she crept up the stairs and poked her head into the attic. She listened. She did not hear bats flutter, but she did hear breathing.

"Who's there?" she called, a very brave, bald woman poised on the third rung from the top, her thoughts racing as quickly as her heart was beating. She tried to remind herself that this was the Vineyard, where crime rarely happened because it was so tough for perpetrators to escape.

"I'm going to get my husband now," she said, "so don't try anything that you'll regret." She lowered herself on the ladder, when a small voice called out.

"Mom? It's me." *Me*, of course, was Riley.

"Riley?" Hannah asked, and hoisted herself again. She climbed into the attic. Riley sat on the floor in front of Mother Jackson's trunk. The lid was open. Hannah's heart skipped a beat, then two, then three. "What are you doing here? Why aren't you in school?" She did not ask Riley how much digging she'd been doing through the memorabilia.

Riley closed the trunk. "Did Grandma Jackson know you were going to be a doctor?"

Hannah breathed a long, deep breath, moved to the rocker and sat down. The rocker creaked from age and miles of sleepless nights with Hannah's own three babies, and Evan before that. "Yes. No. I don't remember, honey. I don't know if I told her." She watched her daughter, who kept her eyes fixed on the trunk.

"Grandma Jackson said I'd be a great actor one day,"

Riley said. "She said I have her talent. All I have to do is want it."

The rocker creaked again. "She was right, Riley. You take after her."

Running her fingers along the cracked leather strapping, Riley said, "There's no one to run the theater now. I suppose I'll end up like you: stuck on the island with nothing but a bunch of old, dead dreams."

The theater Mother Jackson had begun was dark, that was true. But how could Hannah explain that life was not a "bunch of old, dead dreams"?

"I didn't give up my dreams, honey. I changed them, that's all."

"I don't want to be anything but an actor," Riley replied. "I don't want to be a teacher and I sure don't want to be a mother and I don't want to end up decorating flowerpots. You can say what you want, but the way I see it, you gave up, Mom. Maybe I have, too."

"It's not your fault the theater closed, Riley. You can act again someday. In school plays. Maybe you'll go to college in Boston and you can act there. Or maybe you'll be the one to get Grandma Jackson's theater up and running once again." Hannah didn't know if her words were helping, but it was nice that they were having a real conversation like two adults might have, or at least a mother and a daughter who respected one another.

Riley stood up and tucked her shirt into her low-riding skirt. "Never mind," she said, then walked past her mother toward the stairs. "I suppose it doesn't matter." She went down the ladder before Hannah had a chance to say it *did* matter, it really did, that everything Riley thought and said and did, mattered a great deal to Hannah because she was her daughter and she loved her very much.

But Riley was gone and Hannah was left sitting in the

rocker, staring at the old steamer trunk that once had held great dreams, but whose lid now was closed.

"I'm not going back," Miguel said to Katie.

They walked along Main Street in Vineyard Haven, toward Owen Park where they'd left Ina.

"You must," Katie replied. "You must let me do this my way."

"We have been doing things your way—or your father's way—for two years. Now it is my turn."

She hooked her arm through Miguel's. She had cried most of the time he'd been there. She had not meant to. She had meant for them to make love, but somehow, she could not. She could not let him touch her breast, because surely he would know. He knew the shape and form and every sensation of her breasts: He knew her flesh as if it were his own. She could not let him see the scar of the incised skin.

She could not bring herself to tell him.

He cannot be trusted, according to her father.

And Ina's words, *Your father's decisions are usually best for you.*

Would Katie never escape Cliff Gillette's influence?

And so Katie could not make love to Miguel. Instead, she had cried. And blamed it on her hormones, on the poor, innocent baby who'd done absolutely nothing wrong.

"No," she said, because she couldn't let Miguel stay on the Vineyard any more than she could make love to him. It was as if she needed every ounce of energy to fight off temptation demons, those that were real and those that were simply in her mind.

"He hasn't canceled Central Park. What are you going to do?"

"I don't know," she said. "Pray that things work out, I guess."

"If you don't show up, the press will say you're as crazy as your mother."

She wished he hadn't called her mother crazy.

"They'll say you're undependable," he added quickly.

As if she hadn't thought of that.

They walked silently a moment, then he said, "I can convince your father to postpone the concert."

She doubted it but asked him, "How?"

"I'll say that if he won't cancel, then we will elope. Then I'll say that I'll tell the media we had to elope, because the last time you were pregnant he made you have an abortion."

She breathed in little, shallow breaths and wondered why she could not get more air. "Miguel," she said softly, her hand dropping from his arm, "you wouldn't do that, would you?"

He cannot be trusted. Her father might as well have been there, walking on the other side of Katie, whispering in her other ear.

"I want you, Cara Katie. I'm sick of playing this game."

A game? If this truly were a game, which of them was winning? "But he's my father," Katie said.

"And what am I? A man who only wants you for your money and your name?"

She walked along in silence. She wished he hadn't said that, either. She wished he hadn't reminded her of her own lingering doubts.

At Owen Park, Ina was waiting, a book resting in her hands, her brown bag empty and flattened on the bench, a cluster of tiny birds at her feet nibbling on the remnants of a sandwich.

The woman stood up when she saw them approach. "I counted the seagulls," she said, "but I lost track."

Katie tried to smile. "There will be more in summer," she said, "when the tourists come."

"And you?" Ina asked, her eyes jumping from Miguel to Katie. "Will you be here as well?"

Katie nodded. "I must, Ina. I must stay here until the baby's born. So my father cannot make me change my mind."

"He can't do that now. It is too late."

She slipped her arm from Miguel's. She looked at him; she hoped he'd help her respond. But a young couple was walking by. They wore T-shirts and shorts—too early for the season. The girl had high, firm breasts; Miguel's eyes moved to them. He did not look at Katie.

She turned back to his mother, sensing Miguel's rebuff, feeling once again his odd manner of detachment when she needed him. "It's quiet here, Ina," she said. "The baby will like that."

"And Miguel?"

Katie did not look after Miguel. From the corner of her eye she knew he had begun to walk toward the dock, toward the boat.

"I don't know about Miguel," she said. "I must get through this first." She was trying to be kind, but with each step he moved away from her, the distance between them grew.

"There is more to this story, is there not, Katie-Kate?"

If only Ina had not called her that. If she'd not used the pet name Katie's father had made up, the name she'd never liked but never complained to him about. If only Ina had not called her that, she might have confided in her; she might have told her about the breast cancer. But the name only served to smother Katie once again, as if the only thing that mattered was to please her father, as if she were not a person in her own, grown-up right. As if she were not responsible to make her own decisions about her own life.

Katie raised her chin and said, "That's the whole story, Ina." She folded her arms across her billowed stomach. "Soon the baby will be born. Life will begin again."

Ina shook her head. She took one last look at Katie, gave her a sad, lingering hug, then she caught up with her son who had already reached the dock.

And Katie remained standing, hands in her pockets, in the park, watching until the ferry pulled away, making sure Miguel did not get off.

TWELVE

Waiting. If there was one thing Katie was learning from breast cancer, it was the fine art of waiting.

Waiting until the baby was born. Waiting until radiation could begin. Waiting until her checkup Tuesday, when Doc would reassure her that all was still okay.

"No need to worry," Doc had said the last time.

No need to worry, except about Miguel. And Katie's father. And her career.

No need to worry about anything but everything.

She strolled up Circuit Avenue in Oak Bluffs in search of a store that was open for the season. Hannah had called that morning—Saturday—and said she wasn't feeling well and was not up to shopping, if Katie didn't mind. Maybe next week?

More waiting, but what did it matter? Katie, after all, was not going anywhere, except downtown Oak Bluffs that was as bleak and deserted as the middle of January, which, on second thought, was good, because no one would harass her. It was odd, however, to be without her shadow, Brady. Odd and lonely. Kind of sad.

She passed the ice cream shop, the fudge shop, the

saltwater taffy shop where soon tourists in shorts and T-shirts would line up with their dollars. But right now the shops sat idle, as if they were waiting, too.

She tried to turn her thoughts to how exciting it would be once the baby came and she'd learn if it was a boy or girl. She'd told Hannah she wanted to be surprised, but the truth was that she hadn't wanted to know in case something awful happened. But now, with only weeks left . . .

A girl—Michele?

A boy—Miguel?

Miguel.

She turned up the collar of the old denim coat that was easily penetrated by the sharp spring wind that whipped off the ocean, crossed Beach Road, and danced up the hill. She passed Linda Jean's, which was open, because it always was open, wasn't it? She considered going in for a cup of hot tea, but she could see too many patrons on the other side of the glass, at the counter and at tables, sharing muffins and coffee and laughter and conversation. She could not risk going in; she could not risk being recognized.

KATIE GILLETTE, PREGNANT AND ALONE ON THE STREETS OF MARTHA'S VINEYARD, the headlines might proclaim.

She shuddered as she thought of one headline, years ago, that she'd seen by mistake: JOLEEN A MESS IN MENTAL HOUSE. Her father had told Katie the press was having a "field day" with her mother. The only thing Katie had known about "field days" was when her class at school went to Central Park to run and jump and compete against one another.

Now she wondered if they'd have a field day with her, too, and if they'd proclaim her a mental mess as well.

Keeping her head turned from the window as she slowly passed the restaurant, Katie felt an ache in her belly that she recognized. It was an ache of loneliness; the kind she'd felt as a small child when she was friendless, because how could the daughter of Joleen bring friends home to play?

And then it was not Joleen onstage but Katie, her life becoming a glass storefront like Linda Jean's, where those around her were with people and had lives, but Katie was shut out, on one side or the other.

Eastaways was open. Katie quickly ducked inside the clothing store for distraction. She found herself standing in the children's department, where miniature shirts and pants and overalls hung on tiny hangers, neatly new and crisp.

"May I help you?" a clerk asked.

Katie adjusted her sunglasses. "I'm looking for baby things."

"Over here," the woman said, and Katie traced the woman's steps through racks that had to be too close together because real estate on the island was at such a premium.

When they reached "over here," Katie quickly stopped. "There," she said, "what's that?" She didn't have to ask: She knew a pink-sequin leotard when she saw one. "I'll take it," she said.

The woman looked perplexed. What would an infant do with a pink-sequin leotard? Katie could not, of course, explain that the leotard was for her, that she would dismantle it and use the pink sequins for her journal, an appropriate "souvenir" to symbolize the first part of her life.

In addition to the leotard, Katie picked out a cuddly white blanket and a thick hooded towel and three adorable baby outfits. She could not get over the softness of the things; just touching them to her cheek stirred her excitement and reinforced that her decision had been the right one.

Sí, she thought, I am ready to be a mother.

With or without Miguel.

With or without breast cancer.

As she stood at the register while the clerk rang up the items, Katie noticed a silly purple hat up on a shelf. It had a large, silk gardenia and a wide, floppy brim.

"I'll take the hat, too," she said with a smile. Perhaps it wasn't too late for Katie to make some friends, after all.

"You're crazy," Hannah said with a laugh when she opened her front door and Katie stood there modeling the big purple hat. "Don't you know the kids are home from school today—including my fourteen-year-old daughter who feels a need to mimic you and my eleven-year-old son who wants to marry you?"

Katie groaned. She'd forgotten that her presence often caused quite a stir. She swooped the hat from her head and handed it over. "I know you've been holding out for a grotesque purple hat. I bought other things, too. Baby stuff. Show and tell."

"Baby stuff? Oooh, my favorite things." Hannah laughed again and plunked the hat atop her wig. "Let's go out to the greenhouse. Just let me get my coat."

In the daylight of the greenhouse, Katie could see that Hannah's peachy skin had lost its natural sheen and had dulled like a photograph printed on nonglossy paper. But the wide purple brim helped bring out a small radiance, and Hannah seemed genuinely pleased that Katie had come.

Hannah dragged some crates into a corner and they sat down.

Katie looked around at the flats of leafy greens that

poked through squares of soil. "What a wonderful business," she said. "To always be surrounded by newness and life."

"Ha," Hannah laughed. "It's my husband's business, not mine, and it means I won't see him again until the first frost."

Katie smiled and asked, "You have a happy marriage, don't you?"

"Sometimes," Hannah replied. "Most times."

"Miguel wants to marry me."

"The father of your baby?"

Katie nodded. "I need to think about it after the baby's born. After my radiation's done."

Hannah twirled a new green leaf between her fingers, a geranium, maybe, or a marigold. "What does he think about that?"

"He still doesn't know about the cancer. I need to do this myself."

"Why?" Hannah asked.

Katie stared at her a moment.

"I can understand that you don't want the world to know," Hannah continued, "but your boyfriend?"

"My father knows." As if that made it okay that Miguel did not.

Hannah nodded again.

"I guess I don't want the chaos a wedding would bring. The media. The publicity."

"You'd rather be alone."

"To make my own decisions. Besides, I don't know if I want to marry him."

"Then that's the best reason not to get married."

"Were you sure, Hannah? Were you sure about your husband?"

"Evan? Oh, yes. I was very sure."

The rich greenhouse air was quiet for a moment. "Hannah?" Katie asked. "Am I being selfish?"

"Maybe," Hannah said. "But maybe that's okay. Sometimes being selfish is what helps us to get strong."

Katie thought about Joleen, about how Cliff once said she was the most selfish woman on earth, as if she'd had her breakdown on purpose, just to wreck his life. But had her mother needed to be selfish in order to survive the ordeal that her life had become?

"Katie," Hannah said quietly, "I'm being selfish, too. I've decided to take a medical leave. I've turned my lesson plans over to a substitute."

"Hannah, that's great news, you need to give yourself a break."

"Just as you do. If I've learned one thing, Katie, it's that you need to do what your heart and your head tell you. And don't forget that what's going on right now *is* just right now, and that it will all have changed in a month or two or three. And that will be okay, too."

Katie stopped herself from crying, because this was to be a happy visit. She put a hand on Hannah's arm and said, "You know what, Hannah? I hope I can be half as good as the kind of mother you must be."

"Ha!" Hannah laughed, though Katie hadn't meant it to be humorous. "Come on," the woman continued, "let's see the treasures in those mystery bags. I hope they're as nice as my hat."

What kind of private investigator left a message then went incommunicado for days?

A week had passed since R.J. called with his vague message: *Sorry I missed you.* Except to go to the support group meeting and pick up some food, Faye had not left the house. Even Mouser was getting bored with her presence.

Day Seven since his call, she wrote in her journal, the one outlet she had for staying mildly sane. She had tried escaping through work; she had tried escaping through cleaning the house and going through old photo albums. But it was the journal that kept her focused on her mission and her mind off the cancer. As much as she hated to admit it, Rita had been right.

I'm sitting in Greg's bedroom. It's no longer Greg's bedroom, of course. I wonder why I had no problem changing his room, but I could not touch Dana's. Maybe Greg was right. Maybe I blamed him for her death and I wanted him out of my life and I needed to enshrine her, goddess that I know she definitely was not.

Would I have done that to my own son? Was it truly my fault that he left?

She looked around the room.

Over there, by the window, Greg had hung his posters of swimmers and divers. Of Greg Louganis, his hero.

She rested the end of her pen on her bottom lip. Why had she never asked her son if he was gay? She'd known since he'd been fourteen, since she'd seen him look at a young man on the beach, and somehow it had been as if a comic-book lightbulb had lit up over her head. *Your son is gay,* the lightbulb said.

Why did I never tell Joe? She continued to write. *And why did I never tell Greg that I knew? Would things have been different? Would Dana still be alive?*

"My friend, Bruce, was with us," Greg had said the night of the accident. "We'd gone below deck."

Faye had not asked what Greg and Bruce were doing while Dana was being swept overboard.

Joe had assumed they'd been playing poker, because he

was Greg's father and not the kind of man who would be good at accepting that his son was gay. Unmanly. One of those.

She dropped her pen on the notebook and stared at the last words she'd written. *Would Dana still be alive?* So she did blame Greg for her daughter's death. She did blame him, even though she knew Dana was at fault.

Was it because she had to blame someone?

Had it been easier to blame Greg than Dana—or herself? The woman who, when cheated on, engrossed herself in work and stopped being a mom as well as a wife?

She closed her eyes and pushed down the lump in her throat. She wished with all her might that the phone in the hall would ring, that it would be R.J., and Greg would be on his way home.

But the phone did not ring, and Faye was alone in the silence with the ghosts of her children that lingered in the house, and with the gut-wrenching guilt that sometime between then and now, her son might have died a painful, sad death from AIDS.

"The kids are driving me crazy," Rita confessed to her husband while they lingered over steamers and chowder at The Chart House in Tisbury. Charlie had come home from Nantucket for the weekend, and Hazel offered to baby-sit so they could go out. Rita picked The Chart House because it wasn't in Edgartown where they'd know everyone, not that it much mattered because they'd already seen about a dozen people they knew. It was the Vineyard, after all, and it was still off-season.

"Good," Charlie replied, a lilt to his voice, "it will keep you out of trouble until I come home to build the Women's Center." This time he did not add, "Unless you screw it up."

Instead, he smiled. God, she loved that smile. How was it possible that one pair of turned-up lips and one set of teeth could still make Rita feel all safe and warm and good after how many years?

Forever, of course. Since she'd first accused him on the elementary school playground of looking like Lumpy on *Leave it to Beaver,* and since he'd first said, "Yeah, well, your freckles make you look like Howdy Doody's sister," and she'd gone home in tears that she'd made sure were well-hidden.

"You're a pain in the ass," she said now.

He laughed.

She set down her spoon, then she laughed, too.

He reached across the table and took her hand. "I miss you, too, honey. But this is a big project. It requires both Ben and me to be there. It means a lot to the island."

"The *other* island," she sneered, meaning Nantucket, which might as well have been East Patagonia—where Rita hadn't been, either—because it would have required a boat or a plane to get to, and anything that even hinted of motion made her throw up.

He laughed again. "What's with you tonight?"

He was right, of course. Normally Rita was not one to complain; she was the rock, the one who lived each day with gusto and let no baggage get in her way. Lately, however, she felt a tiny bit off-center. She wondered if it was because of the support group. She wondered if it was because of Faye.

"Do you remember a tragedy that happened several years ago, where a child died here on the island? In an accident or something?"

Charlie looked at her blankly, or not-so-blankly. He could, she realized, have been thinking about Kyle—her Kyle, their Kyle.

"Other than Kyle," she said, and tried to smile a half-smile.

He picked up another steamer, pried open its shell, then rinsed it in clam broth. "I'm sure there have been many tragedies involving kids," he said. "No different than anywhere else." He popped the clam into his mouth. "Why?"

Rita shrugged. "There's a woman in the support group . . . she lost a child more than a decade ago. Something about it . . . about her . . . is bothering me."

Charlie shook his head. "Someday maybe you'll run for mayor of the island," he said with another broad smile. "You get too involved, honey. You need to learn to stay out of other people's problems."

She blinked. "Oh. Right. The way you do. At least I'm only 'involved' with a few women, not half a damn island who doesn't even deserve you."

He wiped his hands on his napkin, then slid them under the table and rested them on Rita's knees. The touch of his fingers made her shiver and smile at the same time. "Charlie Rollins," she said, "you're flirting with me."

He pressed his palms into her knees. "Yeah," he said. "And after dinner I'm going to drive you down to Menemsha and we're going to park by an isolated beach and I'm going to make love to you in the backseat."

It wouldn't be the first time. With a houseful of kids and a mother to boot, Charlie had swept his wife up-island more than once. Rita smiled and finished her chowder, grateful that he'd traded in the old Toyota for the minivan that had all that room in back.

THIRTEEN

Faye's phone rang at nine-forty-five. Her eyelids sprang open in a synchronized spring; her heart found its way to her throat. She was still on Greg's bed; she had fallen asleep.

Ring.

She bolted from the bed.

"Don't you dare hang up," she shouted and skidded on the hardwood floor into the hall. She grabbed the receiver just before the machine would click on.

"R.J.," she panted. It was hard to get a breath with one's heart up in one's throat.

Instead of R.J.'s hello, she heard a short pause, then, "Faye? Is this Faye Randolph?"

It was a man, but did not sound like R.J.

"Who is this?" The question was edged with quick annoyance.

"We've never met, Faye. We should have, but didn't." There was a light laugh. "It's Adam Dexter from Nashua. Your sister's friend."

The pulse-pounding she'd felt earlier now moved to her temples. "Yes," she replied. "I know who you are." She supposed she should apologize for standing him up, but right now she was angry that he'd invaded her privacy, that he'd jolted her from sleep, that Claire obviously had given him her phone number.

She was angry he was not R.J.

"Well," he said in the awkward airtime that followed. "I'm calling because I have business this Tuesday in Falmouth. I thought we might get together for dinner. Or lunch."

"Falmouth is on the Cape."

"Yes. I could take a ferry.

"I doubt you'll get a reservation this late."

"I could take the passenger ferry. We could meet in Oak Bluffs." Pause. "If you want."

For all of her flightiness, Claire meant well. Faye did not doubt that her sister was concerned, that her efforts to connect Faye to a man were for what she deemed the "right" reasons. With a small sigh that Faye hoped Adam did not hear, she said, "There's a restaurant called Seasons, up on the hill. They make a great lobster roll." If R.J. called in the meantime, she could only hope there would not be a conflict.

They agreed to meet at one o'clock. He said he'd be wearing a blue windbreaker and Carrera sunglasses.

Faye returned to Greg's bed, but did not sleep most of what was left of the night.

Katie had said she hoped she'd turn out to be half the mother Hannah was, which was what sparked Hannah into getting up Sunday morning, making thick cinnamon French toast with powdered sugar and homemade strawberry jam, and planning a family day that even Riley might not protest.

"Let's go to the mall in Hyannis," she exclaimed as she passed the jam crock to Evan. Casey and Denise shouted "Yea!" and "Yes!" and "Cool!" Riley almost smiled. Evan seemed stunned.

"I don't know, honey. I'm so far behind with work . . ."

"It's only one day," she said, but he shook his head.

"Sorry. I really have to get the flats ready for the bank." He had a lucrative contract to provide the flowers and shrubs for all six branches of Island Federal Bank, a generous customer that paid in thirty days.

But Hannah didn't care about money right now. She hated to play her trump card, but saw no other choice. "We need a day together, Evan. And I need to forget about this stupid breast cancer and have a good time with my family."

He did not reply, because what could he say?

"Four against one," Casey interjected. "You lose, Dad."

"It's Sunday," Evan remarked, albeit feebly, "we won't get across."

Hannah smiled. "Bill Langforth works at the docks on Sunday. I've already made a call."

"Please, Daddy?" Denise pleaded, her little pink cheeks dusted in white powder.

"Yeah, Dad, let's go," Riley added, and Hannah folded her arms and decided that if she'd managed to win Riley's approval, she must be a better mother than she thought, after all.

They held hands: Hannah and Evan, Evan and Denise, Hannah and Casey. Not Riley, of course, but nothing was perfect.

They ate whole-belly fried clams and French fries and cole slaw off paper plates at a restaurant by the water. They laughed at Casey's bad imitation of the grumpy, middle-aged waiter who must have—they decided—forfeited a life spent at sea, to marry the boss's daughter, who insisted he serve fish, not catch it.

They spent an hour at the arcade in the mall, while Riley happily went off on her own with a grin on her face and two twenties in her pocket. Evan had provided the money; no sense in her spending what she had earned baby-sitting.

They bought new sneakers for Casey and a backpack for Denise and ice cream cones for all of them. At five o'clock they walked to the fountain where they'd agreed to meet Riley. Surprisingly, she was already there, with a pile of bags and a Cheshire-cat grin.

"Well," Hannah said, "looks like forty dollars can go a long way."

"Sales," Riley said, then opened a bag. "Look. Is this awesome or what?" She pulled out a tank top that surely would cling. It was black and had rhinestones that spelled "vamp." Hannah did not know that Riley's generation had ever heard of that word.

"Well," Hannah said brightly.

Another bag produced a similar top, that one in turquoise with glitter reading "too cool."

"Well," Hannah repeated, and Evan—hooray!—came to her rescue by jokingly saying, "Be careful, Riley. Your friends will want to take them from you."

"No chance," Riley said, then produced three pairs of large, dangling earrings and two velvet chokers.

"Wonderful, honey," Hannah said, to which Riley made no comment but seemed content enough.

Casey insisted they stop for miniature golf—Evan got stuck under a lighthouse, Hannah, at the windmill—and they made it to the ferry just after sunset.

Crossing Vineyard Sound, the waters were calm and the family was tired. Sitting next to her mother, Riley dozed, then slowly rested her head against Hannah's shoulder.

And Hannah smiled.

And then Hannah realized that not once the whole day had she thought about breast cancer or chemo. Well, not hardly once, anyway.

"I'm meeting him for lunch tomorrow," Faye said at the meeting Monday night. "At Seasons."

"A date," Hannah said. "Well, that's exciting."

"What are you wearing?" Katie asked.

"Oh, it doesn't matter."

Rita watched the women as they sat in their circle. She suspected it *did* matter to Faye what she wore, but that the woman was too upper-crust to admit it.

"The truth is," Faye continued, "I'd rather not go. I don't want a man in my life at the moment. I have a few other things to deal with right now."

"If you wait for the right time, it will never come," Hannah said.

"She's right," Katie added. "What's he like, anyway?"

"He's a friend of my sister's. Which is part of the problem." Her long fingers knitted themselves into one another. "I doubt that he's really my type."

Rita glanced from Hannah to Katie, who seemed to have bonded with an unspoken purpose: to convince Faye that Adam Dexter might answer all feminine prayers.

"Is he rich?" Hannah asked.

"Is he cute?" came from Katie.

"Does he believe in generosity to worthwhile causes?" Rita popped out with, because the Women's Wellness

Center could always use another benefactor, especially one with a name.

"Stop it, all of you!" Faye cried good-naturedly. "I only agreed to meet him because my sister is so angry with me. And I only told you because, well, because I don't know why. Maybe to prove there is life after breast cancer."

"We already knew that," Hannah replied. "What we still don't know is what you're going to wear."

Faye was right, Adam Dexter was clearly not her type. He wore a yellowed, white shirt and outdated blue tie, had nondescript eyes and nondescript, receding hair, and his teeth seemed too big for his mouth. He was a purveyor of superior (according to him) software systems for the marine industry, he supervised seventy-eight others like him at ports throughout the world, and, if he had a lot of money, Faye surmised he kept it to himself.

She ate half of her lobster roll and hoped he would have to leave soon, when he asked, "So. What's it like to have cancer?"

Just as she considered throwing her plate at his face, Faye was distracted by a small commotion at the front door. In walked three women: one wore a lime turban with synthetic blond curls, one had on a black wig that looked like Cleopatra's, and one sported a huge purple hat with a plump white gardenia parked on its brim.

"Table for three," the one in the lime turban loudly announced, "and make it snappy. We're starving." She flashed what appeared to be a ten dollar bill. As she waved her arm, her hand caught the edge of the turban, tipping it to one side and revealing a clump of red curls underneath.

Faye did a quick double take, then sucked in her cheeks

as the women pranced past her table and made themselves at home behind three potted plants.

The purple-brimmed woman peeked through palm fronds and stared straight at Faye. "Don't you just hate it when you have to wait for a table?" The palm fronds snapped shut and Faye suppressed a wide smile.

She turned back to her date. "Actually," she said, "having cancer is remarkable. It opens up your world to wonderful, loving people you otherwise would not have known."

She returned to her lobster roll and ate it with gusto, while, from the other side of the plants, she heard the three zany women order their lunches.

Dear Diary, Katie began, as she sat on the sunroom later that afternoon, with tea and one of the scones Faye had baked. It had been Rita's idea to surprise Faye at lunch, to bring some laughter into her life. "All in good fun," Rita had said, and from the look on Faye's face, Rita had been right.

Katie had gone home happy as well, and was inspired to work on her journal. Among her Saturday purchases was a special, spiral-bound journal. It had a cloth cover that had a picture of what looked like the lighthouse in West Chop, though the book was made in China.

On the first page Katie pasted a half-dozen pink sequins. She decided she would not include any of Joleen's music: This project was her own, not another reenactment of her mother's muse. There had already been too much of that in Katie's life.

Dear Diary, she reread, as if the words somehow would help her put her priorities together and ease the longing for Miguel.

She *tap-tapped* the ballpoint on the edge of the notebook and looked out the window and down to the sea. The spring snow was gone now, leaving behind the startled purple and yellow heads of a few crocus clusters out on the lawn. She looked across the grass, past the tangles of beach roses waiting to burst forth with their fragile blossoms—all pink and white and wrinkled from salt spray, yet heartier and healthier than their petals would appear.

One summer Katie and Joleen had gathered beach roses and together they made rose hips—nature's vitamin C.

"Prevents the scurvy, you know," her father had cackled and her mother had laughed and her father placed a blossom over one eye like a patch. "Ho, ho, ho in a bottle of rum," he chanted, and they pretended they were the pirates from the legend of two hundred years ago; pirates who chewed the rose hips, then spit the seeds overboard and watched them wash up on the beaches of the Vineyard, where, against all odds of the harsh sea, they took hold and flowered and propagated, whatever the heck that meant.

Katie rested her hand on her stomach. She prayed that, like the beach roses, her baby would be healthier than its small size might suggest.

Inside the kitchen, the phone suddenly rang. The ring was loud and unfamiliar. She looked toward the studio where her mother worked, but, working or not, Joleen would not answer the phone.

The phone rang again.

Katie pulled herself up and went to the counter where the answering machine was. If she didn't pick up the receiver, would that mean she truly had become Joleen?

On the fourth ring the machine kicked on. Katie stood first on one foot, then on the other. The machine clicked, reversed, then clicked again. Then there was a voice, a familiar voice.

"Katie," the voice said. "Katie, this is Brady. I hope you're there. We need to talk."

Brady? She was not surprised that he'd tracked her down; she felt a splash of guilt that she'd not phoned him to say she was safe.

"Katie," he continued. "Oh, Katie. Please call me. There's been an accident."

FOURTEEN

An accident?

She grabbed the receiver. "Brady?"

A sliver of silence slipped through the line. An accident. Oh, God, was it her father? Was it Miguel?

"Katie," Brady replied. She braced herself against the counter. Tears sprang to her eyes.

"It's Ina," he said. "Oh, Katie, Ina was killed late last night. Stabbed by a mugger a block from her apartment."

Ina?

He paused.

She paused.

"She's dead," he said.

Katie did not hear herself scream. It must have been someone else, because she was not a screamer; Katie Gillette was too sensible to scream.

It might not have been her, but somebody screamed. She dropped the receiver and stood, staring, as Joleen rushed in from the studio and retrieved the phone receiver. Then she turned her back to Katie and spoke into the phone in tones that were hushed.

Uh-huh.

I see.

Oh, dear.

After a moment Joleen hung up. She gently helped Katie onto a chair.

"It's okay, it's okay," Joleen said over and over as if Katie hadn't heard her the first time.

She shook her head. "No," she heard herself say. "It's not possible."

Joleen sat next to her and pulled her chair close. She took Katie's hands and rubbed them with hers. "It happened very fast," Joleen reported. "She was on her way home from your father's. She had taken the bus."

Katie frowned. "She couldn't have been at Daddy's," she said. "He has a different housekeeper now. Ina worked for me, not him. She must have been at Miguel's. He lives in a small apartment downstairs in our building. He wanted to be close to me. He said that when we got married we could live there if I wanted. It's small, but I like it there. It has a nice fireplace . . ." She knew she was rambling, but as long as Katie talked, she did not have to think about the phone call or its message.

Ina?

Dead?

Joleen moved closer and wrapped her arms around Katie. It was an awkward hug, years delayed in coming, but it was a mother's hug, nonetheless. "Ina was at your father's," Joleen repeated. Her words were tedious in the slow-motion air, her voice was hesitant as if she, too, were crying.

"Why was she at Daddy's?" Katie asked. "Ina knows I'm here."

And then Joleen's moist eyes flashed away—out toward the backyard that sat in the sunshine, where the beach roses waited to turn to pink and then red, to turn to vitamin C that was so perfect for the scurvy. And then she asked, "Didn't you know? For years, Ina Enriquez has been your father's mistress. I thought everyone knew. It was the reason I left."

Her mother brewed more tea, but Katie could not drink it. She sat, helpless, on the chair, wondering why she could not reach Miguel, wondering why he had not called her himself. *He's angry with me,* she realized. *He's angry because I would not let him stay.*

But his mother is dead.

His mother was my father's mistress.

My father's mistress?

She held her arms around her baby-belly and rocked back and forth. Lunch with Rita and Hannah seemed a lifetime ago. A lifetime—Ina's lifetime. How could Katie have laughed and had such a good time when Ina was already dead?

By dusk, neither Katie's father nor Miguel had called. Katie could no longer stand it. Against Joleen's advice, she phoned the apartment, the apartment bought and paid for with the profits of Joleen's "Goin' Home," the apartment maintained with Katie's voice and Katie's flash—as directed by her father.

Brady answered.

"I don't care what he's doing, I need to talk to my father."

"He's, ah, he's taking care of the funeral arrangements," Brady replied.

"I don't care if he's embalming the body. For Christ's sakes, Brady, let me talk to him."

She had not spoken to her father since she'd packed her suitcases and informed him she was going to the Vineyard.

Cliff had said, "I can't believe you'd rather be with her."

She'd thought of a million responses after she had left, but at the time all she said was, "Daddy, I'm sorry, but this is what I have to do."

He'd put on his favorite black jacket and gone out of the apartment so he would be the one who'd left her, not the other way around.

She wondered now if he had gone to Ina, if all those other times he'd gone to Ina, too.

He picked up the phone. He sounded tired. "Brady shouldn't have called you."

"Brady is my friend," she said. "He knew I should know. Ina was my assistant, Daddy. She was my baby's *grand-mother*."

Cliff did not reply.

"I'm coming to the funeral," Katie said.

"Absolutely not." Though Cliff needed to be in control, his words were rarely sharp-edged. This time they were. "The last thing we need is scandal. We do not need you to show up in public, pregnant."

She could have said that at least breast cancer was not so obvious, but now was not the time. She could have said that the world would know in a few weeks anyway, so what was the harm? She could have said those things, but all Katie could think of was that Ina had been his mistress, and it had cost their family. She bit her lip. "If you were so worried about scandal, you shouldn't have been screwing Ina all these years."

He did not deny the accusation. Her insides knotted up. "Is that why you said I couldn't trust Miguel? Or that I couldn't trust Ina? Was it because you were afraid I'd learn your dirty secret? Or didn't you think Ina was that important, in which case it might make me even angrier?"

Cliff said he would speak with her later when the shock had worn off and when she could be reasonable.

Reasonable? Was it unreasonable to expect that certain people—like your father—would not do certain things behind your back? Was it unreasonable to expect that certain people—like your father—would not deceive certain others—like your mother—then try to cover it up as if your mother had been the crazed one, as if your mother had been the loser?

Miguel must be at Ina's, where the neighbors would have gathered, where friends would have convened.

She slammed down the receiver, then dialed Ina's number. She did not know if her heart was pounding from rage at her father, vengeance for her mother, or out of both anger at and grief for Ina, the woman she'd loved, too.

A woman answered. She spoke in Spanish.

"Miguel," Katie pleaded. "*Por favor.* I need Miguel."

The phone was set down; Katie could hear talking, low murmurs of voices hushed by anguished shock.

Finally, he said, "Hello?"

"Miguel," she said, then her tears flowed openly. She forgot about her father; she forgot about her mother. "Oh, God, Miguel, what happened? Why didn't you call? Are you all right?"

He did not speak right away, then he said, "She never listened. She never listened and took a taxi. Why wouldn't she listen?"

He cried.

She cried.

"I'll be there," she said. "I'll leave the island today."

"No," he said. "It is not a good idea."

Katie blinked. "Don't be silly, Miguel. I will be there for you. I . . . I loved her, too."

The volume of low voices seemed to have been turned up. "No," he said again. "My mother would not want such craziness. We will do this quietly. It's bad enough the police already know who my mother was."

"That she was my assistant?"

"That she was your father's whore."

Maybe she'd heard him wrong. Maybe he hadn't said the words that had gone straight to her wounded heart. But the silence that followed told Katie that yes, he'd said it. "Miguel," Katie replied, "I didn't know about them."

He laughed a short snort. "Isn't it ironic? I guess the Puerto Ricans are only good enough to sleep with, but not good enough to marry."

"Miguel, that isn't true . . ."

"Forget it. I've known for a long time. I tried to stop it years ago, but then we met and I figured, what the hell."

She did not know what he meant by that, and she did not want to ask. She bit her lip again; she felt her cheeks grow warm.

"Anyway, I guess my mother loved him, stupid that she was. He's making the funeral arrangements because he said she would have wanted that and I'm not going to argue. Let him pay for it, why should I?"

If he expected an answer to that question, Katie did not offer one.

"It's going to be a private funeral. No one but family, a few close friends, and him."

"I am family. I'll be there."

"No."

"But . . ." She hesitated. "Don't you want me there?"

"I want you where you are," he said. "I want you safe from the media and safe from this asshole world."

She hung up the phone, stared at her mother, and said with clear conviction, "This is total bullshit."

"I don't know what to do," the woman who had once been larger-than-life now said to Rita, who'd never been anything except a small-town island girl with a small-town, island life. It was after seven in the evening and the twins needed a bath. Hazel was in the living room, fixated on a rerun of *The Golden Girls*. Mindy was at the church youth group, hopefully behaving better than Rita had behaved when she'd been in junior high and had learned that some things like smoking and boys were more fun than scriptures and verse.

"She stormed around the house all day. I tried to talk to her, but she said she had to think. Instead of eating supper, she packed her suitcase. Now she says she's going to call a taxi if I won't bring her to the airport."

Rita wished she knew Katie better. Sometimes it was still hard to separate the sweet, soft-spoken girl from the tawdry icon on Mindy's bedroom wall. "Are you going to take her?"

"What else can I do? I told her I'd check the flights. Instead, I'm calling you. Please help me, Rita. I'm so afraid this will hurt the baby. I'm so afraid it will make the cancer . . . well, that it will somehow make it worse."

Rita had no idea if it would or not. She was still trying to digest all that Joleen had told her, that the grandmother of Katie's baby had been mugged and now was dead; that Katie wanted to attend the funeral; that she'd been told not to, but would not comply. In Katie's sequined sneakers, Rita would most likely have reacted the same way.

Rita closed her eyes and wondered if all women were so stubborn and if that's what made them strong.

"I have an idea," she said quickly, glancing at the twins

who were at her feet, busily emptying a cabinet of large pots and pans, and thanking God that her own life had taken a huge turn for the better. "Tell her that you'll bring her. But don't go to the airport. Meet me at the hospital in the Emergency Room." If anything happened to Katie, Rita thought it would be best if they were where she could get help. "I'll try to reach the others from the support group," she added. "Maybe together we can convince her to stay here."

"Should I call the doctor?"

"Doc plays poker at the Hall Tuesday nights." Some things a Vineyarder just knew, like the ferry schedules and the tide times and the way to shuck a clam. "I'll call him if you want."

"It's up to you," Joleen replied. "Can we meet in half an hour?"

Rita hung up the phone and wondered if she'd ever learn not to get involved. She glanced at her watch; she must call Hannah. Then Rita remembered she didn't have Faye's number; she couldn't look it up, because she didn't even know the woman's last name.

Rita asked Hannah to please let Faye know. After the crisis, she'd ask Hannah for Faye's number. Surely someone at the phone company would trace it for a last name and an address. Then Rita might learn once and for all what had happened to Faye's child and maybe why the woman seemed so hauntingly familiar. Maybe she'd even find out if Faye was their benefactor, not that it should matter, but, after all, Rita was nosy, so of course it did.

In the meantime, Joleen rushed Katie into the Emergency Room, both clad in sunglasses though it was now after dark, both wearing wide-brimmed straw hats way ahead of season. Rita and Hannah stood up to greet them; Faye had not yet arrived.

Katie looked surprised to see them. Rita shushed her and steered them to a small conference room that was square and airless. It occurred to her that this was a place where bad news was delivered: *I'm sorry, Mr. and Mrs. Jones, but your son has been eaten by a shark or killed in a car accident . . . or . . . or I'm sorry, Mrs. Faye Blank, but your child has been . . . what?*

Rita pushed away her thoughts and hugged Katie Gillette. "I'm so sorry," she whispered, then hoped it wasn't her words that made Katie cry. Hannah cried, too, then took her turn hugging the girl. Joleen stood in the corner, hand to her mouth, an observer in a tableau of the comforting of grief. She removed her sunglasses: Rita was not surprised the woman looked like shit. Superstar of the seventies and eighties, now no different from them.

They sat down. Then in walked Faye, who looked as if she'd just stepped off the pages of a catalog for the well-groomed woman over fifty. Rita was struck by the odd thought that though Faye was not much older than she was, somehow she seemed so much more mature.

Sophisticated, Hazel probably would say.

Snob, Rita would have added, though the woman had seemed to enjoy their unexpected luncheon spoof.

Katie wiped her tears. "My mother said we had to stop so Doc could give me tranquilizers before I go to New York."

"Your mother lied," Rita said. She folded her hands on the table and leaned close to Katie. "We're going to help you through this, Katie, but we don't think you should do it by going to New York."

Katie blinked. "But you don't know what's happened."

Hannah spoke next. "We know Miguel's mother was horribly killed. And we know other things: that the media thinks you're recuperating from fatigue, that you're at an unknown location, resting your body and your beautiful voice."

Katie just stared from one to the next.

Faye stepped toward the table. "Sometimes it's best to let sleeping dogs lie." Rita wondered what Faye's dogs must have been and how hard it had been for her to let them do that.

Katie turned to Joleen. "You brought me here for this?" she asked. "So they could talk me out of going?" She stood up and put her hand on her belly. "Thanks for your concern, but no thanks on the advice." She looked back at her mother. "Are you going to take me to the airport or must I call a cab?"

Just then, Doc appeared in the doorway. "No one's going anywhere," he said with authority. "The winds have kicked up and the flights are cancelled."

Collective sighs sighed around the room, except from Katie who stood, tense.

"Which does not," Doc continued, "mean that Katie can't go in the morning. In fact, I recommend it. Grief is usually unhealthy until it's faced."

The women remained silent; Katie said, "Thanks, Doc."

He held up his hand. "Which is not to say that you should make the trip alone." He looked toward Joleen. "If you don't feel up to it, then I suggest someone else accompanies Katie." His eyes scanned the small room. "Support groups are successful because they find strength in numbers."

Which must be why today nobody pees without one, Rita thought.

FIFTEEN

Rita had offered to drive the minivan, but Faye had insisted on the Mercedes. It wasn't like Rita not to take control, but in order to avoid rocking the precarious boat, she'd agreed. All she had to do now was make it across.

She smiled as she looked toward Cape Cod on the horizon and knew that she would, after all, do just about anything not to rock any boat that she was on: despite being a Vineyard girl, Rita could get hopelessly seasick even on a clear day like this one, even when the waters were calm. She wasn't much better when sent aloft in a plane. Both of those things accounted for the fact that she'd only been off-island a few times in her life, and then only when under duress—when she was pregnant with Kyle; when Hazel was living in Florida and insisted Rita visit, *just once, Rita Mae*; when Jill was in England and needed her.

What Rita could not do for herself, she could manage for others, which was why she now stood on the deck of the old workhorse, *The Islander*, counting down the journey's forty-five-minute trek.

"It's such a beautiful day," Hannah said from beside her, the hair of her blond wig catching the light breeze. Earlier, she'd quietly remarked to Rita that it was a shame the occasion was too somber for her purple hat, that she loved the way people looked at her and smiled when she had it on. "It's great to be on the water on such a sunshiny day."

As much as Rita agonized over large, rocking vehicles, she was even more uncomfortable when perky people rode them. "Oh, it's a blast," she replied, then looked at Hannah and realized that, though it might be a "sunshiny" day, the woman's skin was sort of gray. Of the three breast-cancer patients, Hannah was the one Doc suggested should stay home. "Nonsense," Hannah protested. "We're sticking together. That's what real friends are for."

Friends? Was that what they'd become? And did that include Rita, though she was cancer-free? She decided that it did. "I'm going, too," Rita had proclaimed, and so there she was, hoping she didn't look as sickly as Hannah surely felt.

"Are you okay?" Rita asked, because how could she not?

Hannah said yes and seemed to mean it. "I'm excited, though. I've never been to New York City."

"You're kidding," Rita said. "Well, neither have I." She didn't know much about Hannah, other than that she was a teacher and hadn't grown up on the island or Rita would have known her or her family or some friend of a friend. With less than fifteen thousand year-rounders on the entire Vineyard, sooner or later one got to know everyone, or at least someone who did.

"I'll bet my daughter would love to see the city," Hannah said with a short laugh. "She wants to be an actress. I'm not sure how much to encourage her or how much to protect her."

"How old is she?"

"Fourteen."

"Tough age."

"No easier than twelve." She gave a soft smile. "Mindy's in my science class."

Rita looked back toward land, toward Nobska Light that inched too-slowly closer. She wondered how much Hannah knew about Mindy other than that Rita and Charlie were now her legal guardians.

"She's a nice girl, Rita. Very bright."

Rita nodded. "We adore her." She didn't say it because Hannah was her teacher; she said it because it was true.

"Well, I used to adore my daughter, too. Lately it hasn't been easy to please her."

"It must be her age," Rita said. "My mother didn't say anything right until I was over thirty." *Mothers*, she thought. *Daughters*. Had Faye lost a daughter? Rita had almost inquired the day before at their lunch, but the mood was too light to darken with sorrow. "Hannah," she asked now, "has Faye told you about her child? The one she lost?"

Hannah shrugged. "No. I get the feeling it's hard for her to talk about. I think more than the cancer, it makes her really sad."

Sad? Yes, Rita knew what that was.

"I think I'll check up on our patients," Hannah added, turning from the rail. Faye and Katie had stayed below deck: Katie masked in sunglasses and an auburn wig from the patient services department. "Are you coming?"

Rita glanced back toward the lighthouse. *Close enough*, she supposed, that she could take the risk. She sucked in her breath and followed Hannah across the deck and down the wet, iron stairs. Then, right there in the doorway, Rita was gripped by haunting déjà vu—an unsettling sensation that she had been there before, that she had done this, that it had not been a good thing. It was a sensation far worse than any possible seasickness.

. . . .

The years washed away like high tide on a beach. The scene that remained was frozen in Rita's mind's eye, an unwanted frame from an unforgiving time machine. Rita had stood there, right in that place where she stood now. Faye had been sitting on a bench, her aristocratic nose buried in a book.

"I'm not feeling well and I have to sit down," Rita had said to the boy seated next to Faye, whose first name Rita hadn't known back then. She had only known that the woman was Joe Geissel's wife, and that Rita had spent the summer screwing Mrs. Geissel's horny husband with high hopes for a hefty commission.

Oh, God, Rita thought now, as she slumped against the wall. *So that was why Faye was so familiar. Her hair had not been gray back then but . . .*

Rita could not move; the blow immobilized her. Her mind flashed back to that summer she and Kyle were in trouble, when she'd have done anything to stay financially afloat. Joe Geissel and his wife owned prime property in West Chop; the Internal Revenue Service was hot after Rita's real estate firm. It had not mattered that Joe was married. It had not mattered that he was a cigar-smoking, Boston Irishman of dubious morals, because Rita's hadn't been so great back then, either.

But now it was years later and there she was, the scorned other woman once again on a ferry with the wife of her former lover, this time not as an adversary, but as a friend.

A friend?

Oh, God.

Her stomach lurched. *The child,* she thought. Had Joe lost a child? Had he told Rita? No. There had been no children around, no signs of any children. And if he'd said they had lost one, she would have remembered.

Hannah was smiling and motioning for Rita to go to where they sat.

How could she? Could Rita pretend not to know who Faye was? Could she still lead the group while secretly knowing the inside-out of Faye's husband, from his scent to his sound to the size of his, God help her, dick?

And, worst of all, did Faye know who Rita was? Had she known that first night of the group? Was that why she'd walked out?

"I'll meet you at the car," Rita called to Hannah. "We're almost to Woods Hole." On shaky, uncertain legs, she managed to pry herself from the wall and descend the next flight of stairs, down to the boat's bowels, where, with some luck, she might be asphyxiated by the carbon monoxide of the sardined cars and trucks before the big ferry hit land.

Right now death would come as a relief, Hannah thought. She had taken her antinausea medication, had stayed away from anything chocolate, which had been making her sick, and had done her darndest to stay out of Riley's way before leaving home that morning. Still, as they climbed into Faye's car and waited out the last push to the pier, she was feeling bad enough to consider not going.

Katie would, after all, be fine without her. The girl did not need an entourage to attend a funeral.

Hannah sat in the back beside Rita, who had left the door open on her side.

"Listen," Rita said, with one foot in the car, the other plunked outside on the gray-painted concrete floor of the boat. "I've been thinking that you really don't need all of us, Katie. Too many people will only cause more chaos. It would be better if I stayed behind."

The boat swayed a little in the wake of the tide. "Oh," Katie said. Just *Oh*, nothing more.

"It's not that I don't want to go," Rita continued, "but we make a rather obvious group . . . four women, one pregnant, two country-bumpkins . . ." If she was trying to make a joke, nobody laughed. Instead, Katie started to cry.

"Oh, God, I'm sorry," Rita said quietly, "but the truth is, I'm not very good on city-soil. Out of my element." She rubbed her hands together and nodded her head, agreeing with herself, though no one else was. "Faye, would you mind popping the trunk so I can get my suitcase?"

Faye, however, stared straight ahead and did not pop the trunk, and all Hannah could think of was that now there was no way that she could get out, too. She clutched the door handle and wished she could be more outspoken like Rita and not always the one who ended up doing things she rather would not.

"Get back in the car," Faye suddenly said. "We're in this together, Rita, like it or not."

The big engines were cut; they sat there in silence. Then Rita pulled her other leg into the car and firmly closed the door. "You're right, Faye. I'm sorry. Of course, we'll all go."

The boat bumped the pier and the large cavity opened, and Faye started the Mercedes as they waited their turn to get off.

After a long and fairly silent road trip from the ferry, they finally reached The Paramount, an art deco hotel in Times Square where Faye had made reservations. Though far south from the neighborhood where Ina lived, the hotel was small and comfortable, a respite from the noisy havens of business travelers, according to Faye, and who would argue with her?

Hannah seemed astonished that the hotel didn't have a sign; little, however, surprised Rita anymore, including that Katie did not know where the service would be held.

"I'll call some funeral homes," Faye announced when they checked in.

Rita thought for a moment, then said, "I think I know a faster way."

Faye scooped her credit card off the registration desk. "Then by all means, be my guest," she said, and Rita was happy to oblige.

They registered for two rooms: Rita and Hannah in one room, Faye and Katie in the other. Rita was grateful that a wall would separate the scorner from the scornee.

Once inside, Hannah said she'd like to rest; Rita found the phone and went to work.

It only took a minute to reach the Vineyard's Sheriff Hugh Talbott on his cell phone.

"I need the name of a good Manhattan cop," Rita said to Hugh. "Someone who might know about a murder downtown."

"What are you into, Rita? Does Charlie know about this?"

She smiled. "Just looking for the funeral of a friend of a friend."

Hugh made a sound that was neither a laugh nor a sigh. "Sam Oliver," he said. "I don't know his number, but he works out of Brooklyn." He explained that Sam had ties to the Atkinson girls from the Vineyard, did Rita know them?

"No," she said, "not really."

"Well, if you hit a dead end, feel free to call back. Maybe one of the Atkinsons knows how to find him."

She thanked him and did not add that the last thing she wanted was one of those rich girls involved in her life. She already had Faye, and that was one too many highbrows in her middle-class book. She told Hugh she owed him a batch of her fudge, her famous penuche that was renowned on the island.

Captain Sam Oliver was not difficult to locate.

"The woman was killed by a mugger late Monday night," Rita told him after mentioning that his name had been given to her by a friend of the Atkinsons, because, after all, it never hurt to drop names. "It happened in Washington Heights. Her name was Ina Enriquez."

Captain Oliver said to sit tight, that he'd call her back.

She sat on the bed, waiting, trying not to think about Faye in the next room, or how Rita would get through the next couple of days, pretending nothing had changed, that her past hadn't finally come full, ugly circle as she'd always feared it would.

She could have used a few acting lessons from Hannah's daughter, but she should have thought of that sooner. She could have dyed her hair, but it was too late for that, too. She could dream up a story about a twin sister who'd been sent off-island to mend her errant ways. She could have, should have, would have.

Thank God the phone rang before she made herself insane.

"Mason-Allen is the home in charge of arrangements," Sam Oliver said. "West Seventy-ninth and Eighth Avenue. The service is tomorrow morning at eleven."

Rita hung up and made another mental note to send a batch of penuche to Captain Oliver, too.

. . .

They met on the mezzanine at seven o'clock for dinner. Katie said she was afraid to call her father. "If he knows I'm here, he'll be furious."

Hannah wanted to offer some advice, to help, but she was hardly an expert when it came to men, fathers or otherwise. So she sat back and listened, glad she had napped and now felt much better, glad she had a semblance of an appetite and could enjoy the fruit-and-veggie plate Faye had ordered for them.

Katie nibbled on a strawberry. Her wig looked as foreign and phony as perhaps Hannah's did. The only consolation was the dimness of the lights, which also helped soften the fact that Hannah wore turquoise while the others all wore black, as if it were a secret credo of the city that Hannah had not known.

"My father has always had to be the one who's in control," Katie continued.

Hannah's father hadn't been like that. Her mother had been the one . . . especially after Daddy died . . . Hannah tried to think of something else, but she could only picture Betty Barnes with that jet-black hair like Riley's.

"It turns out my father and Ina were having an affair for years," Katie was saying. "He deceived me as much as he deceived my mother."

"Well," Rita said, "that must piss you off."

"All I can think about right now is getting through tomorrow. No matter what Ina did, she was my assistant, she was Miguel's mother, and for a long time she was more like a mother to me than the one that I had."

"Which is why we'll go to the service," Faye said. "It's in a funeral home, so chances are they won't throw us out."

They ate a small meal in trepidated silence. Hannah

wondered if the others, too, were trying to think of something pleasant and fun to say and if, like her, they simply could not.

After dinner Faye suggested a walk along Broadway.

"The lights of Broadway," Hannah said. "Wouldn't my Riley be *wicked* excited."

They had all laughed at that—well, at least a little—then they went outside into the night air. But on the yellow-cab-lined street, they hadn't walked more than a block under the dazzling, amber-red-orange glow when Hannah stopped on the sidewalk and let out a startled yelp.

Ten stories up, between two huge billboards—one proclaiming that Pierce Brosnan's choice of a watch was an Omega, the other promoting *The Phantom of the Opera* and *Les Misérables*—Katie's image flashed down in radiant, pink-sequined splendor.

JULY 4TH, the poster promised. CENTRAL PARK.

Katie came to a halt beside Hannah and followed her gaze with her eyes. Then the girl quickly turned and darted through a walkway that led to an entrance of the Marriott Marquis.

"Oh, God," Katie said after they'd scurried after her into the lobby and rode up the glass elevator to the lounge on the eighth floor. "This is way too real. Look at me. How can I do that concert? Even if the baby does come early or on time, how can I possibly prepare? What about the cancer?"

Hannah, for one, could not offer a solution.

They sat by the bank of convex windows overlooking Broadway, overlooking the enormous image of Katie in pink, complete with the rhinestone tattoo of a rose on her left cheek.

"My father's in denial. And I've been right there beside

him." No one responded right away. Katie looked around the table and said, "My world's unraveling. What am I going to do?"

"Tell the truth," Faye said. "Tell him it's impossible."

Katie picked up the small, paper sign that had been tented on the table, a picture of a frothy beer on one side, a wine list on the other. She folded up the edges into a nervous accordion.

"You can always run away," Rita said and ordered a rum and Coke, easy on the ice.

"Running away never solved a thing," Faye responded.

Hannah looked back at the gazillion bright lights. How many times had she seen this image of Times Square on *The Today Show* and *Letterman* and *Good Morning, America*? How many New Years' Eves had she watched the ball drop right there in that very place where the Cup o' Noodles sign stood steaming even now?

She thought about Riley, about her dreams of becoming an actress. Would Hannah have the courage to help her make them come true? Even if it meant that Riley would have to leave the safe harbor of the island?

"I disagree with Faye," Hannah said suddenly. "Sometimes running away can solve everything. I ran away. It changed my life."

The waitress returned and set down their drinks. Hannah took a sip of her Kiss Me Kate, a strawberry-colored fruit drink that contained no alcohol. She didn't know how alcohol would mix with chemo, and besides, she'd always preferred whipped cream to scotch, anyway.

And then she told them. Without even an ounce of liquor to loosen up her tongue, Hannah Barnes Jackson told them about how she'd grown up in Texas, the daughter of a cattle-rancher and a social-climbing mother, who now sat in a San Antonio prison, doing twenty years to life.

"My father died when I was twelve," Hannah continued. "My mother worked like crazy to keep the ranch intact so the money would be there for me to go to medical school."

They all were rapt. Hannah supposed she would have been, too.

"We had a foreman named McNally. I graduated from college and went to medical school in Boston. My mother was so proud. Then she learned McNally had been stealing from her for years. There was no money left: He had gambled it away. She lost the ranch. The night that she found out she took a shotgun from the cabinet and killed him. She didn't even give her story to the jury. Not that it would have mattered: McNally and the jury all were white. My mother was—is—Mexican."

It was very quiet for a lounge that overlooked Broadway. Then Rita spoke. "Holy shit," she said.

Yes, Hannah echoed, holy shit.

"You don't sound like you're from Texas," Katie added.

Years of practice, Hannah explained.

Faye held up her glass. "Here's to your mother," she said. "What a gutsy lady."

"But what about you?" Katie asked. "What about medical school?"

Hannah took another sip of her drink. "I'd always wanted to be a doctor. But I left school during the trial. I was so ashamed. I was afraid that they'd find out."

"Do you ever see your mother?"

She paused for a moment, because this was the hard part. "No. I was so upset I got into my car and drove down to the Cape. I took the first boat to the Vineyard. No one ever tried to find me, not even for the trial."

All eyes were on Hannah: Katie's problems no longer were on center stage, though Hannah now wished they were.

"You never went back," Katie stated.

Hannah shook her head. "And no one has been the wiser. At least until now."

"Surely your family knows," Faye interjected. "Your husband, your kids . . ."

"No," Hannah replied, "they don't know a thing."

An odd silence fell over the small, round cocktail table and for the first time Hannah was afraid that, sooner or later, her life, like Katie's, might unravel, one thread at a time.

SIXTEEN

Katie had listened or had tried to listen to Hannah's confession. Sometimes it was difficult to be sympathetic when all she could think of was, well, herself.

She lay on the small bed in the dark hotel room and pulled the crisp white sheet up to her neck. It smelled of bleach and cleanliness and laundry hung out on the line, the way her mother did it on the Vineyard, way back before Katie had to think about death and life.

Shouldn't she cancel Central Park? Shouldn't one of them face reality, despite the media?

Her thoughts drifted to Ina: What would she have advised? Would she have agreed that this time her father's decision was not the best for Katie? Or had her love for him been completely blind?

Ina.

Her father.

She tried to picture them together, then decided that was not a good idea.

And now Ina was gone. Ina, Katie's friend, who had betrayed her by keeping such a secret. And yet Cliff had said Ina could not be trusted to be told about the cancer. Maybe what he really meant was that he could not trust himself: If anyone else knew about Katie's cancer, the door to his denial might have been forced open.

He might have had to cancel the concert. And the dream once denied him by Joleen.

Suddenly Katie felt a cool hand on her cheek.

"Katie? Are you all right?"

She opened her eyes. In the darkness of the room she could make out the woman's silhouette, slightly bent over the bed. It would have been nice if it was Joleen, but it was not.

"I'm okay, Faye. Thanks."

The hand moved across Katie's cheek. "You've been crying. Do you want to talk about it?" She sat on the edge of Katie's bed.

"I don't want to go tomorrow. I'm sorry we came."

"Because of Hannah's mother?"

Hannah's mother? Oh. She'd already forgotten about her. How could Katie be so self-centered? Had her father made her that way as well as making her a star? "Life is so screwed up, Faye. My life, anyway."

Faye sighed. "Most lives are."

Katie laughed. "I'm a rock star who's pregnant and has breast cancer and is hiding from the world. My father's mistress probably pretended to be my friend for the sake of their affair; my boyfriend probably pretended to love me because it was a gig that paid well; and my father probably kept both of them because they kept me in line, kept me singing my mother's old songs and convincing me I was good. I wonder how much extra he paid them for that." She considered what she'd said, surprised so much pain had spilled out. "Yeah," she added, "I guess that would qualify as screwed up."

Faye snapped on the lamp. "Okay," she said. "Let's see. I

am a woman who's divorced, who had a daughter who drowned and who has a son who's gay, though I haven't seen him in ten years and don't even know if he is still alive. I have a successful business that I now couldn't care less about. Oh, and I've had cancer twice." She was silent for a moment, then said, "Would you like me to go on?"

Katie shook her head.

"Still," Faye added, "some problems can be fixed. If my daughter were still alive, and if she were in your shoes, how should I advise her?"

Katie pulled the sheet over her head. "Tell her to forget about the funeral and go back to the Vineyard and move in with Joleen."

With a gentle laugh, Faye said, "Well, I guess isolation can be a solution. When my daughter died, I isolated in a different way. I obsessed over my business. I pretended to work hard, but I was only trying to protect myself from being hurt again." She paused a moment. "Sometimes it's good to isolate, because it gives you time to heal. The trick is to learn when the healing is as good as it's going to get, and when to get back to the world."

Sliding the sheet away from her face, Katie said, "Sometimes I'm so scared, Faye. I'm scared for my baby and for what lies ahead. And mostly I'm damn scared that I have cancer. I look in the mirror sometimes and say, 'Katie, you have breast cancer.' But it's so hard to believe because I don't look any different except that I'm fat now, not like the girl up on that billboard."

Faye said nothing. Katie sat up and Faye simply held her, though Katie didn't cry. After a moment Katie quietly asked, "So we should go to the funeral?"

"It might be a good place to start finding some closure."

Closure? Yes. The end of one life, the beginning of another. She thought about Hannah and about Faye. She wondered why life had to suck, and how it was that people still went on, guided through it all on the wings of hope. On butterfly wings, like in Joleen's song. "Okay," she said. "But only if you tell me about your daughter who died, and about your son who's gay."

Then she closed her eyes and heard a bedtime story about a girl named Dana, who had loved beach roses, too, and about a boy named Greg, who filled their lives with magic and with laughter and with love.

The women waited until the crowd—and there was a crowd, much larger than Katie had expected—had dissipated into the white-brick funeral home, before they emerged from the Mercedes.

At first Katie thought there must be more than one funeral going on. But as they stepped inside the room marked INA ENRIQUEZ and Katie's eyes adjusted to the half-dark, she realized every seat was occupied. She recognized some people from the industry, including her own roadies, young men and women she did not really know but saw every spring, summer, and fall when they toured the North, South, East, and West.

Many Hispanics were there, too, neatly dressed and somber—neighbors, Katie assumed, from Ina's other life. Katie did not know them, either.

There were flowers, too. Hundreds of yellow hibiscus draped the casket, the altar, the ends of the pews. Had they been Ina's favorite flower? Katie didn't know. One more thing that she hadn't known.

Flanked by Faye and Hannah, Katie let Rita guide them to a small corner at the back of the room. She was glad she'd worn the black lace mantilla that hid most of her face, and the nondescript canvas raincoat that was large enough to cover her distinct pregnancy and succeeded at concealing any starlike delusion.

They had to stand because the folding chairs were occupied. Rita stepped in front of Katie to help block the view not from her to them, but from them to her. Rita wasn't exactly Brady, but the red hair served as a distracting decoy.

Then Katie felt a hand loop through her arm: It belonged to Hannah, the child of a woman who had killed a man. Katie blinked back the thought. She couldn't make room in her heart for Faye or Hannah's pain; it was already overcrowded with her own.

"Is he here?" Rita turned and whispered to Katie. "Your father?"

She peered over Rita's shoulder and squinted across the room. "I can't tell."

The lights grew dimmer and from a hidden place the sound of a piano filled the room: not a dreary organ, but a soulful, rich piano. And then Katie realized that instead of an old hymn, the score was more than familiar: It was an instrumental of her latest top-ten hit. A hit that had been another remake of Joleen's.

Katie thought that she'd be sick. Then her father stepped up to the podium.

She ducked behind Rita's red hair. Her heart started to flutter in disjointed, childlike flutters.

"Ina Enriquez was beloved by many," Cliff Gillette began, "and a friend to all."

Katie closed her eyes as if doing so could erase the sound of her father's voice. She could not believe he was so blatant as to play a song of Joleen's, the woman who'd been tossed aside because of the woman who'd just died. Katie reached out and found Faye's arm. She clung to Faye and Hannah.

"I remember the first day we met Ina," he continued, and

Katie knew the *we* meant Cliff and Joleen. The mourners went silent with rapt attention; the hush of Joleen's name always brought rapt attention. "We were at a vigil for our beloved John Lennon..." Katie wanted to scream. Lennon, she knew, had been killed in 1980. She'd been born in 1982. That meant her father had taken up with Ina two years before Katie had been born, two years that he'd already betrayed her mother.

"I have to get out of here," she whispered to Faye, but Faye must not have heard her, for she simply smiled.

Katie then tugged on Hannah's arm. "Let's go," she mouthed.

As she turned toward the door, her father said, "I'd now like to introduce the pride and joy of Ina's life."

Could she leave without seeing Miguel? Just one look...

Her father left the podium. For a moment nothing happened, then she saw the back she knew so well—the strong, muscled back—move to the front of the room. A warmth flooded through her; she loved him, didn't she? Loved and trusted him despite what Cliff had warned?

As Miguel turned to face the crowd, Katie noticed a little girl standing next to him, holding his hand. Katie had never seen her, but she was quite a beautiful child. She felt a pang of envy that the child, not her, was holding, touching, feeling Miguel's love.

"Ina Enriquez was a wonderful mother," Miguel began. Then he looked down at the child. "She was also a wonderful grandmother to my little Adelaide."

Katie squinted as if that might help her hear what she thought she'd heard.

"If it weren't for my mother, Adelaide would not have had a good upbringing. But she loved my Adelaide as if she were her own. Now I only hope I can raise my daughter in a way that would have made my mother proud."

Katie's mouth went dry. Her knees grew weak; she was too stunned to respond. She watched as the little girl knelt down and kissed the casket.

Faye's,

Hannah's,

Rita's eyes all turned to Katie.

She ripped her hands from them, pressed her palm against her mouth, and pushed through the crowd, rushing through the door and out onto the street.

She ran up Seventy-ninth Street as if she, too, were being chased by a determined mugger. She ran because she feared that if she stopped, she might throw up on the sidewalk or, worse, she might race back to the funeral home and shout about deceit of father and of lover, and about the perils of trusting anyone in life or death. She ran because she feared that if she did not, she might resort to murder, the way Hannah's mother had done.

She would kill Miguel first.

Then her father, for surely he had known.

When she reached the corner, Katie slowed and clutched the sharp pain in her side. Then she heard footsteps running up the walk. She knew the sound, the heavy sound. It was not her father and it was not Miguel. The footsteps belonged to Brady, protective, steadfast Brady, who'd never done her any harm.

Just as he caught up to Katie, Faye's Mercedes pulled up along the curb. Katie shoved aside her bodyguard and jumped inside the car.

SEVENTEEN

It always had seemed strange to Faye that fantasy had the power to keep one going, that dreams of what might be could often be sufficient to sustain a genteel disposition and an ability to cope. She'd watched it happen with her mother, who'd raised her girls to think they were aristocrats, when they were the daughters of a mere professor and his wife.

As Faye said good-bye to Katie, the last of her passengers, she realized that the worst part was when fantasy was shattered, when reality demanded notice, as Katie's had these past few days.

Faye's parents had been lucky: Death had entered before pain. Claire would be lucky, too; it's how things worked for her.

But for those like Faye and Katie, fantasy was short-lived.

Knowing these things was one thing; but as Faye drove home from Joleen's, she could not hide the hope—and yes, the fantasy—that when she pulled into her driveway, a car would be waiting there. The license plates would be from Avis or from Hertz; Greg would have rented it at the airport when he'd flown in from San Francisco or wherever.

He might not be in the car. He might be walking on the beach. She'd walk down the small path through the grassy dunes and see him in the distance. He'd be more handsome now, if that were possible. His boyish looks would be gone; he was a man now. He'd have the golden aura of a California tan.

Then he would notice her. And he'd move up on the beach, and he would stand in front of her, waiting for acceptance or rejection.

And Faye would step forward and embrace her son.

And together they would hug and they would cry.

And then it would be over, the waiting and the guilt and the ache inside her breast that had nothing to do with the cancer, or had it after all? Had the emptiness within enabled disease to settle there?

At last, the driveway was in sight. Faye inhaled a tiny breath and slowly made the turn. She drove past the scrub oaks and the pines and past the thick web of budding pink beach roses that crept and stretched and crowded empty spaces, because this was the Vineyard and that's what beach roses did.

She came into the clearing just beside the house. But no rental car stood waiting; no car was there at all.

"He called six times," Joleen reported when Katie went into the house. "He" must have been Miguel. If it had been Katie's father, Joleen's announcement would probably have been in unhinged syllables instead of hesitant, slow words. "Would you like to hear his messages?"

Katie dropped her bag and stood there, limp. She did not cry; she could not cry; she had cried most of the trip back to the Vineyard. *They must be sick to death of me*, she thought about the others. *They must wish they never met the selfish, whining child.*

She shook her head. "The bastard has a daughter," she said. She walked into the sunroom without enthusiasm. She sat down on a rattan chair. "He never told me." She put her hands over her stomach. "He told everyone at the funeral. Didn't he think I would find out? Didn't he think the media would pounce on that?" She looked up at her mother, surprised that tears were in Joleen's eyes.

"Maybe he was in shock," Joleen said. "Maybe he wasn't thinking clearly."

"But what about Daddy? He knew. He knew and he didn't tell me, either."

Joleen sat down beside her. "How old is she, the little girl?"

Katie shrugged. "Six. Maybe seven."

"Did you see her mother?"

Her mother? God. Katie's belly churned. That thought had tumbled over and over with every mile Faye's Mercedes had traversed along Interstate 95. "For all I know, he's married."

"Could he have been that deceitful?"

She could not believe Joleen was asking such a stupid question. She placed her elbows on the arms of the chair and propped her head up with her hands. "I want to stay here for a while after the baby's born. Would that be okay?"

The telephone rang. Katie closed her eyes. Her breath turned rapid, angry, short.

"Cara Katie," his Latino accent called. "Please. Come to the telephone."

She did not move; neither did Joleen.

"I know you were at the funeral," he said.

It didn't matter how he knew.

"I do not know what you saw or heard or did. But please know that I love you and I am going to make this right."

A jumble of words echoed through Katie's mind: *I want to show the world you're mine . . . What am I? A man who only wants you for your money and your name?* Had he ever tried to prove otherwise?

"I wanted to tell you," he continued. "So many times I wanted to . . . I would have told you before our baby's born."

Her aching head began to throb.

"It was all your father's fault," he said. "He knew about Adelaide. He made my mother stay in her old apartment, to take care of her."

Her father's fault? Not Miguel's at all? Did he think she was that gullible?

"Please," he begged, "don't punish Adelaide. She's just a little girl."

Something snapped inside her. She thought about the little girl that she'd once been while her father had been married to her mother and sleeping with Ina, too. She wondered if her father had ever used her as an excuse for his bad behavior.

With more energy than she thought she had, Katie lunged for the phone before Miguel could utter another syllable of sweet deceit.

"When?" she demanded in a firm but steady tone. "When did you plan to tell me? On our wedding night?"

"Cara Katie, please . . ."

"What about her mother?"

He paused, then said, "She is in Puerto Rico."

"Is she your wife?"

"Katie, please . . ."

"*Is she?*"

In the silence that followed, Katie grew oddly calm. Perhaps she'd expected this, or something like this, all along. She looked over at Joleen and could only think that now another woman had been deceived by a man.

"Katie, you do not understand."

But, finally, she did. She understood that her father and Miguel were in this together, consciously or not, maliciously or not. As long as the truth was kept from Katie, she would stay with Miguel; and Cliff could continue to manipulate both Miguel and Ina and maintain the well-controlled machine that had become his—their—life. She did not ask what would have happened if she'd agreed to marry the man who apparently was not divorced. Instead, Katie lowered her voice.

"And you didn't care if the media found out before I did."

He did not reply.

Then she asked the question she needed to ask. "How much?" She paused. "How much did he pay you?"

"What?"

"My father. How much did he pay you to help me get over Jean-Luis? To keep me happy and recording, to keep me up onstage?"

Miguel did not answer.

"Listen to me, Miguel." Her voice was steady, dispassionate. "You stay the hell away from me. You stay the hell away from my baby. And if you set one foot on this island, I'll have you arrested for stalking a celebrity and you'll be thrown in jail. I don't expect that would be a good thing for your daughter, now that your mother's dead." The telephone receiver met the cradle with a thud. It did not shake or tremble, it simply sat as if in shock.

·   ·   ·

"Of all the rotten, son-of-a-bitching luck," Rita sputtered to Hazel once she finally was safe inside her house and felt like she could breathe again.

Hazel put her finger to her lips. It might be afternoon nap time, but the walls still had giant, toddler ears.

With an exasperated sigh, Rita put the teakettle on the stove. She hadn't planned to tell her mother about Faye and Joe and her.

If Charlie had been home, she'd have been able to forget it, to shove it back, way back, into one of the many files of her not-so-pleasant past. But he'd gone back to Nantucket and that left her with Hazel, and Rita had to talk to someone.

"Of all the son-of-a-bitching luck, that woman in the group—the one whose kid died—it turns out she's the wife of a guy I used to date. I met her many years ago under not the nicest circumstances."

Hazel shook her head and Rita plunked a tea bag into a ceramic mug that bore a big map of the Vineyard and a title EDGARTOWN, 1980. Kyle had bought it for her for Christmas when he'd been only ten.

"I'll tell Doc in the morning that he'll have to find someone else," she continued. "There's no way I can do the group now."

"What about Katie?" The voice didn't come from Hazel, but from Mindy, who was standing in the doorway looking quite perplexed.

Rita moved her gaze from the girl back to her mother. How was it that she often forgot that Mindy was in the house? Perhaps because, at twelve, Rita had not been quiet and endearing, but a scrapper and a pain and always under foot.

Hazel kept her eyes on Rita. "She asked if you went to New York for that woman's funeral."

"Ina Enriquez," Mindy said. "Katie's personal assistant."

Rita went back to the stove and poured the water. "Mindy," she said, "you know I can't answer questions about the support group. It's private, remember?"

"You're telling Hazel." She moved into the kitchen and sat down at the table. "Please, please, Rita. I promise I won't tell anyone. What was the funeral like? Did you see Miguel? He is such a hunk."

Rita did not have to see Mindy's eyes to know they were wide and bright and loaded with anticipation. With futile resignation, Rita joined the other generations and sat down at the table. "The funeral was as funerals go. People sniffling, either because they were in mourning or because there were too many flowers in the room."

"Did Katie give a eulogy? Did she sing a song?" Mindy, of course, did not know of Katie's estrangement from her father or from the "hunk," Miguel, despite that she was pregnant with his child and soon the world would know. Sometimes the shift in morals was still hard for Rita to digest when she thought about her Kyle and how she'd had to hide him the first few years of his life, just so he'd be accepted later on.

"No," Rita replied. "It was a small ceremony." No use telling Mindy things she didn't need to know.

"Oh," said the disappointed fan.

Rita was reminded of how Joleen's music had carried her through the rough times, how she'd set Joleen up on a polished pedestal, worshiping from afar. It might have been absurd and immature, but it had given Rita strength. Idols, perhaps, were still important.

"We saw a billboard of Katie, though," she said. "In Times Square. It must have had ten thousand lights made to look like sparkling sequins. And the rose tattoo on her left cheek is lit with small, pink flashing bulbs."

Flecks of light and color danced in Mindy's innocent eyes.

"The billboard is for her concert in Central Park on July Fourth."

The dancing eyes slowed with suspicion. "But what about her baby? And what about the cancer? How can she stand up in front of half the world and sing if she's still pregnant and she's sick?"

Rita sipped her tea and thought, *So much for innocence.* "I'm not sure that the concert will actually happen."

Hazel stood up. "They should cancel it," she said. "Young people today try to do too much. They don't take time to stop and smell the flowers."

Mindy looked at Rita. Rita winked. "We'll see," she said. "If there's any way, I'm sure Katie will go through with it." Stranger things, she supposed, had happened.

"Then you have to keep doing the support group," Mindy whined, and Rita was startled, because for a moment she'd forgotten about Faye and Joe and that other nasty stuff. How the heck had she forgotten that so fast?

"You have to, Rita," Mindy prodded as she moved forward on her chair. "I bet you'll get free tickets, maybe in the front row! You'll get free tickets, won't you?"

Rita took another sip of tea and wondered how you told a twelve-year-old that there were more important things in life.

But were there?

Was Joe Geissel more important? Was Faye?

Was the Women's Wellness Center? Well, maybe that one was.

Though she'd only lived on the Vineyard just shy of sixteen years, Hannah knew enough to know there were things you didn't talk about, like the scandal that had touched Rita's state-appointed daughter, Mindy, or the fact that Katie's mother was pretty much a hermit. Hannah supposed it was the same way no one ever spoke about Evan's former pot addiction, though many islanders must have known and wondered about the details.

"Not that gossip doesn't happen," Mother Jackson had explained to Hannah, "but we keep it to ourselves."

Hannah lay in bed, exhausted from the trip, feeling gray and glum and not herself, whoever that was now. She remembered it had taken her a long time to trust what Mother Jackson said was true, that islanders didn't discuss one another's dirty laundry, at least not to outsiders. She hoped the group followed that creed and wouldn't spread the news about her incarcerated mother.

Still, Hannah knew the time had come to tell her family, in case one of the women leaked the word, in case her husband or her kids learned some other way, in case Hannah died.

She closed her eyes and tried to push away that thought, but the way she felt today verified the possibility.

"Surprise!"

Her body jerked because, yes, she was surprised, surprised that Casey and Denise barged into her room: Casey carrying a covered dish and Denise clutching a cluster of blue hydrangea that Evan must have forced to flower early in the greenhouse.

Denise bounced on the bed and Hannah clutched her stomach to ward off the unexpected motion. She tried to smile. "What's this?"

"For you," Denise said, handing her mother the blossoms, their stems bent and damp from the determined grip of seven-year-old hands.

"We made your favorite," Casey announced, removing

the cover of the dish and presenting Hannah with something quite mysterious that smelled sort of like peaches. She tried not to mind that Riley was not with them.

"Yum," she cooed, as if this were the grandest gift ever given any mother. "But it's not my birthday."

"We missed you, Mommy." Denise's small arms entwined themselves around her neck.

Her wig tipped to one side. Hannah hugged her daughter and wondered how her children could ever understand about her mother and the things that she had done. Tonight, she thought, she'd tell Evan everything. Then tomorrow they could tell the kids. Together they would find the words.

She ruffled her daughter's hair, then gently fixed the wig. She smiled with gratitude for her two younger kids, for their lives and their innocence, and for keeping her—for the most part—sane. Then she quietly folded her hands and asked, "Did anyone bring forks?"

The call had come that morning. Faye stood in her dining room and once again pushed the button on her answering machine, half in disbelief. Was there someone she could call—Claire?—to share the news?

Not that there was any news to share. Not really. Not yet.

And not that Claire would be so god-awful glad to hear from her once she learned that Faye had thanked Adam for lunch but told him not to call again. She was not interested. She did not want to date. Her fault, she said, it had nothing to do with him. Ha.

Suddenly something else was more important anyway.

"Faye," the recording began. "This is R.J. Browne."

Her heart skipped a beat again, though surely this must

be the tenth or twelfth time she'd played the message since arriving home that afternoon.

"I have good news. I'd like to talk to you in person, and I could use a short vacation. So unless I hear otherwise, I'll see you tomorrow on the Vineyard. No need to pick me up; I have a reservation on the ten-thirty ferry." He paused, then laughed. His laugh was nice, friendly. "No trouble getting a reservation. You can tell it's not quite summer."

The machine beeped and Faye remained in place, staring off at nothing in particular, hearing only those four words: *I have good news*.

"Mouser," she said quietly, not because the cat was anywhere in sight, but because it made her feel more sane to talk to someone, something, other than herself, "Good things are going to come our way." The yin and yang of life were finally on her side, and she would not,

would not,

would not,

think of anything but that.

After dueling with Miguel, Katie took Joleen's suggestion and went for a long walk on the beach. She was surprised the ache inside her wasn't worse: perhaps she'd cried all her tears on the way back from New York; perhaps what she felt now was simply relief. Sadness, yes, but also relief. Without Miguel, she'd no longer have to wonder; she'd no longer have to feel that tiny, not-quite-right spot that had to do with him and her. Still, it wasn't fair that her father had always known.

Your father's decisions are usually best for you. Ina had said, and Katie had once believed it. Maybe it had been true when she'd been twelve or twenty, even. She thought about how close she'd come to having another abortion. And then she realized she was an adult now; it was time to stop blaming Cliff Gillette for her success or failure. And to stop depending on him for the same.

She stopped and closed her eyes and listened to the mournful cry of gulls. Then she slowly wondered if her cancer was a gift, a strangely wrapped endowment that had given her the chance to stand up on her own.

Katie returned to the house to find that her mother had made soup: thick, hearty chicken soup the way she'd made it when Katie was a little girl and the family was a family.

"The baby's going to love this," she said, and felt already nourished because Joleen had made the gesture. She noticed that the table was set with pottery and cloth napkins and a burst of wildflowers as a centerpiece. "How nice," she said, because it was. *I could get used to this*, she thought.

"Sit down," Joleen commented, "we need to talk."

Katie sat and Joleen brought a tureen to the table. She ladled her creation into bowls, then went back to the counter and returned with a bulky envelope. She sat down. "Eat," she said, so Katie ate. The soup was warm and wonderful.

"After the baby's born," Joleen said halfway through the meal, "you cannot stay with me."

Katie set down her spoon. "What?"

Joleen shook her head. "It's my life, Kathryn, out here on the Vineyard. It's not a life for you."

Because she knew her mother must be joking, Katie laughed.

But Joleen did not.

"You and your baby will always be welcome here," Joleen continued. "Summers, winters, anytime. But not to live.

Not as your permanent home." She did not look Katie in the eye.

Katie lowered her gaze to the chicken soup. She no longer had an appetite. She thought about the times when she'd longed for her mother to be with them, but Cliff explained that Joleen was meant to be alone. She had not believed him then. She'd thought it was her fault.

"You don't want us," she said.

"I want you to have your own life. You deserve much more than being stuck here on an island."

Katie tried to stop the tears from dropping from her eyes. She wanted to say something, but somehow she could not.

"Kathryn," Joleen continued, "your father made me who I was. When he came along, I was just a teenager—a salesclerk in a store in Akron that carried art supplies. I painted watercolors that no one ever saw and wrote simple poetry that no one ever read."

Why was she talking about him, the man who had deceived them both?

"No one's perfect, Kathryn. Not him. Not me. But your father loves you. Don't doubt that for a minute."

Too late, she should have said but didn't.

"What your father did to me was painful," Joleen continued, "but always, always, it takes two. That last summer we were together, I did not have a miscarriage. I had an abortion."

Katie had suspected that, but had never asked.

"It was my idea, not his," Joleen added. "I couldn't take the thought of another child being born into the spotlight; I couldn't take the scrutiny of my marriage, that had by then become a farce."

Katie reached across the table and took her mother's hand.

Joleen shook her head. "I was not the kind of wife your

father wanted. I loved writing my music, but I hated the attention. You, however . . . you light up the stage and everything and everyone around you."

"I can't write music the way you do, Mother. I'll never be as great as you."

"We're different people, Kathryn. I never could perform the way you do. It's you who gives my music life. Better than I ever did or could."

Was that true?

"But how can I go back to Daddy after what he did to you? After what he's done to me?"

Joleen slid the envelope across the table. "Who says you need your father? These are the songs you found. And a few more, too."

The room was filled with silence, except for the foghorn off the sound. Katie looked at the envelope but did not take it in her hands.

"When all your troubles are behind you," Joleen said, "you can start again with these. With my music and your talent, you'll light up the world again."

EIGHTEEN

"As angry as I was, I don't think I wanted McNally dead," Hannah whispered in the darkness to her husband, who lay beside her in their bed, listening with great patience while she told the story. "In jail, maybe for a long time, but not dead. Do you know what I mean?"

It was a moment before Evan said anything. He was not what one might call an "immediate responder," especially when the subject was as thought-provoking as this. Finally he said, "Jesus, Hannah, did you ever tell my mother?"

She frowned. She'd just told him that her mother killed a man because he'd robbed Hannah of her future and robbed them of their life. Why was his first concern about his dead mother? "I never said a word to anyone until now." She did not add that she'd told the women of the group.

"Oh," he said, and that was all.

"Why?"

"Because I'd like to know if she'd think that we should tell the kids."

Hannah felt a sinking feeling. "They're our kids, Evan. I want them to know."

"I'm not sure I do."

The Vineyard night was cool and damp. It drifted through the sheer, white curtains and settled in the gully between them on the bed. "What if they find out another way?" she asked.

"We live on an island, Hannah. We're protected from the real world."

She did not say that cancer was part of the "real world," and they hadn't been protected very well from that. She rested her hand against her forehead, she closed her eyes. She tried to force away a picture of her mother doing penance in the library or laundry or wherever inmates worked, dressed in an awful orange jumpsuit with numbers on the back. She wondered if, in all these years, her mother had been diagnosed with breast cancer and if she had survived.

"I'm sorry, Hannah," Evan continued. "But try to understand that this is all news to me. I can't believe you've kept it to yourself, something as serious as this."

Hannah did not remind him she'd not known about his pot-smoking until they'd been married for ten years.

"I think the kids are too young to know," he said. "Maybe in a few years we might tell Riley." He rolled onto his side, his back now facing her, discussion closed.

"She's old enough now." Hannah did not tell him that their daughter was old enough for many things, including sex, which Hannah had learned from a bathroom wall last year at school. BEST ISLAND BLOW JOB, the crude graffiti read, RILEY JACKSON. Aghast with horror, sick with shock, she had confronted Riley. Surprisingly, her daughter laughed. "Maybe I'll get an award at the next assembly," she'd said. Then added, "I hope you know it's not true." But Hannah didn't know, not for sure. So she tried to talk to Riley about AIDS and birth control, but Riley said she already knew about that stuff. It might have helped if Mother Jackson had been alive for some advice.

"Be reasonable, Hannah," Evan said into the night. "The kids have too much on their minds right now. They're worried about your cancer. This would upset them more."

Taking a deep breath, Hannah held it for a moment. She moved her hand down to her breast and touched it through her nightgown, and thought about the lump that was buried there, would be there until the chemo was complete and her mastectomy was done. Then she realized Evan had not said, "Oh, honey, I'm so sorry," or "God, Hannah, how strong you were to overcome all that," or even "Have you ever thought about going to her now and trying to reconcile?" But Evan had not said those things, and Hannah was left to wonder why women married men, when their heads and hearts so rarely seemed to be in the same place.

Rita's need to know had surpassed mere curiosity: She needed to find out if Faye was behind the new Women's Wellness Center. Only then could Rita decide how big the stakes would be if she resigned from the group. If she left, Faye could renege on the money and the island women would lose. If Rita stayed, she'd have to face that woman every week, maybe more, because they were "sticking together," because "that's what real friends are for."

It was always possible that Faye did not remember Rita, fat chance of that.

The only way to learn the benefactor's name would be straight from Doc. Of course, he'd never tell her because of that god-awful confidentiality, but he must have something somewhere, a letter or some notes. Which meant Rita would have to break into Doc's office, then riffle through his files.

She really had no other choice.

Six o'clock in the morning was a lousy hour to leave the house, but it should be a safe time to show up at the hospital and not run into Doc. Rita had awakened Mindy and asked her to listen for the twins. She explained that she had to check on one of the women in the group who had a minor problem—no, it wasn't Katie—but that she'd be back before Mindy left for school.

The good part was no one was on the road, so Rita made it to the hospital and into the empty parking lot in record time.

It was dimly lit inside the corridor, the air filled with the hollow sound of nothing happening, poised on the precarious rim of a day that had not yet awakened.

Rita tiptoed down the hall on furtive feet, as if she had no business being there, which she, of course, did not. She moved past the vending machines and down the doctors' wing, all the while her heart beating more quickly than she supposed was healthy for a heart. Was this how common thieves felt just before the heist? Their aorta pumped with adrenaline, fueling each villainous step?

OBSTETRICS AND GYNECOLOGY. INTERNAL MEDICINE.

The small plaque had been screwed into the metal door decades ago, as had the strip below it that read: ROLAND W. HASTINGS, M.D.

Rita was always caught off guard when she saw the name. Somehow she had never pictured Doc as a "Roland," just a simple "Doc." The fact that he had a first name made him seem too ordinary, and to the people of the Vineyard, he was anything but that.

She assumed the doorknob would be locked, for which she was prepared to implement the bobby-pin-break-in method she'd perfected through the years to gain access to the cottages she'd been hired to clean—cottages that belonged to people who had lost their keys or had them stolen or who'd taken them home to Pittsburgh or Cincinnati or somewhere too far to get them, because the next renters would show up in an hour.

This door, however, wasn't locked. The handle turned, the door pushed open, and Rita went inside.

It was dark. Faye woke up, startled from a dream, another of those dreams in which Dana called out, but Faye could not reach her.

She touched her neck; it was wet with perspiration. She wondered why the dreams had come back now. Was it an aftereffect of the radiation?

She felt the soft plop-plop, plop-plop of Mouser's feet on the comforter, followed by the gentle nuzzling of his body against her side.

The pain eased a little and Faye remembered that R.J. would arrive that day, and she would learn where Greg was and how soon she could see him—if at all—again.

She closed her eyes and tried not to think about her children, but instead about what she would wear and if she should make lunch for R.J. and why she felt a need to bother.

Rita closed the door behind her, careful that it did not rattle but made only a quiet *click*.

She blinked twice, then twice again, waiting for her eyes to adjust to the darkness. She'd been in Doc's office many times: She tried now to remember where his large wooden desk was positioned; where the sofa sat uninvitingly, its pimples of foam stuffing jutting out in many places; where the ancient file cabinets were aligned against which wall, burdened as they were with the stories of the lives and aches and pains and deaths of so many islanders.

Reaching into her bag, Rita withdrew her pocket flashlight. She stared down at the shadow of the Eveready in her hand. It had made sense when she'd thought of it last night; all she could envision now, however, was an arc of light sweeping through the dark, alerting the night watchman or the janitor or even a nurse who might be passing by, that someone was in Doc's office and it looked like a burglary.

It was bad enough she was somewhere she did not belong. Arming herself like Jessica Fletcher or Miss Marple would only serve to call unpleasant attention.

With a snort of laughter at herself, Rita tossed the flashlight back into her bag, then fumbled against the wall until she found the switch. She flicked it on and Doc's office quickly came to life: desk and sofa and the wall of files.

Geissel. Faye would be listed under Joe's last name, wouldn't she? The child had died pre-Rita, before Faye and Joe's divorce. Most likely *Geissel* would have been the name of record.

She stole her way to the files and scanned the rectangles of oak tag tucked into the slots. Thank God Doc had not yet automated: He might be modern enough to see the need for a Women's Center, but when it came to paperwork, he believed the old ways were the best.

The drawer marked F–H creaked open, its runners complaining against the weighty contents.

Gallagher.

Gardiner.

Garvey.

Rita hesitated. Julie Garvey? Would a quick peek reveal

if Julie Garvey had her face lifted the way everyone suspected? Would Doc have that information in the file?

Rita Mae, she could almost hear her mother scold.

"Oh, all right," Rita muttered, then continued.

Gates.

Geary.

Geissel. *Geissel.*

She held her breath, as if this were a great surprise and
not the reason that she'd come. Stuffing her hand between
the jam-packed manila folders, she began to lift out the
Geissel folder. Just then, the office door opened and someone sucked the air out of the room.

"Rita?"

Well, of course it was Rita. Who else on the damn Vineyard had hair the color of overripe tomatoes?

"It's me, Doc," she replied, turning, half-relieved that it
was him and not a guard who had a gun. The other half of
her was quickly racing to sort out her thoughts, trying to remember what she'd figured she could say if she got caught,
which it appeared she had. "I didn't expect to see you here
so early." Which went without saying, as Doc probably
knew.

"What are you doing in my files?"

Would forty-nine years of knowing someone help cushion the indiscretion of a single act? "Doc," she said, closing
the file drawer, cursing herself for coming at six o'clock and
not five-forty-five, "I had a crisis with one of the women in
the group."

"Those files are confidential, Rita." He moved toward
her and insinuated himself between Rita and the filing cabinet—*his* filing cabinet—and his confidential files. "You
should have called me," he added. "You shouldn't be sneak-
ing into my office."

"I didn't exactly sneak, Doc. The door was open. I

turned the light on." Thank God he could not dispute either of those things. She hoisted her bag onto her shoulder. "I thought it was too early to call you." She laughed a short laugh meant to sound caring. "It's Faye," she said. "I don't know what to do."

Apparently convinced that she was not up to no good, Doc relaxed his eyebrows to their normal place above his eyes and not scrunched into his nose. "Faye Geissel?" He said the name as if there were more than one Faye on the island who had breast cancer, just as if there might be more than one Rita with red hair.

"Yes, well, I know her as Faye Randolph." Rita breathed again, glad that she'd averted his thoughts from her dastardly deed. "Apparently she had a child that died." She said a quick prayer to Kyle, asking for forgiveness for exploiting him again, and added, "like my Kyle. Well, not the same way, of course. But one who died."

Doc stared at Rita. He leaned protectively against the cabinets. "Rita, you know I can't talk about my patients."

"But Doc, I'm only trying to help. She can't seem to open up about the tragedy. I think I can help her because I've been through it, too."

He sighed. "Rita, you're not a professional. Just try to be their friend. If you're concerned about any of them, tell me. I'll talk with them directly. It's not up to you."

She wanted to say that she knew she was not a professional. She wanted to remind him she'd been doing him a favor to facilitate the group because he'd been hard up and she had trouble saying no. Then she figured she'd be better off to leave well enough the hell alone. But as Rita turned to leave, she could not stop herself from saying, "Doc, one question. Is Faye the one who's putting up the money for the Women's Center?"

He laughed. "Rita Blair," Doc said, because to him, she'd

always be Rita Blair, "I swear you are as incorrigible as your mother."

Coming from Doc, Rita took that as a compliment and left Doc's office, grateful that her heart had found it's way out of her throat.

Riley wasn't in her room when Hannah went to wake her. Her books were gone; her bag was gone. It wouldn't be the first time her daughter left for school too early, to meet her friends and hang out on the corner, as if this were a real city and not one where her parents could possibly see her.

It doesn't matter, Hannah repeated to herself as she went downstairs to make breakfast for Evan, Casey, and Denise.

The only thing that matters is what's right for you, Faye had said when they were in New York, before the funeral turned all attention once again onto Katie.

She supposed that Faye was right, but it was easier said than done. Still, it was nice that none of them berated her for abandoning her mother.

Write down your feelings in your journal, Rita had suggested. Hannah doubted she should include lingering fantasies about John Arthur, which resurfaced whenever she was angry with her husband, or the fact that she was trying to ignore that the road race was this week.

Don't forget the other stuff, Katie added, *like pictures of your kids when they were babies, or, if you have one of you as a baby.*

Rita had laughed. *All Katie thinks about these days are babies.*

Hannah didn't know what happened to the photos of herself as a child, let alone a baby. There only was the picture in her high school yearbook . . .

Popping two slices of homemade bread into the toaster,

Hannah thought about the yearbook that she'd saved from San Antonio and hidden at the bottom of Mother Jackson's trunk. Perhaps now was a good time to look at it again.

GUILTY. MURDER TWO.

The front page of the newspaper had yellowed. It cracked along the edge where it had been folded; the ink had chipped from some of the bold black headline.

Yet the words were unmistakable.

> SAN ANTONIO—A local rancher and mother was found guilty yesterday for the brutal killing of her foreman, Edward McNally. Elizabeth Barnes was sentenced to twenty years to life after pleading no contest to a charge of second degree murder

. . . and on and on the article continued. Hannah read every word as if she'd never seen the clipping, as if she'd not spent the first year after the trial reading and rereading the newspaper every night until she could read no more, and then she put it in her yearbook and promised herself she'd never look at it again.

She'd kept her word until now. Even when Mother Jackson died and Hannah found the false bottom of the trunk, she hadn't looked either at the yearbook or the clipping. She'd simply transferred them with her birth certificate and old biology book from her bureau drawer to the place where they'd be safer, far from unknowing eyes. She should have thrown them out back then.

She sat on the rocker in the attic, the yearbook open on her lap, the paper in her hands.

She never should have kept them. Why had she ever kept them?

A sound came from the corner by the eaves under the window.

Was it *Riley* again?

Hannah didn't move. Another bat? A mouse?

She sat and waited. Silence fell again.

I've got to get rid of this once and for all, she thought, yet still she clutched the paper, as if she knew that once it was gone, it would be . . . gone.

Again, her gaze drifted across the fading type. "Twenty years to life," the district attorney said. Then she read the last line that she'd not noticed before, because before it hadn't mattered; it had seemed so far away.

"Twenty years to life, with early release on good behavior."

Good behavior.

Early release.

Slowly Hannah counted from the date of then to now.

Sixteen years.

Early release.

Oh, God, she thought. *Was sixteen years enough time for her to be let out?* And, if so, would Betty Barnes one day soon be at Hannah's door, exposing Hannah for the liar and the fraud she was, the kind of selfish daughter who had left her mother when she'd been needed most?

NINETEEN

If fresh cod was in the refrigerator and a bottle of Chardonnay was chilled, Faye would be prepared to invite R.J. to stay for lunch.

She checked her watch: eleven-thirty. It had been a busy morning. Tired though she was, Faye had made a quick trip to the market, straightened the downstairs of the house, run the vacuum and dusted. Other than her sister, Claire, and the brief visit from Doc, it had been a long time since anyone but Faye and Mouser and occasional maintenance people had been inside the Vineyard house.

At first she'd hesitated to wear a pair of jeans, despite that they were Donna Karan. Faye had never been comfortable in jeans—coarse blue denim somehow seemed so unfeminine to one who'd been raised in Boston, the aristocrat of nonaristocrats. Still, unlike her linen or her silk-noir pants, the jeans did not wrinkle and they seemed much more in keeping with the island. She did, however, add a short-sleeved, silk sweater. Now that it was May, long sleeves were not needed.

May. Were the days ticking by more quickly because she was approaching the downside of her life?

Standing in the living room in front of the large bay window that looked out to the sound, Faye supposed she was obsessing over clothing and death because those things might be preferable to what R.J. might say.

She leaned against the grand piano that no one had played since Greg had left.

Did he still play piano?

Did he have a good and happy life?

Was he in love?

Ask again later. The triangle in the black fortune-telling ball came to her mind. How many times had Greg and Dana sat on the back porch and played that child's game, asking a litany of questions from will they be rich and famous to will Dana marry Eddie and would she have a lot of kids.

They had not asked if Dana would die before she came of age.

Mouser jumped from the windowsill, then came the sound of gravel churning in the driveway. Faye stood up straight and tucked her silver hair behind her ears. *Oh,* she thought, sometimes the worst part of being on the Vineyard was that there was too much damn time to think.

He drove one of those big SUVs that reeked of masculinity, and that for some women, Faye supposed, was a final statement of feminism that shouted, "Hey, I have power, too."

R.J. Browne, however, did not need a vehicle to define his sexuality. He merely turned off the ignition, opened the door, and—voilà—testosterone oozed from all his pores. Faye quickly thought once again that *if only* she was ten years younger . . . Then she smiled at how that thought would horrify her sister who would no doubt see it as further proof that Faye was hopeless when it came to men.

"How was the crossing?" Faye asked as she led R.J. into the house, because that's what one asked anyone who'd just come over on the boat.

"Fine," he replied. "Uneventful."

They commented on the beautiful day and that maybe summer would be early this year. She did not mention Greg; she remembered when she'd been a young child, eager to share with her father some exciting, childhood news, how her mother made her wait until "he caught his breath."

She supposed that was what she was doing now, letting R.J. catch his breath.

"Iced tea?" she asked. "First of the season."

He shook his head. "I won't stay long," he said, taking a seat on the couch. "I left my friend in town to shop." He laughed. "Not all the stores are open yet," he added, as if Faye didn't know that.

"Soon," she replied. "Memorial Day." She tried to act pleasant, not to feel or show disappointment that R.J. had *a friend*. Well, what did she expect? That he felt any chemistry with an ancient, dried-up woman? *You're not the only woman over fifty searching for a rich man*, Claire had said. Claire would not have guessed that Faye did not care if he was rich. She sat down next to R.J. and forced a smile. "Are you staying over?"

He nodded. "For a few days. At Mayfield House in Vineyard Haven."

With his friend, of course.

"You gave me a good excuse to make a trip out here," he continued. "This break has been much needed." His grin was wide and happy; distracting herself was work.

She folded her hands and wished she'd worn her linen

after all. "What about Greg?" she asked abruptly. "I take it you found my son?"

He propped his elbows on his knees and tented his fingers together. "Yes, Faye, I found him. He is doing very well."

She closed her eyes. A slow, light dizziness floated through her head. She gripped the cushion of the sofa. She took a deep breath. "Where is he?" she asked, opening her eyes.

"Phoenix," he replied. "He owns a restaurant there with his partner, Mike Tanner. Actually they own two restaurants: one in Phoenix, one up in Sedona. They call them Crawdaddies."

A restaurant. Two restaurants. Greg had always loved to cook. But his partner must have money: Greg only had five hundred dollars when he left. Five hundred dollars and one suitcase. He'd left his rich-boy clothes at home. "What kind of restaurants?"

"Cajun. They make a great étouffée," R.J. added with another laugh.

"You went there," Faye said. "To Phoenix." She'd been to the city two or three times on business. She'd been there and she hadn't known . . .

What if she'd eaten at his restaurant . . .

R.J. was nodding. "I went there to be sure that it was him."

Of course, she thought. She wished she'd poured herself some iced tea, because her mouth was suddenly dry. "Did you talk with him?"

"No. I talked to Mike Tanner. I asked if they were from New Orleans, because the étouffée was so good. He said he was from Chicago and his partner was from Boston."

"Did . . . did you see him? Did you see Greg?"

"Yes. The next day I drove up to Sedona." His voice lowered and his tone grew soft. "He was at the restaurant, Faye. He's quite a handsome boy."

She sat there for a moment and did not know what to say. Then she remembered R.J. had done exactly what she'd asked. *Once I know where he is,* she'd said, *I'll decide what to do next.* She smiled a tentative smile, because it had been too long between words.

She asked how she could find him.

R.J. handed her a paper that had been folded in his pocket. "This is the name and number of the restaurant in Phoenix."

Faye stood up and extended her hand. "Well, thank you, R.J. Once again you've proved your worth."

He paused a moment, then stood up and took her hand. He held it lightly. "My pleasure," he said, then kissed her cheek.

And then R.J. was gone. Faye returned once again to the sofa by the window, where she sat down and touched her fingers to the place he'd kissed. Her tears spilled down her cheeks and dropped onto her white silk sweater.

"I can't do it anymore," Rita said to Charlie on the phone that afternoon. "It's too much responsibility on top of the kids and Hazel." He had called after lunch, which he rarely got to do because he was so busy.

"In a few weeks I'll be home for good and we can have a real, old-fashioned talk," he said. "Can you hang in 'til then? You know how Doc depends on all of us at one time or another."

The hurricane of '92.

The overload of tourists in '95 and '96 when the Clintons came to town.

The year—Rita did not remember when it was—that

the flu outbreak had been so bad that there were patients in the halls of the hospital.

Despite that he was a gynecologist, in times of need Doc was the elder statesman of health care on the island, and when too many needed him, he always needed others to help do the laundry, make the coffee, mop and clean the floors. The island had been its own, dependable support group long before support groups were in fashion, no matter what Hazel said.

"It's not an emergency, Charlie," Rita explained. "The breast cancer support group is just . . . women."

"I'll bet it's an emergency to them." Having known Rita all her life, Charlie knew the best ways to get to her. She hadn't planned to tell him she was abandoning the group, but it was Monday, so he had asked. "Besides," he said, "there are only three of them. How much trouble can they be?"

Rita pulled her feet up on the couch. She studied her plain, unpolished toenails. She had not left them unpolished that summer she'd spent Wednesday afternoons with Joe: She'd done anything and everything to keep herself looking good, because Joe was where the money was and Rita was using him. "It's not them," she admitted, because sooner or later she admitted everything to her husband.

And then, with Mindy off at school and Hazel at the Center and the twins playing merrily on the playmat on the floor, Rita confessed to Charlie the summer of Joe Geissel and her sins against the man.

When she was finished, Charlie did not say a word at first, then he commented in a low, not unhappy voice, "And I thought you were a virgin when we married." Which was, of course, a laugh, because they'd only been married two years now and he and Rita had first had sex in high school and she'd had Kyle as a result.

"But how can I look this woman in the face?" Rita added. "What if I was the reason for their divorce?"

He did not say, "Well, what did you expect?" or anything to make Rita feel even more like the low-life form she already knew she was. "Does she remember you?"

"With this hair of mine, how could she not?"

"Still, you don't know for sure. Maybe she's forgiven you. Then again, with breast cancer and all, maybe you're the last thing on her mind."

Rita did not say anything.

"And maybe," Charlie added slowly, "you should think about something else. It seems she's in the group because she wants the help of others. Maybe this is your chance to make it up to her."

One thing that always drove Rita crazy about her husband was that he was so patient and so kind and, often, so preposterously right.

Dear Diary, Rita wrote, because what was good for one goose was good for another. She'd waited until the twins went down for their naps, then settled at the kitchen table with a small notebook and a pen.

A long time ago I was broke and I was scared. I'd raised a kid all on my own before most women did that sort of thing.

Chewing the tip of her pen, Rita reread what she'd written. It was true, of course, that she'd raised Kyle long before being a single parent was in vogue. She'd raised him and sometimes it had been damn hard.

Of course, her mother had been a single parent when she'd raised Rita, too. But that had been different. Rita had a father who'd taken off long before she was old enough to remember him, or so her mother had said, and who would have had the nerve to ever question Hazel?

Rita went back to her writing. *I have no excuses for the things I did back then. Things like sleeping with men I did not love and who did not love me, simply because I needed attention or I just needed sex. Once I did it because I needed money. I am especially ashamed of that, because I'm afraid my actions might have broken up a marriage. Anyway, I'm just writing this to say I'm sorry, in case anyone is listening.*

She closed the book and set down her pen. She'd never been one who liked writing, but she had to admit that something, somewhere deep inside her, felt a little better now.

If she could screw up her courage, she'd read her words tonight to the group. And maybe Faye would listen, and maybe Faye would know. And maybe Rita's apology would be accepted, and they could get on with the business of why they were really there.

God, sometimes Rita hated being married to Charlie Goodie-Two-Shoes Rollins.

"Did you do it?" Katie asked Hannah after the three women had decided not to wait for Faye, because by seven-thirty it was fairly clear that she wasn't going to show up. "Did you tell your family about San Antonio?"

Rita tried to act interested, when, in fact, she was angry that she could have saved her breath and her paper and her ink. She would not read the passage in her journal tonight: There was no point in her salvation falling on irrelevant ears.

"I told Evan," Hannah explained. "He's angry that he didn't know. He insists that we're not going to tell the kids."

"Hiding things from the ones you love will only hurt them more," Katie spoke quietly and shook her head.

Hannah nodded and continued, "And now I'm worried

because I realized my mother could be released sooner than I thought. What if she's already out? What if she tries to find me?"

Rita knew she should say something wise and insightful, never mind that she was, after all, a nonprofessional. *Just try to be their friend*, Doc said. But right now she didn't have the patience. Instead, she twisted on the plastic chair, looked up at the round white clock with the large black hands, and wondered if this evening would ever end.

The big sun was magnificent as it swashed its stripes of pink and orange across the wide horizon that stretched above the Elizabeth Islands. As often as Faye had watched the sun set on the Vineyard, there was nothing quite as special as seeing it from the air.

She did not know if, physically, she could make the trip. Radiation and the adventure to New York had completely worn her out; she only felt a need to sleep.

But how could she sleep, knowing where Greg was, knowing that the time had come for them to put aside the past and try and find their way back to each other?

She had called Claire. If her sister could go with her on this journey, maybe Faye might have the strength that it would take. But the perky message on Claire's answering machine said, "Sorry you missed us; we've skipped out of the country." It was May; Claire and Jeffrey must be in Paris.

Faye and Joe had gone to Paris once, when the kids were still young and they still had been in love. Despite Joe's rough, uneducated edges, Paris had softened him: They'd held hands as the elevator climbed the Eiffel Tower; they'd stood in awe beneath the Arc de Triomphe while reading the names of war dead; they'd ascended Montmartre just to see the artists in the square, busy at their easels, though Faye knew the *Mont* was now a tourist attraction and the artists' works no longer were considered so noteworthy.

The small plane banked now and made its way toward LaGuardia International. And Faye began to wonder what had happened to her family and what had happened to the man whose hand she'd once held with joy, though her mother had warned her that Joe was not their kind. Randolphs, after all, did not marry contractors, no matter how much money they had amassed, no matter that Joe's firm was involved with many major buildings in the city.

"Damn Irishmen," the Widow Randolph had said in her declining years. "We never should have allowed them to move into our town."

Faye, however, had not listened, because Joe thought she was a goddess and told her many, many times that he could not believe his luck in finding her. Coming from a household where her younger sister had collected all the men except their father, Faye found the Irishman quite irresistible.

Of course, everything had changed the night Dana was killed.

And now, there was Faye, divorced and alone, twice-stricken with breast cancer, a commercial, if not personal, success, seated on a small plane headed for LaGuardia where she would board a larger one that would take her to her son.

She rested her head against the seat back and wondered if the slight tremble that had come into her hands was one of trepidation or if that was an aftereffect of the radiation, too.

TWENTY

When Riley had not come home in time for dinner, Hannah was annoyed. Her daughter knew the rule: dinner together as a family except in times of fire, flood, or medical emergency. The kids and Evan laughed about it, but abided nonetheless. They did not know how important "family" was to Hannah, or that it was because, without them, she had none.

So Hannah had been annoyed, but not as angry as when she went home after the group meeting and found Evan pacing in the kitchen. "I need you in the shed," he said, which was where they went to discuss something in private.

Casey looked at Denise and rolled his eyes and Hannah followed Evan out back to the greenhouse.

"Did you tell her?" Evan accused once they were inside and he'd closed the plastic-covered door behind them.

Hannah inhaled the soil scent. "Tell who what?" But even as she asked, Hannah simply knew.

He folded his arms at his waist as if holding in his anger. "Riley. Did you tell her about Texas?"

Hannah moved to a row of peat-moss cups that showed

tall, greening sprouts of summer flowers—impatiens, perhaps—that should be ready by Memorial Day. Her chemo would be finished, and she'd be scheduled for surgery. The lavender, pink, and coral flowers would be in full bloom; she would not. "Of course I didn't tell her, Evan. But not because I agree with you." She did not add that she might have told her out of spite, but Riley had left for school too early that morning.

"She's not home yet," he said. "I assumed you'd told her and she's angry and decided to stay with one of her friends."

Why did he assume that Riley would be angry? What if, unlike him, Riley understood? She stopped poking at the green leaves. "Wait a minute," she said. "Riley's not home yet?"

"No."

"She hasn't called?"

He puffed his cheeks, then pushed out a whoosh of air. "It's worse," he said. "I think some of her things are gone."

Hannah steadied herself on the makeshift shelving. She stared in disbelief. "What?"

Evan unlocked his arms. His hands fell to his sides. He tipped his head up to the ceiling and silently closed his eyes.

Hannah took a step back. "What are you saying?"

He looked tired, gray, and older, as if he were the one who was undergoing chemo. "I guess we need to call her friends," he said. "She must be with one of them."

Hannah kept staring at him. Then she sort of laughed. "Oh, Evan, stop overreacting. This is simple teenage rebellion. Riley hates me because I have cancer, that's all. She thinks if she asserts her independence everything will be all right." As she said it, Hannah tried hard to believe it.

"No," Evan said, "there's more."

Whether from instinct or experience, Hannah had a

sudden urge to press her palms against her ears and block out the words that he'd say next. Whatever they were going to be, the words would not be good.

"Her clothes are gone," he said, and she knew that she'd been right, she did not want to hear this, not now, not ever. "Donna Langforth stopped by tonight and asked if Riley was sick, because she didn't go to school today."

And Hannah did exactly as she wanted. She threw her palms against her ears and ran out of the greenhouse, the plastic-covered door slapping shut behind her.

She ran upstairs because she did not know where else to go. She ran upstairs and wanted to close her bedroom door and rip off her hideous wig and climb under her covers and never leave her bed. She wanted to do those things and yet, in order to get there, Hannah had to pass by Riley's bedroom.

Which, of course, she could not do. She could not pass by without going inside. Without seeing for herself that Riley's things were gone.

Her cropped tees: gone.

Her hip-huggers: gone.

Her favorite clogs: gone, too.

Worst of all, her backpack with her favorite CDs— Britney, *NSYNC, and, yes, Katie Gillette—gone.

Hannah leaned against the white bureau that she and Mother Jackson had stenciled with bunnies and baby lambs right after Riley was born. Three or four times she'd asked Riley if she wanted the bureau changed: Her daughter had said no; she liked it as it was.

She hadn't taken the bureau, of course, but it seemed she'd taken everything else that mattered, at least to her.

. . .

The last time Rita had driven to Joe Geissel's house in West Chop truly had been the last of many times, when she'd gone practically with hat in hand because she'd learned that, on top of everything, she owed the IRS twenty grand. She had not told Joe, of course, because Rita Blair was far too proud. Instead, she'd tried to make him list his summer house with her so the commission would bail her out.

When he'd not agreed she'd gone after his wife.

The next day he'd shown up on her doorstep, spewing obscenities at her like, "What the fuck do you think you're doing?" when he'd known what she'd been doing all along.

"I thought you wanted to sell your house," Rita had maintained.

"I hadn't planned on getting a divorce in the process," the angry, red-faced man replied.

"You should have thought of that before you slept with me."

He had steadied his eyes on her and said he should have been more careful in his choice of partners. Then the zinger came when Joe added, "I thought I could trust you."

With all the men who had come and gone from her lonely, lonely life, Rita had never done anything to warrant anyone's mistrust. With those words that Joe sputtered, she'd realized just how low she'd gone, just how scared she had become.

And now, in the darkness, she was headed along Beach Road, straight toward Joe Geissel's house again, this time not for heated sex, but for a confrontation with his wife . . . because Rita knew if she was ever going to sleep again, she needed to clear this matter up. She could not have Katie or Hannah or the whole damn island of women yet to come, miss out on the Women's Center because she'd been so stupid long ago.

Rita only hoped that Faye was home and that she was not too late for amends.

Katie wondered if she'd ever see her father again, and if she did, what she would say.

You destroyed our family, then you said it was my mother's fault.

You paid people to be nice to me so I'd do everything you said.

My whole career is a joke.

I hate you for what you've done.

But did she really hate him?

She sat in the living room at the piano, looking over Joleen's songs, plunking out a note, a chord or two. Joleen had gone to bed; Katie had tried that, too, but a nagging ache inside her stomach kept her from falling asleep. Perhaps she'd had too much herbal tea at the meeting, perhaps the baby was feeling the same angst that Katie was, a gnawing loneliness that she'd been lied to by so many she had trusted, except, of course, Joleen, who'd simply never told her about Cliff and Ina, who'd never warned her to watch out for herself.

Her eyes moved from the keyboard to the telephone that sat on the table by the sofa. What was her father doing now, with his lover buried in the ground? What about Miguel? Had he run back to his daughter's mother and begged for her forgiveness?

She plunked another chord. Tears ran down her cheeks.

Closing the lid of the piano, Katie rested her forehead on the top. She wondered what would happen to her father if she never sang again.

A small cramp gripped her stomach. Katie hugged it

tightly and looked at the phone again. He'd been a good and decent father who had worked hard for her career, who protected her from others by paying Miguel to love her.

She supposed it wasn't criminal.

It was, however, painful, like the pain she felt right now that did not leave her stomach.

Then a long cramp squeezed her gut. She stood up quickly; and an odd warmth oozed between her legs. A whimper cried from deep inside her. She did not have to check to know the warmth was wet and it was blood.

"I know it's late, but I need to speak with Lindsay," Hannah said into the phone.

Lindsay Jordan's mother—a woman Hannah barely knew—said she was sorry, but Lindsay was asleep. She asked if she could help.

Hannah wound the cord around her fingers. The Jordans' house was the eleventh that she'd called and there was the remotest possibility that Riley had gone there, because they lived out in Aquinnah where Riley rarely went, simply because it was too far.

"My daughter, Riley," Hannah said, her voice slipping into a cracking, garbled sound. She lowered her head. She could not stand to hear one more person—one more mother or one more father—say "Sorry, I haven't seen Riley today." Hannah shook her head and said, "Never mind, Mrs. Jordan. I'm sorry to have bothered you." She reached across the round, maple kitchen table and hung the receiver up on the wall.

"That's it," she said to Evan, who sat across from her, his face as pale as hers, his body now as ravaged with dis—ease as Hannah's was with cancer. He turned back to the papers and notes and the phone book that lay open on the table.

He flipped the pages, searching for another schoolmate's name, another number, another address of someone who might know.

"Forget it, Evan. We've been through everyone. Everyone who might know where she's gone."

"No," he insisted. "We must have missed someone . . ."

"She didn't show up at school today. No one except Carlie Daggett has seen her since school on Friday. And Carlie saw her leave the library Saturday afternoon. She came home after that, remember?"

Evan nodded, though Hannah would have bet that he did not remember. Details such as that seemed unimportant at the time, when you had no idea you'd be called upon to remember each iota of every minute and each coming and going of every child at a later time.

"She isn't hurt," Evan said. "You don't think she's hurt?"

"She ran away, Evan. She's fourteen and she's confused right now. I will not believe that she's been . . . hurt. She ran away, that's all." *That's all.* As if it weren't the big deal that it was, as if it was as harmless as going to the beach to look for wampum or to dig for clams.

"We need to call the police," Hannah said the words that she'd been trying to avoid.

Evan moved his eyes away from her. "I guess," he said.

They sat there for another moment, as if neither wanted to be the one to do the deed, to make the act official that Riley, indeed, was gone.

Rita was dead asleep when the telephone rang. She woke up with her heart hammering in her throat, with the dreaded fear that something bad had happened—Charlie!—to someone she loved.

She raced into the hall, because she'd never had an extension put in her bedroom. She collided with Mindy who rounded the opposite corner simultaneously. Their eyes flashed at each other; they reached for the receiver. Rita got there first.

"Rita?" a breathless voice, a woman's voice, quickly asked.

It could not be about Charlie. Please, God, don't let it be about Charlie . . .

"Yes?"

"Rita, it's Joleen."

Joleen. It was not about Charlie. The hammering inside her eased a tiny bit. She ran her hand through her mass of hair, then put her arm around Mindy's small shoulders and held the child close to her.

"Joleen," she said, "is something wrong?"

"It's the baby. Katie's baby."

"Oh, no," Rita moaned, loosening her hold on Mindy.

"I've brought her to the hospital. The doctor isn't here yet. She's bleeding, Rita. I'm sorry to bother you, but Katie's really scared."

"Of course she is."

"Can you come over? I tried calling the woman, Hannah, but her line's been busy. And I get nothing but an answering machine on the other woman's line."

The other woman, Rita thought and could not bring herself to think of the irony in that. Yes, Rita knew that Faye was not at home. *Returned to Boston,* Rita had deduced a short while ago when she'd found the house locked up and dark, when her plan to apologize had been thwarted because *the other woman* wasn't home.

She blinked her selfish thoughts away. "I'll be there," she said. "Give me ten or fifteen minutes." Quickly she hung up the phone. She took Mindy by the shoulders and looked squarely in the girl's eyes. "I have to go out for a little while. Will you keep an eye on Hazel and the twins?"

Mindy looked at Rita with those knowing eyes. "What happened to Katie?"

Rita brushed back a lock of hair from the worried scowl on Mindy's face. "I can't say anything, honey, you know that. But I'm sure she'll be all right."

"What about the baby? Is it about the baby?"

Rita kissed Mindy on the cheek. "Please, honey," she said. "I'll tell you everything I can when I come home."

TWENTY·ONE

"We've called her closest friends and even some who aren't," Hannah explained to Sheriff Talbott, who had come with Officers Harrington and Solitario because the Vineyard made the safety of its children a top priority. At first they'd sat in the living room, but then moved to the kitchen because that was where the phone was and because it was more comfortable there.

Hannah poured coffee for the men and sliced a cranberry-orange bread, not that anyone would eat it. She sat down next to Evan, who had barely said a word except to shoo Casey and Denise back to bed. Hannah would have bet, however, that the two younger kids were sitting on the stairs, straining to hear the grown-ups' conversation. It was a trick they'd learned from Riley several years ago.

Riley, the smartest of their children, the most clever, the most difficult to raise.

Riley, with the black, Mexican hair.

"We'll need a list of names," Hugh Talbott said, "and addresses if you have them."

"You won't go to the houses tonight will you?" Hannah asked. "It's so late . . ."

"Your daughter's missing, ma'am," Officer Harrington added. "Time can be important."

Hannah looked away from him. She picked up a slice of bread and put it on a napkin. She wondered if she felt worse now than when Doc Hastings said that she had cancer, and decided that she did. Faye had said cancer paled compared to losing a child. Hannah wanted to scream.

"This is a difficult question," Hugh asked quietly, "but have you noticed a change in Riley's mood lately? Any behavior differences?"

Hannah stared down at the slice of bread, at its chunks of nuts and berries, the things that, before the cancer and the chemo, had always tasted so good; morsels of calories and fat that had helped stuff down her feelings and help dam up the hurt.

"Our daughter is fourteen, Sheriff," she said. "Her mood changes from day to day. But lately, yes, she's been more quiet than usual. And more rebellious, too, if that makes any sense."

Hugh nodded as if it made sense to him.

He thinks she's taking drugs, Hannah deduced. She sighed. She pushed the napkin away. "It's not what you think," she said. She told him about her breast cancer and about the loss of Mother Jackson. "When I say I'm not going to die, Riley does not believe me. She's been very angry at me for getting sick." Now that Hannah had said it out loud, it made total sense. But Hugh and the policemen just looked at her as if she were dreaming.

They asked a few more questions, drank their coffee, then said they'd do their best to find her.

Then Hannah went to bed, but not to sleep. Evan said he'd be in the greenhouse if any word came through.

.   .   .

Rita wondered if she held the record for the person who'd spent more off-hours in the hospital than anyone else on the island, except the nurses and the orderlies who worked the oddball shifts. She walked into the emergency room, hating the familiar smell, hating that she knew exactly where to go.

The receptionist—Diane Leyfred, a woman Rita had known for many years and never liked—would not let Rita see Katie until she went down to the "very private" room and checked it with Joleen.

"Regulations," Diane said. "We used to only have to worry about the media in these situations. Now there are other concerns. You understand."

Not exactly, Rita thought, but knew that now was not the time to challenge anyone.

Diane took her sweet time.

". . . Excessive trauma to the baby . . ." Rita clearly heard the familiar voice of Doc Hastings' say when she finally was granted clearance into the designated "very private" room.

Not that anyone, including Rita, would have recognized the superstar. Katie was huddled under the sheet, her frightened eyes peering out just above the hemline, her hair tied back from her pale face. Joleen didn't look a whole lot healthier.

All eyes turned toward Rita. "Evening, Doc," she said. It was the first time that she'd seen him since he caught her in his files, the naughty child who'd been scolded by someone else's parent. "Katie," she said and went to the side of the bed. "How're you doing?"

Katie's small hand escaped from beneath the sheet and reached out to Rita's.

"She's had a scare," Doc said, "but I think she can go

home in a few days. We're going to do some tests and an ultrasound. My guess is that the stress that Katie's been under may have been the cause. In any event, the crisis seems to have passed without harm to the baby. We'll know more in the morning when the ultrasonographer is here."

Rita did not ask if an ultrasonographer would be available around the clock if—when—the island had the Women's Center.

Katie's eyes filled with tears. "I probably have to stay in bed for the rest of my pregnancy."

Doc smiled. "It's not so long," he said. "A few more weeks."

Rita squeezed Katie's hand. It was damp and cool. "I'll have to dig into my bag of goodies and see what I can find to keep you occupied." She turned to Joleen. "Any chance we can have our meetings at your house?" From the corner of Rita's eye, she detected an approving nod from Doc. Perhaps she'd just atoned for her office break-in sin.

"I'll even bring refreshments," Rita added, because she was on a roll. Maybe Hazel could help her bake them. Or Mindy. Yes, Mindy would love to do something for Katie Gillette.

"Of course," Joleen replied, the recluse opening her home for her daughter's sake. "I'll fix a bed up in the sunroom. Then Katie won't be stuck upstairs."

Rita smiled at Katie. "Can you be counted on to stay in bed for weeks?"

"Maybe fewer than we thought," Doc said.

Fewer?

Though none of them said anything, fewer weeks could mean much more: less chance of complications; an earlier chance for radiation; and, of course, there was the billboard in Times Square that read: JULY 4TH, CENTRAL PARK.

. . .

Just before noon, Hannah took a shower. Casey and Denise were still in bed, as she'd suspected they'd stayed up late listening on the stairs until Hugh Talbott and his officers had left. Hannah said she didn't want the kids to go to school on such little sleep. The truth was, she was terrified to let them from her sight.

In the shower, she soaped up her bald head as if it still bore hair, a small, but significant gesture that she made daily for herself. *The hair will grow back*, the gesture said. *The hair will grow back and you'll be well again*, not that it mattered now.

After rinsing off her head, she lathered both her breasts. When she massaged the tips, both nipples tingled in response, the right one unaware it had been invaded by disease.

How was that possible, she wondered? She held each breast in one hand; she kneaded the soft soap bubbles under, around, on top, fully, firmly. Again. Again.

It felt so good, Hannah paid no attention to where her lump lay in dreaded wait. Instead, she moved her sudsy hand between her legs, her parted thighs. She thought about John Arthur and his muscled, sweaty body, his soft, sweet smile, the way he held the Gatorade. She gently rubbed herself, moving back and forth against her hand. She felt her warmth rise slowly, a familiar, heated glow. She rubbed a little harder . . .

. . . and then she remembered Riley.

"Damn!" she shouted. What the hell was she doing? Masturbating in the shower while her daughter was missing? What was wrong with her? *What was wrong with her?*

Hannah burst into angry, shameful tears. She covered her breasts and then her eyes with her wet, wandering hands, and then she shivered and she shook while the hot needles of the shower pelted down on her.

When Faye finally reached Phoenix it was late at night—later, even, according to her internal clock that was two hours ahead, and could have been three, but Arizona was a holdout and did not do Daylight Saving Time.

She rented a car at the airport and asked the clerk to recommend a decent hotel that was not hard to find. He checked availabilities and directed her to The Buttes, a magnificent creation carved into a rock mountain that Faye knew she'd appreciate more in the morning when she wasn't overtaken by exhaustion.

In the morning, however, as the sun rose over the jagged rock and sparkled off a waterfall outside her window, Faye's tiredness had been replaced by grim anxiety.

Standing at the window, the sash of her silk robe pulled tight, she followed the cascade with her eyes, as it trundled to the lagoonlike pool that twinkled aqua in the sun.

How had it happened that a boy who'd been raised so close to the ocean had chosen to escape into the desert?

Perhaps because of Dana and the accident. Or perhaps he'd needed to shut out everything related to his family and his past.

Closing her eyes, she let herself think about what she and he would say and do. What did a mother say to a son after a decade of silence?

What if he wouldn't see her; what if he wouldn't talk to her?

Rejection. No. She would not, could not think of that.

Turning to the small desk, she picked up the phone book. Crawdaddies was the name of Greg's restaurant—Greg and a man named Mike Tanner, who might be his partner in the business and in life, too, for all Faye knew. She ran her finger quickly through the section. There it was. A big display ad that boasted THE NEW ORLEANS OF THE SOUTHWEST.

She stared at the ad and kept the book flat open. Then she sat and began her vigil until lunchtime, which she supposed would be the best time to place the call.

"We've checked down at the docks." Hugh Talbott's voice drifted up the stairs.

He was there. Hugh had come back. *Dear God,* Hannah prayed as she stood in the hallway outside her bedroom, clutching the robe she'd just put on, *please let the news be good.*

"And?" Evan asked.

It seemed that it took an eternity before Hugh replied. Why was everything so slow? Why did Hannah feel as if the whole world had slowed down like the carousel in Oak Bluffs at the end of a long ride?

And if everything was so slow, why was her heart beating so fast?

"And a girl matching Riley's description boarded the six-fifteen morning boat yesterday."

"To Woods Hole?"

"Yes. The good news is that she was alone. Which rules out kidnapping," he paused, then added, "or other things."

Other things. Hannah supposed that meant things like drug dealers or pimps. She quickly tied her robe and hurried down the stairs. Thank God she'd put her wig back on when she'd come out of the shower.

"She has no money," Evan said.

"She had some. She paid for her ticket in cash. One way."

One way. Proof that she had no intention of returning. Hannah sucked in a breath. "Where did she go once she got across?"

Hugh shrugged. "That's what we'd like to know. I sent Harrington and Solitario to check things out. But I need to know if Riley knows anyone over there. Did she ever mention meeting anyone from the mainland? Maybe on-line?"

"We don't have a computer for the kids. When they need to use one, they do it at school or at the library."

"What about friends? Any on the mainland? Any family over there?"

Hannah shook her head. "No. No friends. No family."

Maybe it was the long way Evan looked at her that made her start to feel the nausea. Maybe it was the way he turned his head away, as if knowing, knowing this was all her fault.

"Not that we know of," Evan added, and he was right, because they didn't really know.

And that's when Hannah got the sickest feeling in her stomach, a feeling so upsetting it made chemo look like a day at South Beach in Katama. Her thoughts floated back to the morning—had it been only yesterday?—when Riley was not there when Hannah had gone to wake her. Then, in a dreamlike, swirling motion, Hannah thought about the night before, when she'd confessed her past to Evan as they lay safely in their bed.

Safely, she'd thought.

Safely in their room.

But had Riley been listening against the wall or at their door? Had Riley heard Hannah's confession about San Antonio?

Oh, God, she thought, *was that why Riley was gone?*

She heard herself cry out; she grasped the banister too late as the blood drained from her face and her still-damp, showered body slid down to the hardwood floor.

•   •   •

He lived halfway down a canyon in a house of cedar and tall glass through which Faye supposed Greg could see the sun rise and set against the red, red rocks and feel the healing peace of the Indian legends as they wove whispers through the pines.

It was late afternoon before Faye found her way up north from Phoenix, before she drove into the town known for its magic and its aura and its bell rock that rose up high above the land and its cathedral carved into the mountain where soft chants of monks could now be heard.

She did not stop to witness these things, of course. She had read about them in the tourist guide while awaiting time to pass until she could call Crawdaddies and ask if Greg Geissel was there or what time he could be expected.

"Greg's up north this week," a disconnected female voice replied.

"Sedona?"

"Yes. He's in Phoenix every other week."

She asked and was given the address of Crawdaddies up north.

"But you won't find him there tonight," the female added. "They're closed up north on Tuesdays."

Faye tapped her pen on the desk. She quickly said she was a friend from back East, and was only in town for a day. Did Greg have a home up north as well?

In Boston, no one in their right mind or even in their wrong mind would give an unknown caller the home address of their boss. But Phoenix was not Boston, Faye reminded herself as she parked the rental car a distance from the house, far enough away so he might not see her first, despite the bank of windows that greeted everything and everyone outside. As she stepped out of the car, Faye noticed that the air was cooler here than in Phoenix; dry and dusty, but cooler, more peaceful.

She traversed the red clay road in her Bali pumps and wished she'd brought her sneakers from the Vineyard, perhaps even her jeans. Then she suppressed a smile: Had she become a true islander after all?

When she reached the front walk, Faye stopped and took a breath: It was laced with flecks of throat-closing anxiety, despite the clean, clear air, despite the calm serenity that loomed around her.

She looked into the driveway, where two cars were parked—a BMW and a Mercedes. If one could tell by homes and cars, it appeared that, indeed, her son was doing well—financially, at least—with all the trappings she could snobbishly admit she would have hoped for him.

How had he done so well when he'd left home with less than five hundred dollars?

She pushed away the thought. She took another breath. The time had come to walk up to the door. Tucking her silver hair—hair that was still brown when he had left—she slowly walked up to the door and rang a large brass bell.

Her heart stopped beating—of course it did—and did not start again, even when she heard footsteps approach from the other side.

And then the door opened.

Faye blinked against the sunlight that framed the figure at the door.

She visored her forehead with her hand. "Greg?" she asked, but even as she asked, she knew that she was wrong. The man before her was not her son. It was Joe, her former husband, the father of her children, part of the reason Greg had left so long ago.

TWENTY·TWO

"I always thought gray hair would make you look older."

It was good that Joe spoke first, because Faye was caught too unawares to know what to say, her jumbled thoughts uploading question after question, all a variation of "What the hell are you doing at our son's house?" But Joe might misconstrue that into thinking he had the upper hand, so instead Faye simply said, "My hairdresser says it isn't gray but silver."

Joe reassessed her head as if he'd last seen her yesterday and not four years ago, when they'd faced each other in the courtroom and the judge had granted the divorce. Faye knew that once the shock had passed, she'd be angry that he was acting so nonplussed.

"I have not, however, traveled across the country to talk about my hair." She wondered if his blasé reaction was merely a defense tactic to cover up his shock. She could not remember if that was something Joe would do. Over time she had worked hard to erase all sentiment of her husband from her mind.

He blinked. "How are you, Faye?" he asked with the kind of interest that seemed genuine.

"I'll be better when I'm out of the heat," she replied. "And when I've seen our son."

"Yes," he said, "of course." He stepped aside and Faye walked past him. He smelled of sandalwood, a scent that she'd once bought him. She wondered if he'd worn it when he'd been with Rita Blair.

"I'm sure you know I'm surprised to see you here," she said.

"And you," he said.

She walked to the wall of windows and stared out at the rusty canyon, wishing she were somewhere else, anywhere but there.

"He's not here right now," Joe added. "Greg."

She nodded, because what did she expect? It was the way life went for Faye: never easy, never smooth.

"He went to town, but he'll be back soon. You can wait here if you'd like."

She did not know if she could do that, if she could stand in the same space as her former husband and not kick and scream and claw at his face because he'd never told her that he knew where Greg was—unless . . . Had he known all along?

Chances were Riley was safe. She'd not been bound and gagged and raped and had her throat slit until she'd bled to death. She'd not been a victim of any of the other million scenarios Hannah could have conjured up if she'd not known all along that Riley had run away—that Riley was simply making a statement to her mother that she hated her.

Hate, Hannah could deal with.

Rape or murder, she could not.

But if Riley had overheard Hannah's confession, could

that have made her angry enough to run away . . . to San Antonio?

Don't be ridiculous, Hannah scolded herself. Riley could not have gone to Texas. She did not know Betty Barnes' name. She did not know where the woman was locked up.

Besides, Evan had said, *She has no money.* Yet Hugh said she paid cash for her ferry ticket.

She had no money.

Unless . . .

There was one possibility.

Which was why, after the sheriff left again, Hannah climbed into the attic, to Mother Jackson's trunk.

The beaded purse was gone.

The Silver Certificates, gone.

Certainly the cash was enough to afford passage to the Cape, and for a time thereafter, until . . . until what? How far ahead was a fourteen-year-old capable of thinking and of planning? Did she expect she could find work without a permit or did she think the cash would last forever?

Hannah noticed that Scout's overalls from *To Kill a Mockingbird* were rumpled in disarray, not the way Hannah would have left them when she was there . . . when? Just the other day . . .

Oh, God, she thought.

Oh.

No.

And all Hannah could remember was when she'd gone up to the attic and she'd read the old news clipping and how she'd thought she'd heard a bat.

Oh.

God.

Wishing she did not have to do what she had to do, Hannah slowly began to remove the trunk's contents and set them carefully on the wide floorboards around her.

Please, please, she whispered into the air as she took out one playbill after another, one folded poster, one covered, leather box.

At last she reached the false bottom. She stopped; she said one last prayer. Then Hannah lifted the lid of the compartment.

She groped around the small space. Nothing; nothing was there. Not her yearbook or her birth certificate. Not the old biology book. Not the news clippings from the trial. Everything was gone. Riley knew it all.

Did God have some sort of checklist that He used for everyone, a certain preset number of problems that each person must endure?

Before the breast cancer, Hannah might have felt she'd been through enough, that no benevolent God would make her go through any more pain for one lifetime. She remembered walking home one night after a play. She was holding Riley's right hand and Evan was holding Riley's left, and she felt filled with so much gratitude and love that she figured her quota of hard times must finally have been met. She thought God must be pleased; her suffering was done.

She might have even felt that way until her diagnosis, despite losing Mother Jackson, despite her growing difficulties with Riley. Those were ordinary, everyday problems. They did not compare to Hannah's early life that she'd hidden in the trunk.

She thought of that now, as she went out to the greenhouse where there was a telephone, an extension Evan had put in to take his calls for work. He was not working now.

On her way downstairs from the attic, Hannah had seen Evan sitting in the living room, staring at the television though the set was not turned on. Riley's disappearance had made her husband motionless.

Hannah had stopped in the kitchen and taken her pocketbook from the broom closet. She'd opened up her wallet, and removed the torn section of yellowed paper with a number written on it. Even in the darkness of the obscure corner of her wallet, even though the ink had faded over time and the creases of the paper had nearly broken through, Hannah could still make out the phone number that had been written so long ago.

She'd hoped she'd never have to call it.

At Evan's small desk in the greenhouse, she shoved aside a stack of order forms that needed tending to. Then she picked up the receiver and drew in a long breath.

Oh, God.

Oh, God.

Was that the smell of pot?

For a moment, Hannah did not breathe. And then, in that moment, she decided some things no longer mattered. Not what the neighbors thought or didn't think, not breast cancer, not whether or not her husband was smoking pot. The only thing that mattered was finding Riley.

Hannah picked up the receiver and firmly dialed the numbers.

Texas Department of Women's Corrections.

On one hand, it had been so long since Hannah had heard a Texas accent that she nearly did not understand the operator's drawn-out words. On the other hand, or with some other, innate sense, Hannah sadly knew exactly what the woman said.

"I'm calling about one of your prisoners." She closed her eyes so this wouldn't seem so real.

"Call her lawyer," the Texan drawled. "This isn't a hotel."

"Wait!" Hannah cried, afraid the woman would hang up. "I don't want to talk to her. I only want to know if she's still there. If she's been released."

"I can't give you that information."

"Who can?"

"Like I said. Call her lawyer."

"I don't know who he is." She might have recognized the name if she could check the news clippings, but Riley had those now.

The woman sighed. "I'm sorry, lady. I can't help you."

"Please," Hannah implored, "the inmate is my mother. My fourteen-year-old daughter has run away, and I'm afraid she's going there. Please. I live in Massachusetts and I can't come down there. I have breast cancer. Please."

During the pause that followed, Hannah feared she'd been disconnected. Then the woman asked, "What stage?"

"Excuse me?"

"Breast cancer. What stage?"

She felt her body sigh. "Three," she said. "I'm almost finished with my chemo, then it's surgery."

"My sister had Stage Three eighteen years ago. She's doing great."

Hannah did not know what to say. She should have felt reassurance. Instead, she wanted only to cry.

"You do everything they tell you, honey, and you'll be fine."

Hannah nodded as if they were in the same room now, sisters in awareness.

"Now," the woman added, "what was the inmate's name?"

Hannah blinked. A tear leaked from the outside corner of each eye. "Barnes," she said, wiping the tears. "Betty— Elizabeth—Barnes."

"Hang on. This might take a few seconds."

So Hannah hung on, her thoughts drifting to the Texas heat and a nameless, faceless woman whose sister had Stage Three breast cancer and who was doing great, but might not be so great if she had a fourteen-year-old daughter who'd run two thousand miles away.

She sucked in another breath and quickly wished she hadn't. That was pot, all right. No mistaking it.

"Sorry," the woman's voice said when she came back on the line, "but Elizabeth Barnes was released last month on good behavior."

"After you left me," Joe was saying, "I couldn't stand it any longer. I lost everything. I had to find my son."

Faye had opted not to sit, but instead remained at the bank of windows, watching the sun do its day's-end stretch over the canyon as it seeped through the twisting juniper trees and the rich dark pines, illuminating the red, high-desert floor.

She could have challenged Joe's words about her leaving him. She could have reminded him that he had pushed her away with his philandering with Rita Blair and all the other women who'd come and gone before and after. She could have said that he did not "lose everything," that she had only kept the Vineyard house and he'd taken the rest. What he'd really "lost" had been his family. As she had, too.

She could have said those things, but what would be the point? Joe would still be Joe and they still would be divorced and Greg would remain the only common thread left between their lives.

"So you found him," she said. "And he welcomed you so quickly?"

Joe laughed. "Not so quickly. I bought a house here in Sedona. It took two years before he said 'hello.'"

Faye felt a smile of some gratification pass her lips.

"Our boy has done okay," he added.

"With a little of his daddy's help, I suspect," she replied, and for some reason hoped her words were not laced with sarcasm, because she'd not wanted them to be.

"No," he said, and that surprised her. "Greg did this on his own, with his partner, Mike. Neither one had a pot to piss in, but they wanted a restaurant, so they worked their butts off. I guess he picked up a thing or two from his old man after all."

He might have added "and from his old lady," but as much as he'd say he wasn't, Joe was a chauvinist at heart. It was their generation; old traditions too often died too hard.

She wanted to ask how he felt about Greg being gay. She would not have expected he'd take it so well. Perhaps "losing everything" had altered his attitude.

"And what about you?" Faye asked. "Do you live out here, too?"

"Part-time. Part-time in Boston. Semi-retired from the business. Not completely, though."

Maybe he'd softened, but apparently he still needed to boss someone around, be a man, tough as nails.

"And you?" he asked. "How is your business?"

"Okay," she answered. "Fine."

"And your sister?"

"Claire is fine, too." She wouldn't tell him otherwise; he and Claire narrowly escaped killing each other on more than one occasion.

"And your health?" he asked.

She did not, would not pause. "Fine."

In the distance she heard the low howl of a coyote. It was followed by another, this one closer, then another.

"Choir time," Joe said, hoisting himself from the dust-colored sofa and walking to where Faye stood. "Every night at sunset, the coyotes sing to one another all through the canyon."

They stood beside one another; they listened. The music was, indeed, a chorus of nature, of highs and lows and in-betweens, a melody of life. Beneath the chorus, too close to her, Faye heard Joe's breath as well.

"He blames himself, you know," Joe said, and he needed no other words.

"Yes," Faye replied. How could she not know that?

And then the door behind them opened, and her son—their son—stood there.

It was one of those rare moments frozen by time and space and emotions not yet ready to be felt, a tableau of life on hold while thoughts made themselves ready to be thought, while voices waited to know what words to speak.

"Mom?" Greg said at last, and Faye felt instantly ashamed that she had not gone first.

She moved toward him.

He set two grocery bags on the Spanish tile in the foyer.

She stopped about a yard in front of him. Was he taller than before? No, he was not taller, but he was fuller, "filled out" her mother might have said, if she had known him, if she'd not died three months before Greg had been born. *Died because her daughter married a rogue of an Irishman*, Faye had often mused with great mother-daughter guilt.

Stepping closer, Faye lifted a hand and touched the high cheekbone of his face. She looked into his aqua eyes that were lidded with dark lashes. Her handsome son still resembled her sister, Claire.

"Greg," she whispered, as the music of the coyotes resonated in the background. "Can you forgive me?"

He stood there for a moment, his eyes scanning her face,

their color turning bright, brighter, from the pools of water rising in them.

And then he touched her shoulders and Faye began to cry, and she was overcome with weakness and the need to just be in the comfort of her only living child.

TWENTY-THREE

The morning of the road race dawned sunny and cool—a perfect day for running, a perfect day for thinking about other things than sickness and missing children.

Hannah, of course, could not, would not go. What would be the point? To hand out paper numbers? To serve juice and cookies at the end?

She'd been awake most of the night. She'd had her chemo treatment—her last and, hopefully, her final. It had depleted her, yet it was difficult to sleep. How could anyone have slept when all the children were not safe at home and the husband had stopped speaking to most everyone?

Sipping her tea, Hannah looked out the kitchen window at the dew that kissed the grass. She closed her eyes and heard the foghorn in the distance on the sound. She thought about her life and how sick she was of it.

Happy, smiling Hannah. She was sick of that façade as well. There was, after all, only one thing that made her smile these days, only one thing that had made her genuinely smile for nearly two years now.

Before thinking much more, Hannah brought her mug over to the sink, rinsed it out with quiet, deliberate tidiness, then slipped her warm-up jacket over her pink fleece sweats, and quietly left the house.

She took the truck because it was the last vehicle in the driveway. As she headed toward Beach Road, Hannah was aware that her smile had returned, that it grew wider with each curve and turn that brought her closer to the place where the race would start: the gazebo at Oak Bluffs.

"I'm here," she'd say to John Arthur, "such as I am."

And he would grin and direct her to the table where she could check the runners in, where he would lean close to her while showing her the paperwork, where she would pick up on his chemistry and know that if he would have her, she would succumb to him that day.

The consequences would not matter. Life was in shambles anyway.

She wedged the truck into a small spot, surprised at how many cars already lined the streets. She checked her wig in the rearview mirror, inhaled a breath for courage, and went out to meet her fate.

Weaving through the crowd attired in T-shirts and shorts, Hannah began to make her way to the registration tables, to the area where banners hung from the gazebo: A–H, I–O, P–Z. Her eyes moved quickly from left to right and back again, in search of the one familiar face that mattered.

"Hannah!" a voice called out. She turned quickly, but it was only David Metzger, a fellow church parishoner, the one whose wife headed up the bake sale. "How are you feeling? You're not running, are you?"

She shook her head. "No, but John Arthur thought I might be able to help out. Have you seen him?"

Metzger scanned the crowd and shook his head. "Nope. Not yet."

"Well," Hannah said, "good luck. Have a good run."

"Hannah!" It was Mary McCarthy. "Gosh, it's good to see you!"

"Hey!" Hannah called back. "Have you seen John Arthur?"

But Mary simply shrugged and waved and darted off, a paper sign printed with a large number 34 flapping on her back.

She recognized Barbara and Jen and Melissa from school; apparently John Arthur had encouraged others to take up running, too. She tried not to feel jealous or insecure. She held her head up high and approached the folding tables, where she spotted Laura Carter, the school nurse. As always, Laura was in charge.

"Laura," Hannah asked bravely, "have you seen John Arthur?"

Laura gestured for her to wait a second while she checked another name off a computer sheet. "No," she said at last. "I don't expect he'll be here."

No?

"Oh?" Hannah asked, hoping she'd concealed her disappointment. "Is something wrong?"

Laura checked off another name, handed out another paper sign. She turned to Hannah. "I guess you haven't heard. He took another job in Taunton. He resigned last week."

Hannah stood but didn't speak. Around her, more people gathered in a line.

"A through H over here," Laura called out to the crowd.

And Hannah kept on standing, wondering what she should do next and if she should just laugh with short sarcasm and thank her guardian angel for stepping in before Hannah had screwed up her life beyond repair.

·　　　·　　　·

Doc kept Katie in the hospital for a week. Rita went to see her every day; Joleen, who wrestled with the constant fear of being recognized, visited her daughter after dark—a time that grew later as each day drifted more closely toward summer.

Rita had meant to call Hannah, to tell her about Katie. But facing a last round of chemo, surely Hannah had other things on her mind. Rita decided there was no harm in waiting.

As for Faye, Rita had driven to the Geissel house three times during the week: no car was in the driveway, no signs of life were visible. It seemed apparent that the woman had returned to Boston, to her other life.

But Rita had no other life, this was it. Which was why, on Monday, after visiting with Katie, listening to the baby's heartbeat ("It's getting stronger, don't you think?" the excited, expectant mother asked) and reassuring Katie that yes, everything would be fine, Rita had stopped by the supermarket to buy ingredients for carrot cupcakes for tonight and for the penuche she'd been meaning to send to Sheriff Talbott and Sam Oliver in New York. Maybe she'd coerce Mindy into doing the baking.

Juggling the bags as she let herself in her kitchen door, Rita reminded herself again that she had to call Hannah and tell her they'd be meeting in Katie's hospital room until Doc released her. She should also, she supposed, call Faye, just in case. She would leave a message for propriety's sake.

Propriety, she thought, setting the grocery bags on the counter. *Under the circumstances, how utterly absurd.*

"Doc is discharging Katie," Mindy said as she greeted Rita in the kitchen. "Joleen called. She asked if you can pick her up."

Mindy spoke as if she were bosom buddies with the rock

star and her former-rock-star mom. Tabloid journalism again. TV "News" Magazines. Still, something didn't seem quite right. "Wait a minute," Rita said. "Joleen called and actually told you?"

With a twelve-year-old's smirk, Mindy said, "Well, she sort of thought that I was you."

Putting her hands on her hips, Rita feigned anger. "And what the heck made her think that?"

The smirk disappeared. Mindy averted her eyes. "Well, I sort of told her."

Rita shook her head. "And I'll bet you sort of told her I'd be glad to get Katie and bring her home, right?"

"She's ready now. Doc saw her right after you left, and told Katie she could go." Mindy moved to the grocery bags and began to empty them.

"Then that's settled," Rita said. "You'll have to make the carrot cupcakes for the meeting tonight."

"Yeah?"

"Yeah. But don't ever do that again, okay?"

The girl hesitated, then nodded. "I didn't mean to, Rita. It just sort of happened."

"Well, I hope it won't happen again."

Mindy smiled. "Sorry. Oh, and before I forget, Joleen asked if you'd stop by the store and pick up frozen peas."

"Frozen peas?"

"Yeah. The kind in a bag. She said Katie will need them."

With a sigh, Rita went into the other room. The thought of driving back to the hospital, stopping at the store, then delivering the patient to West Chop wasn't very appealing. But Katie would be excited and Joleen was depending on Rita and . . . and Rita realized she'd better call Hannah before she forgot again. Hannah and Faye. She'd better tell them they'd be meeting at Joleen's.

. . . .

Rita called Hannah first because it seemed easier. But the voice on the other end did not sound like her. More like an old woman.

"Hannah? It's me, Rita."

Hannah paused so long that Rita briefly wondered if she'd called the wrong number.

"Oh, Rita," the reply finally came. "I didn't recognize your voice."

Rita didn't say "ditto." She quickly filled her in on the near-miscarriage, the hospital stay, the fact that Katie now was confined to bed. "Joleen is going to let us hold our group meetings at her house. Is that okay with you?"

Again, a hesitation. Then Hannah slowly said, "I can't go, Rita. I'm not feeling well."

"Oh, I'm sorry. Is there anything I . . . we . . . can do to help?"

"No. No." Hannah stopped talking. Maybe she was crying.

"Hannah? What's wrong?" Had she had some bad news? Had her cancer spread? Had something happened with her mother?

"Riley ran away," Hannah's words sputtered out. "I don't want to leave the house again, in case the police find out something. In case she comes home."

Rita was relieved. It wasn't the cancer, it was only . . . Riley? The fourteen-year-old?

Hannah spilled the rest.

After listening carefully, Rita wondered if she could apply for a psychologist's license—no schooling required, just a few years on the Vineyard.

"Have you written any of this in your journal?"

"I bought a new notebook. I haven't opened it."

The "Facilitator's Brochure" hadn't mentioned what Rita should do if the participants wouldn't participate. "It might help you feel better."

Hannah, however, didn't reply.

Rita thought for a moment, then said, "Joleen doesn't live too far from you, Hannah. I'll pick you up at six-forty-five. If anything happens, I can have you home in two minutes."

"Oh, Rita, I can't."

"Yes, you can. And you will. Besides, good news never comes until you're not home."

"But, Rita . . ."

"Six-forty-five. No argument. And wear the purple hat." The last comment raised a small chuckle out of poor Hannah. Rita quickly hung up, then grabbed her keys and left to pick Katie up at the hospital. She wondered if, while she was out, she should have "Rita's Island Shuttle" painted on the side of her van.

TWENTY-FOUR

Rita was probably right, good news wouldn't come if Hannah just sat and waited. Today was the eighth day Riley had been gone—eight days and not a word except from the police who reported that the girl vanished once she'd reached the mainland. No taxi or shuttle drivers recalled seeing Riley, no people in Shuckers or Fishmonger's restaurants reported seeing a teenager with a backpack who was traveling alone.

It didn't make sense because it wasn't summer yet and tourists were still sparse. It didn't make sense because surely Riley would not have known where she was going, she would have had to ask directions to . . . where? San Antonio?

Or was it possible someone had picked Riley up?

Hannah stayed at the table next to the phone, her thoughts whirling together with no beginning and no end, or none that made sense. She no longer had John Arthur to think about, to distract her from real issues that needed her attention. It was right, she knew, but it was not comfortable.

She looked at the new spiral-bound notebook that sat

on the counter. It was the same kind of notebook she used in planning her lessons: The kids wouldn't read it if they thought it was schoolwork.

She turned back the cover and stared at the blank, white sheet. She glanced again at the phone that stood mute on the wall. Then, with a sigh, Hannah picked up a pen. And without further thought, she began to write.

Mother, she wrote, because now was the time, *I hate you. I hate what you did. I know you were angry because what McNally did would hurt me, but I hate it that you pulled apart our lives. I hate it that you made me run away from everything and everyone I once loved. Including you.*

A muscle seemed to squeeze around Hannah's heart. She fought off the discomfort and she kept writing.

Things turned out okay for me. I married Evan. She hesitated; she thought about the recent smell of pot and wondered what it would mean for the future. Then she reminded herself that it didn't matter. Less and less seemed to matter every day.

I have three children, each one different from the next. Riley, the oldest, looks like you, though I've never told anyone. She's fourteen now. But maybe you know that already.

You'd think that with all I now have, I wouldn't hate you still.

But I was so embarrassed and ashamed. And I was so helpless, the way I am right now. I hate you because my daughter has run away and I'm afraid she's gone to find you and I don't know what will happen if she does.

I can only say that if you upset her or make her cry, I will personally want to kill you, the way you killed McNally. What with the breast cancer I have, there's probably not much for me to lose.

Hannah rested her pen on the edge of the notebook. She reread the entry and wondered if she should share it at the meeting tonight. It wasn't as if she could send it to her

mother. She didn't, after all, have a clue where Betty
Barnes was now.

Lowering her aching, tired, hairless head, Hannah let
her teardrops fall onto the page.

If reconciliation had a face, it would have been Greg's; if it
had a place, it would have been Sedona. They spent hours
and days forgiving one another: Faye forgiving Greg, Greg
forgiving Faye, Joe forgiving Faye, Faye forgiving . . . yes,
Faye forgiving Joe. They spoke about Dana in good, happy
ways.

How she loved sailing, Faye exclaimed, *before she even
learned to swim.*

And looking for wampum, Joe added.

Claire still wears the ring Dana made for her.

But what about the skunks! Greg said with a laugh. *Man,
she loved to tease them. Remember when one sprayed the side of
the house?*

That was Dana's fault?

We thought it was you!

Joe had already told Greg about her first bout with breast
cancer. She did not tell either one of them about the second.

In the mornings they took leisurely walks; in the afternoons Faye napped at Greg's, while Joe went to his own
house to do the same; in the evenings she and Joe went to
Crawdaddies, where Greg and his staff treated them to de-
lectable offerings each night.

Cajun Rattlesnake? Why not? Faye responded with unbri-
dled gusto. She wondered how it happened that inner
peace opened all possibilities, and that loving life made no
task seem like a risk and no burden too heavy to fear.

For the first time in a long time, Faye wanted to live.

On the morning of the sixth day, reality returned.

She decided to check her messages: maybe Claire had returned from her most recent jaunt; maybe the fact that Faye had found Greg would give her and her sister a new starting point, too.

Four messages awaited, but not one from Claire.

Faye? Hi. It's R.J. Browne. I wondered if you wanted to join my friend and me for dinner. We're at Mayfield House until Wednesday. Give me a call.

Beep. She frowned a tiny bit, pleased that she'd not been there. A dinner date with R.J. and his ladyfriend would not be very cheerful.

Hi, Faye, this is Katie. I guess I'm okay and so is the baby, but I'm in the hospital. Doc says I have to stay in bed for the rest of my pregnancy. How the heck will I do that? Anyway, if you're around, I'd love to see you. I'm so bored! Bye.

Beep. Katie. What had happened? Was she truly okay? Katie seemed so positive, so spirited, so like Dana had been. Did Joleen have any idea how lucky she was?

This is Rita Rollins from the group. Pause. *I wanted you to know that we're meeting at Joleen's tonight instead of at the hospital.*

Beep.

Beep.

Faye, it's Hannah.

The voice was so strained that it was hard to believe it belonged to the kindly woman.

I don't know what to do, Faye. My Riley has run away. A long pause was followed by several sniffles. *Oh, God, I don't even know why I'm calling you. I know you lost your child . . . oh, never mind. I'm sorry to have disturbed you. I'll be fine, I'm sure.*

Despite the desert sun that drenched the wall of glass in Greg's living room, Faye felt a chill rise from her toes.

Hannah's daughter had run away? But she was just a child . . .

"Mom?" The question came so suddenly it shook her from her thoughts. It had been so many years since anyone had called her *Mom*.

"Dad's not going to join us this morning for our walk."

With a smile, Faye shrugged. "That's okay, honey. I'm sure you'll protect me from snakes and coyotes." But instead of heading for the door, Greg sat on the overstuffed chair beside her.

"Mom, do you know about Grace?"

Faye frowned. "Grace? No, I don't know anyone named Grace." Grace? But Greg was gay. Had that somehow changed?

Greg turned his gaze toward the red-rock canyon. "She's a local artist here in Sedona. Silver jewelry; it's really very pretty."

He was trying to say something; what on earth was it?

"Greg?" she asked, because Greg, the little boy, had sometimes needed to be prodded.

He sighed. "Dad's known her about a year or so," he said and that was all, but that was all that was needed.

Oh. It wasn't about Greg. It was about *Dad.*

Faye waited for the flutter of hurt that would start in her stomach and move up to her throat, the way that it had when she'd been confronted with the facts of Joe's other women. This time, however, the flutter didn't come. "Your father's a free man," she said, "there's no need to apologize for him."

"He never thought you'd come back to him."

Faye took his hand, her son's long, smooth hand. And her life and its purpose became crystal clear. "I didn't 'come back to him,' Greg. I came to find you. I didn't even know your father was here. In fact, if I had known, I might have chosen not to come."

Greg lifted his blue eyes—Claire's eyes—up to her. "You're sure?"

"Yes," she said. "These past days have been wonderful for the three of us to be together, but I never had any intention of anything more between your father and me."

"Lots of times he's a jerk," Greg announced, and Faye let out a laugh.

"Don't say that about your father!"

Greg smiled and shrugged. "Well, he means well. Most of the time. He had a hard time at first, about Mike and me." His words trailed off.

"I've known since you were very young," Faye said. "I know that you are gay."

At first he didn't say anything, then he asked, "And that's okay with you?"

She patted his hand. "You are my son. I only want you to be happy. You seem happy with Mike."

He smiled. He took her hand in both of his.

"I have a question," she asked abruptly. "Do you think you could stand it if I was around more often?" She had not, until this moment, known what she would do. And all she knew now was that she wanted—no, needed—to spend her time, whatever was left, near her son.

"What do you mean?"

"I mean, maybe it's time I turned the business over to Gwen. Maybe it's time to sell the Vineyard house. You're settled here; only bad memories remain back there for you."

Greg didn't respond.

"It's okay, honey," she said. "I understand, truly I do. Besides, I'm sure it would be healthier away from that mildewy old island."

She thought that he might laugh, but he did not. Instead, he ran his hands through his thick hair. His blue eyes shimmered. "For years my therapist tried to get me to go back. More than once I almost did. But in the end I was too scared." His voice was poised on the edge of quavering. "Mom, let me go back with you. Let me go back with you and, if you still want, I'll help you sell the house."

"Oh, honey," she said, "but the restaurant . . ."

"I have assistants. And Dad can supervise. Just for a few weeks, Mom. Please?"

"What about Mike?"

Greg smiled. "We've been together for years now. We know the importance of sometimes being apart."

Faye put her thin arms around her son, and drew him close to her. Then she said yes, he could come home if he wanted; he could help her sell the house.

There would be time later to tell him the rest.

When Rita arrived back at the hospital, Katie was sitting on the side of the bed, swinging her feet as if she were ten. The act made Rita think about Mindy, and how youth might be stolen but the spirit could still thrive.

"Remember, straight to bed," Doc warned Katie as his last instructions, "and ice under that arm."

That's when Rita noticed the padding wrapped under Katie's right arm. Katie shrugged it off. "Lymph node biopsy," she explained. "Doc's making sure I get my money's worth."

Rita glanced at Doc. "Just a precaution," he said, and helped Katie into the wheelchair. "Results in three days."

"Precaution," Katie said. "I'm so sick of that word. I'm surprised Doc didn't expect me to leave on a gurney, just as a precaution."

Rita laughed and Doc shook his head and Katie adjusted

her sunglasses and sun hat that Joleen had left, and then Rita and Katie set off down the corridor to "Freedom!" Katie cried.

They went out through the Emergency Room because it was closest to the car. As Rita steered the wheelchair through the double doors, a flash of light nearly blinded her. The sun? Another flash. A glint off the windshields of cars in the lot?

"Go away!" Katie screeched.

Rita threw up her hands.

"Rita!" Katie screamed. "Get me out of here!"

Another flash. It wasn't the sun. It was the flash from a camera. In the middle of the day.

Rita whirled the wheelchair around and shoved it inside the door. She pushed Katie into the triage room, then took off on her well-sneakered feet, bolting back through the door, out into the daylight, charging after the asshole who had dared to take pictures of Katie in a moment not meant for the world.

Pumping her arms and kicking up her legs, Rita saw that her prey was a man in jeans, a gray T-shirt, and a navy-blue baseball cap, which described about two-thirds of the men on the Vineyard at any given time.

"Goddamnit! Get back here, you slimy son of a bitch!" Rita shouted as she crossed the lot, her sneakers barely touching asphalt, her pulse thumping, her mind thanking God that she no longer wore stilettos, had not worn stilettos since she'd become pregnant with the twins.

"You son of a bitch!" She kept screaming, chasing the figure that still carried the camera and was now racing across the street toward the water where a rental Jeep waited. He leapt inside the Jeep, then turned over the ignition just as Rita reached him, banged on the back door, and shouted "You son of a bitch!" one more time, before the Jeep roared away.

Sand and gravel spit at her from under the wheels, and Rita was left standing there with only the baseball cap that had flown from the man's head and was now upside down on the ground.

Rita put her hands on her hips and bent forward, panting, trying to catch her breath, wishing she'd been faster, or at least that she'd been smart enough to look at the goddamn license plate.

But she wasn't faster and she wasn't smarter, so all Rita had was a great sense of failure and two huge questions:

Who the hell had told the press Katie was in the hospital, hiding out on the Vineyard?

And how soon would it be before the whole world found out?

Rita picked up the dusty baseball cap. It had a Yankees logo on the front, which ruled out most every man from there to Boston and back.

TWENTY-FIVE

Mindy sat at her desk, her social studies book opened in front of her, her headphones stuck on her ears, her hands and feet *tap-tapping*, her head nodding to a silent beat.

Rita watched from the doorway. She knew there were a million other ways the paparazzi could have found out. Well, not a million, maybe, but surely from the mailman or from a nurse or from someone at the A & P. There were a million other ways, but something gnawing at Rita's gut told her Mindy was involved. And whether Rita liked it or not, her gut was a trustworthy source.

"I don't care who told them," Katie had said once she was settled in the daybed in Joleen's sunroom. The bed was plump with watercolored pillows and made with crisp, white sheets. Perhaps Joleen was a fine mother, after all.

Rita hadn't said, "Well I care," because she didn't want to admit that, compared to Brady, she was a lousy body-guard. Nor did she want to say she suspected her own daughter—well, not really her daughter, but close enough—might be behind what had happened. As Rita stepped into the girl's bedroom now, she felt as if she'd run the Chilmark

Road Race and, despite hard work and effort, she had finished dead last.

"Mindy," Rita said, as she plucked off the headphones.

Mindy jerked at the surprise interruption. "I'm studying," she said. "I have a test tomorrow."

"We have to talk," Rita said. She sat on the edge of the small bed facing the desk. "Did you tell anyone Katie is on the island?" Straight to the point was the best way for an honest reaction, to see whether eyes flicked guiltily from one side to the other, or whether the body shifted and twisted while struggling to regain some comfort.

If Mindy just sat there, she'd no doubt be innocent. But the girl flicked her eyes, then twisted on her chair, and Rita felt her heart sink to her no-longer-manicured toes.

"I didn't tell anyone," Mindy said defensively. "I promised you I wouldn't, and I didn't."

Rita was reminded of her teenage days of keeping things from Hazel, of not revealing what she had said or done with whom or when. "Did someone ask?" Rita asked, because "I didn't tell" didn't mean someone hadn't asked. Semantics were what counted when one was being evasive.

Mindy turned her head back to her book. Rita's gut gnawed once again. She took a long breath.

"Honey," she said, "please. Just tell me what happened. Katie needs our help."

A quick flash from Mindy's eyes landed on Rita. "I told him to leave, Rita. I didn't tell him anything, I promise."

Rita's heart tightened. "Who, honey?"

With small shoulders that rose, then fell, then rose again, Mindy replied, "Some man. I don't know who he was."

Rita supposed it was the man she'd chased. "Where was he? When?"

The shoulders arched again. "The other day. He was

standing where the school bus lets me off. He said he saw you with Katie on the ferry, and someone on the dock told him who you were. He said he'd give me tickets to the Central Park concert if I told him some stuff. Like where Katie was, what she was doing, stuff like that." She closed her eyes. "Even if you can't get us tickets, Rita, I figured it wouldn't have been worth it to tell him because I'd never get to go because you would have killed me."

How could Rita help but smile? Then she said, "What did he look like?"

"He was an old guy."

Old? Well, to Mindy that could mean anyone over thirty. Or twenty-one.

"He had on a blue jacket. And a Yankees hat."

The Yankees cap. Yes, it was him. "Shit," Rita said, because she couldn't help herself. "What else?"

Mindy's eyes grew wide. "Nothing. I told him to get out of my way or I'd whack him with my backpack and scream for the police. He got in his Jeep and drove away."

Rita laughed and rubbed the child's back. "You did good, honey. Thanks." She was glad Mindy hadn't told the man anything, but she wished there was a way to track him down and help Katie find out what she could expect.

Hannah didn't look well when Rita picked her up. Her skin had that dull pallor once again, and her eyes had lost their color, too, maybe from the chemo, maybe from the fact that her daughter had disappeared. Rita said a quick prayer that Mindy would not do something so terrifying once she turned fourteen.

"Any word?" Rita asked as they drove toward Joleen's.

Hannah shook her head, and her silence said it all.

. . .

The group had been reduced from four to three: one confined to bed; one deeply depressed; the other continuing to fumble as if she knew what she was doing. Rita hoped their benefactor wasn't a fly on Joleen's cottage wall.

As Rita had expected, Faye didn't show up.

"I'm sure she was tired of my whining," Katie said, adjusting the bag of frozen peas tucked under her arm. It was a crude ice pack that Doc and many of his patients swore was more comfortable than the new fandangled stuff and worked nearly as well.

"No," Hannah piped in. "I'm sure Faye didn't want to hang out with someone whose mother committed murder. It wouldn't be exactly 'proper' up in Boston. Not exactly great publicity for her business."

Rita supposed she should tell them about her and Joe. Then they'd know Faye's departure had not been their fault, and it would explain the inevitable demise of Doc's dreams for the center.

From her bag, Rita unpacked a stack of fabric squares, ingredients for another project she'd read about: small, pretty pillows to make and then donate to women having breast surgery. The pamphlet said the pillows helped cushion physical pain that followed some procedures. Rita wondered if someone could make a cushion to buffer the discomfort of simply being a jerk. It would be a product she should be first in line to get.

She set the fabric squares on Joleen's table and tried to choose the words to tell the others about Joe and Faye and her. Then she realized Katie was chattering to Hannah about what had happened at the hospital with the lunatic and the camera. Rita's confession now, thank God, could wait.

"So I expect my face and pregnant belly will be plastered any day now across newsstands from here to L.A. and back."

Rita removed two packs of foam pieces from her bag. Should she mention the man who'd approached Mindy? What good would it do anyone if she dragged the poor kid into it? And why was Rita suddenly at such a loss to know what to do or say?

"Well," Hannah replied flatly, "maybe it won't happen. No sense dwelling on the negative until you know for sure."

Rita knew when a woman was doing her damndest to stay upbeat while everything around her had turned to shit. With or without her daughter, in a short time, Hannah would face the mastectomy; with or without a boyfriend or a father or the peak of a career, Katie had the worry of the baby and then radiation.

Compared to them, Rita's life was a piece of freaking, pink-frosting cake with or without her not-so-nice behavior in her not-so-distant past. She plunked down at the table. Maybe it wasn't a good night to begin a new project. She felt disjointed, out of touch. *Muddled*, Hazel would explain. *Detached*, her friend Jill would say.

"While I was in the hospital," Katie continued, "I decided that no matter what, I won't do Central Park."

Rita took a hefty bite from one of Mindy's carrot cupcakes and decided not to get involved. Was *muddled detachment* suitable grounds for Doc to fire her?

Hannah passed up a cupcake and drank her tea instead. "If you change your mind, it might be too late."

Rita did not know if Hannah was regretful about her daughter or her mother or the fact that she'd chucked a chance to be a doctor because she'd been ashamed and scared. On another night, Rita might have asked. But not on the night that Rita was feeling guilty about Joe; guilty about not telling them about Mindy and the man, for which she somehow felt responsible; and guilty that she didn't have a clue where or how to find a man in jeans, carrying a camera, and missing his Yankees cap.

Then the doorbell rang and Rita felt like she'd been saved.

The women looked at one another.

"I'll get it," Rita said, standing up, because Katie should not leave her bed and Joleen was in her studio and Hannah didn't seem inclined to move.

There were lots of people Rita would have liked to have seen when she opened the door. But, of course, this was her life and that's not how things happened.

Gripping the old doorknob, Rita stepped back and tried faking a smile. "Faye," she said, "what a surprise."

She'd been reunited with her son and had come back to sell the Vineyard house. She'd heard her messages and she said she was concerned.

"Hannah," Faye said, sitting on the edge of Katie's bed, facing the table. "Maybe I know someone who can help find your daughter. A private investigator. The one who found my son."

Hannah's eyes glazed with silent tears. She shook her head. "Evan and I don't have that kind of money. Besides, the police are trying . . ."

"I've known the man for years," Faye said. "He'd do it as a favor to me."

Rita would have liked it better if Faye hadn't turned out to be a decent person. It had been easier to justify those afternoons with Joe when she'd fantasized that his wife was a cold, uncaring bitch.

"Even if he found her," Hannah said, "it's pretty obvious

Riley doesn't want to be around me. She'll be fifteen this summer. How do you chain a teenager to an island or to anyone or anywhere if it's not what she wants?"

Rita recognized self-pity when she heard it. "Listen to Faye," she interrupted, though her eyes did not venture toward the woman. "At least let her friend help."

"But what if Riley's in San Antonio? What if she's found my mother?"

Faye looked at Rita, then back to Hannah, "Then he'll find your mother, too, if that's what you want."

Hannah lowered her head and quietly cried.

Faye put her arm around her. "Hannah, it will be okay. In fact, my friend is on the island. As soon as I heard the message about your daughter, I called him. He's going to meet us for breakfast at The Black Dog in the morning."

Rita gulped another bite of cupcake and wondered if she could go home now.

R.J. hadn't exactly offered to meet them for breakfast. He'd suggested meeting them that evening; he said he'd been trying to reach Faye for a week, though Faye could not imagine why. After all, R.J. had his ladyfriend and they were on vacation, what did he need with her?

She couldn't possibly meet him at night. Daylight felt more professional, less as if she were an older woman who'd been attracted to a younger man who had another lady on his arm, because why wouldn't he? Daylight would make her feel less desperate.

Besides, Faye thought as she escorted Hannah into the restaurant the next morning, Faye was no longer desperate—if the word Claire had used had truly suited her. Greg was back under her wings and under her roof and there was no need for desperation now. Faye Randolph loved again and was loved again, by a son and not a partner, but a son was better anyway, for there was nothing for her to prove, only the opportunity to be herself without any of the expectations that a man like Adam Dexter—or even R.J. Browne—would have of her, starting in the bedroom, because no one except her doctors had seen Faye naked since the first breast cancer and that was how things were going to stay.

Hannah said she'd like to face the water and the pier where the ferries came and went. Maybe she hoped to catch a glimpse of Riley.

Faye sat next to Hannah and braced herself to act happy to meet R.J.'s friend, the woman whose face, no doubt, would be aglow from days of sex with the man who, despite Faye's resolutions, managed to completely turn her on.

"Faye," his voice said softly and, with a ready, manufactured smile, she turned around, because their backs were to the door.

"R.J.," she said, extending her hand, which he took in his large, strong palm and held a bit too long. "This is my friend, Hannah," Faye said, turning to Hannah. When Faye turned back, R.J. stepped aside and said, "And this is my friend, Bob Johnson."

Bob Johnson was not a woman.

He held his hand out and said, "Nice to meet you, ma'am," both to her and to Hannah while Faye sat there, stumped.

Was R.J. gay?

Was it possible for a gay man to give off such . . . such chemistry to a woman?

The men sat down, with R.J. across from Faye.

"So," R.J. said, rubbing his hands together lightly. "We've had quite a week. I actually think I might be fished out for a while."

Faye looked at him and blinked.

"Best time of the year for cod," Hannah said while Faye fought to regain her composure.

R.J. had not been with a woman? The morning he'd arrived, what had he said? That he'd left his friend shopping? Naturally she'd assumed . . .

"Oh, we caught our share of cod," the friend named Bob Johnson replied, and R.J. laughed and Faye just smiled.

The men ordered short stacks of buttermilk pancakes. Faye ordered tea and a small omelet and hoped she wouldn't get any more proverbial egg on her face. Hannah had tea, but said she'd pass on the food.

Then R.J. got down to business. "Start at the beginning," he said to Hannah, who paused a moment then explained about the ferry and that Riley had left with a pile of silver certificates that had belonged to her late grandmother.

Throughout the meal, Faye's mind wandered. Would it be as easy for her to abandon the Vineyard as it was for a fourteen-year-old? It was so wonderful to have Greg in her life again. She wanted to be near him, to share part of his life. But Greg's life was out West . . . Could she really go there? Was she really ready to relinquish the damp and drafty, wonderful beachfront house?

Faye loved the island, had loved it since she'd been a girl.

And what about Claire? Though Faye and her sister had never really seen eye-to-eye, the truth was, Faye would miss her and her chaotic energy, her blasting in and out of Faye's life while arriving or departing en route from another port of call. That was Claire's life: always on the go with Jeffrey, her trust-fund-baby husband, to whom travel and adventure were sort of like a job.

But despite her comings and her goings, Claire had always managed to be there for Faye—through Dana's death and Greg's leaving and through the divorce. And through the cancer—well, the first time.

"Bob has to get back to his wife in Boston." R.J.'s words leapt across the table. She realized he was speaking to her. "But I can stay a few more days." He turned back to Hannah. "I'd like to start by seeing some of your daughter's things. Pictures, a diary, anything like that."

Hannah nodded, then R.J. smiled at Faye. "But I hate dining alone," he added. "Faye, would you join me tonight?"

Was that Hannah's foot that kicked her beneath the table? Faye straightened the napkin in her lap. "I'd love to R.J., but Greg is here . . ."

"She'd love to, R.J.," Hannah said quickly. "Her son owns two restaurants. I'm sure he's perfectly capable of cooking a meal for himself."

Faye wanted to protest, but then decided not to. If she'd learned anything at all, it was that life came and went too quickly not to sometimes say yes.

What a dunce. If Rita had been born any more stupid, she could have tried out for one of those reality-based TV shows where contestants ate rats and worms and God-knew-what in the name of being cool.

She could not believe she hadn't thought about the Jeep until after she'd opened her eyes this morning to the sound of Olivia babbling at Oliver in the next room. Rita had snuggled under the covers and smiled, wishing Charlie had been there to share the delight of their children—theirs!—making lovely children sounds.

She was feeling a pang of longing for her husband's gentle touch when a thought popped suddenly into her mind:

the Jeep! Throwing off the covers, she bolted from the bed. She drove her hand through her Brillo pad of hair, jumped into her robe, and darted from the room. She used the bathroom quickly, the way a mother learns to when she's pressed for time. She ran across the hall, smiled at the twins, changed their diapers one, then two, put on their sweat suits, and hauled them—one per hip—down the steep stairs of the old saltbox that Rita had refused to leave even though Charlie now built mansions with his buddy, Ben, and Hazel had offered to pay for one with the inheritance from her "short-lived but profitable" marriage that had begun on the Vineyard and ended in Coral Gables.

Well, Rita thought, of course she wouldn't give up this ramshackle of a house. After all, she was Rita Blair Rollins, Queen of the Stupid People.

Hazel and Mindy were already at the table: Hazel studying the newspaper and Mindy studying the air around her, as only a twelve-year-old can seem to do.

"We forgot about the Jeep," Rita said to Mindy. She plopped the twins into their highchairs one, then two, and poured coffee into the big mug that Hazel had set out. "It's a rental," Rita said, "which means there are less than a dozen places on the island that it could have come from." She took a big slug of her coffee. "What's more, I'll bet that half the rental places are closed until Memorial Day. It shouldn't be hard—even for me—to track down the guy with the camera who was asking all the questions."

TWENTY-SIX

Hannah hated parting with pictures of Riley: What if Riley never came home? Could R.J. Browne be trusted to give the photos back?

He had dropped his friend off at the ferry, then followed Faye and Hannah to Hannah's house. Evan was not around, maybe he was in the greenhouse smoking a joint. How much more stress could Evan take? How much more could she?

She took photos of Riley off the wall in her workroom; she returned to the living room and handed them over.

"How would your daughter know what to do once she was across?" R.J. asked, as he scanned the shots taken last summer, plus a few at Christmas and Riley's ninth grade class picture. "Did she often go over to the mainland?"

Hannah sat on the plaid sofa. She had told Hugh Talbott these things already, and she would tell a million people if it meant getting her daughter back. "We went every fall to shop for school clothes." She stared at her untouched tea-cup. Faye had been so kind to make coffee and tea, though they'd just had breakfast. Hannah recalled the first night of the group, when Faye had excused herself because she "did not belong" there. Hannah was glad the woman had changed her mind. She took a sip of tea to let Faye know she was appreciated. "We waited to shop for school clothes until after Labor Day, until the crowds thinned."

"Did you take your car across?"

"Yes. We drove up to Falmouth. And to Hyannis, to the mall."

"Did Riley go to the Cape for any other reason?"

"My mother-in-law took her to a few plays. Summer stock in Woods Hole." She told him about Mother Jackson's theater and Riley's love of the stage. Then she told him about the recent Sunday they'd spent in Hyannis. "But I'm sure she didn't meet anyone. It was a last-minute family trip."

R.J. set down the photos. He did not say whether or not he thought Riley was pretty. He did not comment on the streak of bright pink hair in the Christmas pictures. "Do you think she might know how to get from the ferry to, well, to anywhere? For instance, would she have known about the trolley that goes into Falmouth or where to catch the bus to Boston?"

A trolley into Falmouth was news to Hannah. And she did not remember where the bus station was located.

She shifted on the sofa and tried to cover the thinning fabric on its arm. Tears welled in her eyes. "I don't know," she said. "I've gone over and over this in my mind, but I still don't know how she could do it." She did not add that Riley was a smart girl, and that she certainly could have figured out logistics. The part that Hannah didn't understand was, how had Riley mustered so much independent will? Had her anger at Hannah been that powerful?

"She might have gone to San Antonio," Hannah said suddenly.

R.J. raised an eyebrow.

Faye sat beside her on the sofa and put her arm on Hannah's shoulder. "That's a long shot, R.J.," she said. "Maybe you have enough to get started?"

The man stood up. "Sure thing. Faye? I'll pick you up at seven?"

Faye nodded and R.J. said he'd be in touch, and then he left. When the door had closed behind him, Hannah burst into tears. Faye sat and stroked the hair of Hannah's wig as if it were real, as if it might bring her comfort, which it did not.

"Can I do anything for you, Hannah?" Faye asked. "Anything at all?"

"Yes," Hannah finally said. "If you're not busy tomorrow, could you bring me to the hospital? Now that my chemo's finished, they want to do some tests before they schedule surgery."

Faye agreed and did not ask why Hannah's husband would not be taking her; why Hannah did not want to interrupt his self-imposed retreat from his family and from the world.

"It was a guy named Darryl Hogan," the tattooed clerk at Island Jeep Rentals told Rita as he shuffled through some paperwork and pulled out a pink sheet. "Yep," he repeated, "Darryl Hogan."

Rita drummed her fingernails on the counter. She resisted the urge to reach across and grab the paper from his hand. Sometimes even Rita knew what was rude and what was not, and the good news was that she'd found him, Darryl Hogan, and that the low-life media-scum had rented his Jeep from Chuck Lewiston's establishment near the airport. Rita and Charlie had known Chuck from the second grade, when his family moved to the Vineyard from New

Bedford. He was a small and geeky kid, and hadn't changed as an adult. According to tattoo-man, Chuck was, in fact, off-island now, loading up on more Jeeps in preparation for the season. He'd instructed the clerk to "give Rita Blair anything she damn well wanted." Rita supposed it didn't hurt that back in junior high school, Chuck had peeked in her window while Rita took off her bra and he didn't know that she'd known, but she had and she hadn't pulled the shade. Even back then Rita had sensed that Chuck would never be a ladies' man, and his opportunities to see a naked woman might be few and far between.

Her eyes moved down and up from her once-titillating breasts: she thought of how, back then, breast cancer had not crossed her mind.

She pulled out her pen and a small notepad. "What did Darryl Hogan give as a local address?" she asked, because every renter of every vehicle had to leave instructions where they could be reached, not for any special reason except to keep them honest.

"Vineyard Haven. Mayfield House."

She dropped her notebook back into her purse without writing down the name. Why would she be surprised that Darryl Hogan was staying at the same place as that private-investigator-friend of Faye's? Rita's life; Rita's luck. At least Rita knew the owners of the inn; maybe she could get some information from them quickly and get out of Vineyard Haven before she'd have to see Faye more times than she could handle.

Mayfield House sat up on the hill that rose up from the harbor and overlooked Vineyard Sound. It was a big old Captain's house, freshly painted in yellow and trimmed with white, ready for tourist-time. Rita shuddered at the impending crunch of summer as she marched across the gravel drive. *Things could be worse,* she told herself. Faye's Mercedes could have been parked in the lot, but thankfully was not.

Ginny answered the door. She wore a red-and-white bandana tied around her head and had a cleaning rag in one hand, a bucket in the other. It was hard to believe that not so long ago the woman had lived the high life in Los Angeles. She had a daughter who was a famous soap opera star and, rumor had it, Ginny had undergone a plethora of bad marriages before landing on the island and tying up with Dick Bradley, who'd been a widower too long.

All of which only proved you couldn't judge a book by its jeans-and-sweatshirt cover, though Rita knew she was the last one who could stand in any sort of judgment. Besides, she'd known Ginny a while, long enough to know that the woman was for real and it looked as if the marriage was one that was going to "take."

"A guy named Darryl Hogan," Rita said to Ginny after they took a seat out on the porch. "I was told he's staying here?"

Ginny nodded. "He was. He checked out this morning."

"Shit." There she went again. At least the twins weren't around. "Damn. Was he alone?"

"Alone with a bunch of cameras."

Well, that wasn't exactly news. "Did he talk to anyone? Make any phone calls while he was here?"

"I can check." Ginny disappeared inside and Rita waited on the porch, her eyes glued to the driveway, on guard for a Mercedes. A few minutes and no Mercedes later, Ginny returned and gave Rita a slip of paper. A phone number was written on it. The area code was two-one-two. New York City. Home of many media giants.

"That's the only place he called," Ginny said. "But in the two days he was here, he called there seven times."

Obsessive. Compulsive. A prerequisite, Rita supposed, to being a reporter.

She tucked the number in her pocket. "He hasn't returned the rental Jeep yet."

With a shrug, Ginny commented, "He said he wanted to see some of the island sights."

"And he took his cameras."

Ginny laughed. "What the heck does one need with more than one camera?"

Rita stood up. "Probably for the eyes in the back of his head. The son of a bitch is from the rag media. Tabloid stuff. He went after a friend of mine."

Ginny took off her bandana and ran her hand through her short, dark hair. "That explains it."

"Explains what?"

"He wanted to know where Jackie Kennedy lived, where Carly Simon lives, and where John Belushi's buried."

"Shit. What did you tell him?"

Ginny smiled. "I gave him directions to the cemetery in Chilmark."

They had a good laugh over that one, and Rita finally knew what she needed to do next.

When Faye returned from breakfast and from Hannah's, she found Greg in the backyard, sitting on one of the Adirondack chairs that faced the water. She told him about R.J. and about Hannah's daughter and that R.J. had agreed to look for her.

Greg had smiled, then said, "Good. Now sit down."

She sat. "We're going to get dirty," she said, lightly brushing the broad arm of the chair. "I haven't called the cleaning people or the lawn service, to get ready for the season."

A moment passed before Greg said, "I used to love to come here the first weekend of every year, when there was so much activity all around—vacuum cleaners vacuuming, mowers mowing, the smell of disinfectant in the kitchen and the bathrooms—as if the world's filthiest people had stayed here over the winter and we had to rid the place of every germ and dust bunny or perish from the earth."

Faye smiled.

"Dana and I hid under the porch and pretended we lived underground. We brought Geraldo with us and tried to train him to be our lookout for the big, bad adults out in the world."

Geraldo had been Mouser's predecessor, a fluffy black cat that hated being outdoors, that chose Dana's bed as his place, no matter where the family was. "And was he a good lookout?"

"No. He kept running away."

Faye looked off toward the water. It had been a long, long time since she'd thought of Dana without pain; it had been a long, long time since she'd talked about her with another person who had memories of her, too.

"Whenever I've thought of you over the years," Greg said, "I've always pictured you here. I never saw you in the house in Boston, just here, on the Vineyard, where we always were so happy."

"Were we, Greg? Were we happy?"

His blue eyes narrowed in thought. "About as happy as any family can expect to be, I guess. Not as much as some. More than many."

He was right. They had been happy. One season they'd been hooked on playing checkers, another with making jigsaw puzzles. One summer they'd found so much wampum they made "authentic" jewelry, including the pinkie ring Dana had given Claire.

Playing games, hunting wampum, making jewelry: They'd done these things as a family—Greg and Dana, Faye and even Joe.

Faye had assumed that the joy would last forever.

"I knew when Dana started drinking," she said. "I think I knew it from the first night she came home drunk. She was only fifteen, wasn't she?"

Greg's gaze grew distant, melancholy. "Yeah," he said, "I guess."

"I told myself she was going through a teenage phase. I told myself that it would pass."

"It didn't pass."

"I know."

Greg folded his hands. "Sometimes it was my fault. I drove her places, and she'd find a way to drink. She made me promise not to tell you and Dad. She threatened that if I did, she'd tell you I was gay."

Faye nodded. She understood.

He laughed. "Dana would do anything if it meant getting her own way. Most times it was easier to agree than to try to change her mind. I wish it hadn't been like that."

Faye shook her head. "Your sister was a charmer," she said. "She was pretty and smart, and maybe she had too much going for her. She was a lot like your father. Yes," she nodded, "she was a charmer."

A tiny smile curved at the corner of Greg's mouth. "Sometimes I wonder what she would have become. What kind of woman, what kind of person."

A long time ago, Faye had wondered those things, too. In recent years she'd labeled those thoughts too painful and urged them from her mind. "We'll never know, Greg. We'll never know a lot of things."

They sat quietly once again, the sound of hungry sea-gulls circling the sky.

"You're not really going to sell this place, are you, Mom?"

"That depends on you."

"Me?"

"Do you want it?"

"I live in Arizona."

"Right now you do. But what about later, down the road? After I'm gone?"

Greg laughed. "Geez, Mom. Don't talk like that."

She reached across the small V that separated their Adirondack chairs. She took his hand in hers. She summoned all her strength. Then she looked into his eyes and said, "Greg, I had breast cancer again this winter. I think this time I'm going to die."

"Hey, asshole, he's not there," Rita said, stepping from behind a tree in Chilmark Cemetery. She'd waited for an hour and had nearly given up, thought that he'd come and gone or decided not to come at all.

The man angled his camera and clicked the shutter.

She moved a little closer. "I said, he isn't there. It's only a grave marker that says 'John Belushi.' Everyone knows they moved his body on account of tourists. On account of parasitic, sensationalistic scum like you."

He turned the camera toward her. The shutter clicked again. Rita held her hand up to her face. "You're such a jerk," she said. "How much do you get paid to do this shit? To trample other people's lives with your first amendment bullshit?" She reached out and grabbed the camera. She fumbled with the back, trying to get the film.

The asshole laughed. "Nice try," he said, "but no film. It's digital. And by the way, if you're looking for the shots of Katie, I e-mailed them last night."

She dropped the camera. "You bastard."

He laughed again.

"Who do you work for?" she asked.

"Wouldn't you love to know."

"I'll pay you."

"Not enough."

"You don't know that."

"Yes I do." He smirked and bent down to retrieve the camera.

It was all Rita could do to stop herself from planting her sneaker on his face. Instead, she stomped off across the tombstone-sprinkled lawn, reminding herself that at least she had the phone number he'd called not once, but seven times. Maybe when she and Katie learned what rag it was connected to, she'd call that cop in Brooklyn who'd tracked down Ina's funeral. For a little more penuche, he might be willing to pay the tabloid a visit.

They'd spent the rest of the day on the beach, searching for wampum, in honor of Dana. They hadn't found any. After Faye had told Greg about the breast cancer, Greg wanted to call Joe: Faye said please don't, that she had made peace with Joe and that was how it should be.

"Isn't there anything the doctors can do?" Greg had asked after they'd moved from the yard to the sand.

Faye had smiled and held his hand. "It's okay, honey. If I die, at least Dana is there."

But early that evening, as she stood before the full-length mirror in the hall, Faye wondered why she hadn't gone for her last mammogram. Had she been so resigned to die, that she no longer cared?

But Greg was in her life again.

A small twinge fluttered in her heart; she made it go away.

She clasped the silver choker at her throat and examined the way the pewter-colored trousers fell around her legs. They were too big. She had refused to weigh herself; she refused to live with the dread of wondering if she'd wake up in the morning or if she had lost weight or if she'd be tired that day.

Maybe the weight loss was from the cancer, or maybe it was from the fact that she'd been so busy. It certainly wasn't from worry, because Faye knew she'd reached *acceptance* when she'd been faced with that word "recurrence."

She turned back to her outfit, to her evening, because all she could do well now was live in the moment, that moment, right now.

She closed her eyes and made herself focus on the hope that her pretty, short-sleeved cashmere sweater would compensate for the baggy pants.

"My beautiful mother," Greg said as he stepped up behind her. "You have always been so beautiful, even if you've been sick."

She opened her eyes and turned to kiss his cheek. "You don't mind that I'm going out tonight?"

"No. I'm glad you have a date. As long as you're home by midnight."

Faye laughed. "I don't think that's a problem. The Vineyard still has no nightlife except in July or August." She brushed the front of her trousers. "Do these look okay? They're not too loose?"

"You're wonderful. And this guy is very lucky that he found you."

She laughed again, and around those edges of acceptance, joy slowly crept in. Then she felt another twinge, a warning that this would end too soon. She cleared her throat. "R.J. is lucky, all right. He's lucky he found *you*. Otherwise he'd be dining alone tonight at the hot dog stand in Oak Bluffs."

"Mom?" Greg asked, as Faye went into her bedroom and began to switch her things from her black purse to her gray. "What about Hannah's daughter? Do you think he'll find her, too?"

"I don't know," she said. "He confided to me that it won't be very easy; not like with you. Chances are her Social Security number won't have showed up yet at the Internal Revenue Service."

"That's how he found me? Because I pay my taxes?"

Faye smiled and held her palms up to his cheeks. It was so hard not to keep touching his face, his hands, his hair, anything to reassure herself that he was really there. "I didn't ask him for specifics. I only cared that you were found."

"But this girl," he said. "She's fourteen."

"She'll be fifteen this summer." Neither of them had to mention that Dana was fifteen when she had begun her dance with death.

"I've made a decision," Greg said suddenly, or at least it seemed suddenly because Faye did not realize he'd had decision-making on his mind. "I'm staying here with you."

She stopped and stared into his bright blue eyes. "You live in Arizona," she said. "I said I'd sell this place and move out there . . ."

He shook his head. "You don't belong in the desert, Mom. You belong right here. And I belong here with you until, well . . ."

"But your business . . ."

"Mike can handle it. We're coming into summer. Not

exactly tourist season when the temperatures shoot past a hundred."

"But what about your father?"

"He'll be fine, Mom."

They looked at each other. Greg's eyes were the first to fill with tears. "Please, Mom. Let me stay home with you."

She hugged him once again and said it would be all right, at least for the summer, and then, downstairs, the doorbell rang.

TWENTY-SEVEN

"Take down the billboard," Katie said into the phone with more conviction than she'd felt since her decision to have her baby and delay the radiation. She glanced from the phone to her mother, then to Rita, who had wasted her whole day on Katie's behalf, searching for a man and the source of a phone number. Katie could have saved her friend the trouble. She turned back to the phone. "I don't care if you have to crawl up there on your hands and knees and dismantle it bulb by bulb. Take down the billboard, Daddy. I will not do Central Park."

"It sounds like Joleen's been putting ideas in your head," Cliff responded on the other end of the line.

"This is my choice. Once my baby is born, I'm going to have a real life. I don't even know if I'll want to sing again."

"You'll sing again. It's in your soul."

She closed her eyes as if to block the thought. It was the first time she'd called her father since the funeral, the first time she felt strong enough to withstand his manipulation.

Manipulation.

Until now, it had worked every time.

Your mother left us, Katie-Kate.

I'll never leave you, Katie-Kate.

I'll help you own the world.

She had never been sure if she'd wanted to own the world. But it was what he'd wanted for her, or maybe for him, in addition to the money and the fame that her cloned image of Joleen had wrought.

"I can't cancel the date, honey." His voice had dropped now; it was serene and almost sorrowful. "It would cost me a small fortune. You canceled the tour. You canceled the CD. Your old Dad's not in the most solvent state."

Katie squeezed her eyes shut. "That's a lie. Joleen has more money than she knows what to do with. I suspect we do, too. I figure you make me keep working because you don't know what else to do since you screwed up our family and your life."

Cliff didn't deny it.

"Cancel the fucking concert, Dad. Or I'll tell the world my father sunk so low he actually paid someone to take my picture and sell it to the tabloids."

The loud silence that followed, sadly confirmed Katie's suspicions. She looked back to Rita, who still held the paper with the New York City phone number.

"I didn't do it for the money, Katie-Kate. I did it for you. You've been out of the spotlight too long. People might think you're like your mother . . ." He sounded so pathetic, Katie couldn't listen.

"*I'm not my mother*," she seethed. "For once in your life, stop trying to turn me into Joleen. I am your daughter and I'm having a baby and I have breast cancer and *I am not Joleen*. For godssake, Daddy, cancel the concert and stop that awful man from printing that picture." She snatched the paper from Rita. She looked down again at the phone number that the man named Darryl Hogan had called seven times from Mayfield House, the number that did not connect to a newspaper office as Rita had thought, but to a phone in Cliff's penthouse overlooking Central Park.

"No," Cliff replied. "I can't stop the picture and I won't cancel the Park."

They ate dinner at Lambert's Cove as two adults might do, trading conversation about art and poetry and allegories from the Bible that might or might not be true. Faye had forgotten that R.J. had been a minister; she had not, however, forgotten that he was a man.

And when the meal was over and they'd had coffee and Kahlua, it seemed the most natural thing in all the world to go to his room at Mayfield House.

"If you say no, I'll understand," he said.

"I won't say no," she answered.

And before Faye realized what was happening, she was floating up the stairs of the gracious Captain's house and entering a room that was decked in chintz and had a high, four-poster bed and a tall, manteled fireplace where R.J. built a fire.

She knew what he was planning and she prayed he would not stop.

He pulled the comforter off the bed and dragged it to the floor in front of the warmth. "Come here," he said, and so she did.

"I have to tell you something." She looked into the flicker of the newly sparking flames. It was less stressful to look there than into his eyes.

He leaned too close to her; he began to slowly unbutton the buttons of her sweater. She knew that she must stop him before he reached the part that uncovered her tattoo, her stamp that said cancer had been there and, she supposed, still was; she must stop him before he reached the other side and the implant that wasn't really her.

"I know about your breast cancer," he said, lowering his face to kiss her throat. "I know about the first one and I know about the second. I know everything. I'm a detective, remember?"

Then, when her sweater was fully open and her bra unfastened, he kissed her gently all over before removing her pants that were too big, and they made love into the night.

"Make a fist," the lab technician said as she tied the tourniquet around Hannah's arm.

Hannah made a fist and closed her eyes: just because she'd been in medical school didn't mean she liked having tests done on her. She closed her eyes, though, purely out of habit, for she was far too preoccupied to care that the deep prick into her arm would suck the life's blood out of her.

After all, what difference would it make?

If she survived breast cancer, surely she would not survive Riley's having run away.

The needle plunged into her arm, then slowly drew out her blood. She ignored the lightness in her head and thought about her daughter, as she thought about her every minute of her days and nights.

Where was she?

Was she cold and scared and hungry?

Or was she on a bus to San Antonio, high on her adventure, feeling the rush of escape that Hannah remembered feeling so long ago?

It would be easier to let the cancer have its way and take Hannah from this pain. The school could find another science teacher easily enough. And Evan could pull himself together like he'd done before. He could find another, better mother for Casey and Denise, someone without murder in her past; someone who was a better mother than one who could cause a child to run away.

"Okay, Mrs. Jackson," the technician said. "Keep your arm up for a minute."

Mrs. Jackson? Most folks were on a first-name basis on the Vineyard, no matter what the age. Only students called teachers "Mr." or "Mrs." Hannah tried to place the girl in the white lab coat. "Do I know you?"

The girl smiled. "Eighth grade, class of '91. Your science class is what got me interested in biology. And phlebotomy."

Oh, God, Hannah thought. Sometime in the last few years she'd become so old that her former students were now her caregivers. A small eddy of bile pooled in her throat.

The girl looked at Hannah's paperwork. "Next stop, chest X ray. Then you're finished for today."

At least her former student didn't say that the tests were the first of several precursors to the mastectomy. Perhaps losing a breast was as insignificant to the class of '91 as it now was to Hannah.

How could death be so imminent when Faye felt so alive?

She barely had slept. Though R.J. had wanted her to spend the night, Faye could not do that, not with Greg waiting at home. So she'd come home after two, was wide awake before dawn, and went downstairs to the kitchen where she made Irish scones, then bundled some for Hannah, some for Katie, some for Greg. And R.J. Yes, some for R.J.

That had been hours earlier, but her energy had not

waned. For the third or fourth time, Faye thumbed through an old *Redbook* magazine, then finally deposited it back on the coffee table in the waiting room.

She tried to put aside her enthusiasm and focus on Hannah.

Faye had, of course, been where Hannah was now, going through the torture of test after test, waiting, waiting, waiting for results that took too long to come.

The second time around, the tests had been worse: liver, lungs, bone; the cold, metal table where she'd lain for the bone scan, the radioactive dye that made her feel awkwardly alien. The doctors said all the tests had been negative, but Faye did not believe them. Hadn't she been in marketing long enough to know when the consumer was being carefully misled?

"A lumpectomy should do the trick this time," the Boston doctor said. "And radiation will give you an extra boost at the end, to kick it out once and for all."

She sat back in her chair now and realized she'd been relieved once she'd accepted the inevitable, once she'd seen past the doctor's cheery smile and heard beyond his well-crafted words of spin.

Relief ended the agonizing wait for the other shoe to drop.

Phew.

Death was on its way.

Still, Faye had the lumpectomy and the radiation and the extra boost because she had nothing to lose.

She did not have the final mammogram because she did not need confirmation of what she already knew.

Yet now Greg was saying that he wanted to stay.

And R.J knew about the cancer, yet had made love to her anyway.

Dear God, Faye thought with a sardonic smile, what could possibly be better?

Well, for one thing, life.

She glanced up at the clock that ticked away the minutes that she had left to breathe. The clock did not care a hoot if Faye Randolph lived or died.

Only days ago she would have agreed.

But now? . . .

Did she dare risk the knowing?

She wondered if Doc Hastings was in his office. Could he arrange a mammogram for her? And was she truly ready to accept the results?

Rita felt like such a shit. But how was she supposed to know that the phone number Ginny had given her would link the pushy paparazzo directly to Katie's father?

"Let it go," Hazel said with a large, audible sigh. "I warned you not to get too involved with these women."

Rita abruptly stopped the stroller that was leading them on a morning stroll through downtown Edgartown. "Warned me? I believe your words were something like 'Doc needs a Women's Center.' I didn't think of that as a warning. If anything, it felt like pressure from you, too, to take charge of the group."

Hazel shrugged. "Well, it's not your problem. Not that the singer's father tried to sell her out, or that the teacher's daughter ran away." She did not mention Faye.

They walked another block, past the Old Whaling Church, which had been built in the 1800's as a Methodist church, but later became a center for lectures and town meetings and then for concerts. The old church had transformed itself into whatever was required in order to sustain its life on the island.

Survival, after all, was the spirit of the Vineyard.

Rita supposed she was no different. She'd become the leader of a breast cancer support group because that was what was needed. If a sudden need arose for flying circus acts, she supposed she'd try that, too.

"It seems that these women have enough to deal with," Rita said, "without the outside world broadcasting their problems."

"Most people have more than one problem," Hazel said. " 'She has problems.' That's what you hear folks say. Hardly ever do you hear that someone just has one."

Rita sighed and was grateful that she, at least, had one less problem: It had not been Mindy's fault that Darryl Hogan found Katie; it had been the fault of Katie's own father.

She thought about Katie, and about poor Hannah. Sometimes, Rita thought, there were advantages to being raised without a father.

Faye had never been to Doc's office in the hospital. When Dana drowned, Doc had come to Faye; he had been sent by the family doctor back in Boston, whom Claire had called when she did not know what to do with her inconsolable, distraught sister.

He had returned that summer of her first breast cancer.

Faye thought back to those days now as she combed the corridor. Doc had saved her life both times: Could he do it again? Could he tell her that she had more time? Weeks, perhaps? A couple of months, maybe a few?

She reminded herself that the results of the mammogram couldn't be worse than she already assumed.

They couldn't be worse.

Could they be better? Did she dare hope?

Spotting the small name ROLAND W. HASTINGS, M.D. on the metal door, Faye stood up straight and lightly knocked, half-hoping that he wasn't there, knowing she might be better off to stay in her safe place of acceptance, where hope couldn't be false.

"Come in," a voice called out from the other side.

She touched the doorknob. She hesitated. Then she thought of Greg. She opened the door.

"Faye," Doc said and quickly stood up from behind his cluttered relic of a desk. "How nice to see you."

He could have said, "Is something wrong?" because why else would she be there? But Doc Hastings was a kind man, not given to histrionics or to offering a suggestion that all things weren't right with the world.

"Hello, Doc," Faye said. "I need your help."

She sat down on a sofa. He sat in his chair. He leaned across piles of papers on the desktop, his hands folded, his attention undivided, despite the fact that Faye had clearly interrupted him.

"I brought Hannah to have some tests," she said. "While I was waiting, I realized I need a mammogram. I didn't have one after my radiation."

Doc nodded. "How long now since the last dosage?"

"I had the boost almost eight weeks ago."

He took off his glasses and rubbed his eyes. "Any reason you didn't have it before this?" he asked. He could have asked, "Why the sudden change of heart?" but he did not.

Faye smiled. "My son has come home. I want to know how much more time I have." She did not mention R.J.

"Greg is back? Oh, Faye, that's wonderful." He leaned back in his chair and folded his arms. "You must be very happy."

She was surprised Doc remembered Greg's name. "Yes,

but I'd be even happier to know I have longer to live than I think. Or than I thought."

Was that a slight frown that passed over his face?

"You had a lumpectomy," he said, "isn't that right?"

"Yes."

"Stage One. Noninvasive."

"So they said." How could she explain to a physician—a scientist—about feelings that were abstract, about a sense of knowing what she could never prove?

"But Faye—" he began, but she interrupted.

"Will you schedule the mammogram," she asked, "or should I do it at the front desk?"

"I'll take care of it." He rose again. "Is any day better than another?"

"It doesn't matter. As long as it's soon."

They smiled at each other and Doc nodded happily. He walked around the desk and Faye stood up. He took her hand in both of his. Just as he began to speak again, his office door banged open and smacked against the wall.

Faye jumped.

Doc jumped.

Their heads spun toward the door. A man of middle age stood there. He was pale and trembling. And in his hand, he held a gun.

TWENTY-EIGHT

The man had thinning hair; he wore faded jeans and a navy-blue T-shirt and looked quite ordinary. Except, of course, for the gun. Faye's eyes traveled from the small steel revolver back to Doc, who stood as frozen as she felt.

"Evan," Doc said, "what on earth are you doing?"

Evan.

Evan.

Oh, my God, thought Faye. *Evan is Hannah's husband.*

He didn't speak for what seemed like way too long a time. They stood like three old marble statues, Faye and Doc and Evan. His eyes were dazed; his gaze was distant.

"Evan," Doc repeated. "Please. Give me the gun."

Evan looked down at the gun. "I don't know what to do, Doc. I can't take it anymore."

"Killing Doc won't solve anything," Faye said.

Evan blinked. He looked over at Faye as if he hadn't noticed her before. "I'm not going to kill Doc," he said. "Why would I do that?"

Neither Faye nor Doc mentioned one might think otherwise, what with the weapon aimed in Doc's direction.

Nor did they comment that it was no secret Evan had once thought Hannah would get better care in Boston.

"I'm the one who's a worthless piece of shit," Evan said. "My family will be better off without me." For one who seemed so out of it, he spoke with surprising clarity.

"Then why all this?" Doc asked. "Why are you here?"

"I came to say I'm sorry. To right my wrongs before I die."

Before I die? Was he going to kill himself instead of Doc?

"Sorry about what?" A tiny line of sweat formed across Doc's aging brow, though his voice was startlingly calm.

Evan chewed his lower lip. "I blamed you for my mother's death, though it was really my fault." He blinked a long, slow blink. " 'Evvie?' she asked me—oh, I hated when she called me Evvie, it made me sound like such a girl—'Evvie, if I take sick, should I go up to Boston?' I said 'Don't be ridiculous, Ma. You'll live to be a hundred, maybe more.' And so she didn't go. Six months later she was dead."

Faye half-listened to Evan's confession. She could only think of Hannah: How could poor Hannah survive another blow like this?

"Evan," Doc said, taking a small step forward. "It wasn't your fault. Six months would not have made a difference. She'd been sick at least two years before she came to me. Please, Evan. You can't change that. But Hannah needs you now."

Evan swiveled the gun from Doc and pointed it at himself.

Faye inhaled an anxious breath.

"No," Evan replied. "Hannah needs a husband she doesn't always have to look at and wonder if he's doing drugs or not."

Sadness filled Faye's heart—sadness for the unassuming woman, Hannah, the gentle soul whose life had been touched with so much grief. *Who said life was fair?* she remembered Doc once said.

"Talk to Hannah, Evan. Would you like me to help?"

"It's too late," Evan replied, turning his attention back to Doc, the gun drooping slightly toward the floor. "I can't let her see me this way. I can't let my kids see me. I'm just a coward, that's all."

"Balderdash," Doc said, and Faye almost smiled at the word she hadn't heard for nearly half a century. "You come from courageous stock. Your mother was one of the bravest women I've ever known."

"She's dead," he said, "and now my wife might die as well."

Dead. Faye leaned against the file cabinets. Looking at the crumbling man, the word gave her new strength. With a wavering gun being controlled or uncontrolled by a man not in his right senses, she supposed she should have feared for her own life. But Faye already expected death, so did the timing really matter?

Her eyes darted from Evan to Doc, then back again. She stood up straight; her legs tensed, ready to bolt. *Adrenaline,* she knew. At least the cancer hadn't robbed her of that.

She moved more closely, just a bit, so Evan wouldn't notice. Then she gritted her teeth, said a quick homage to Hannah, and vaulted forward. She pounced. She kicked. With two swift thrusts she chopped his forearm. The gun jumped from his hand and clattered to the floor. Faye whisked it up before Evan or Doc or even Faye had fully realized what the hell she'd done.

They stood again in silence, the three unmoving statues; Faye's heart beating quick, soft beats, her breath pacing out her pulse. Then Evan wailed a wail of tears and sagged against the wall.

"Well," Faye said at last, "I guess one of us should phone the police."

Instead of picking up the phone, Doc propped himself against the desk and wiped his brow. Then he said, "No, Faye. I'll take care of things. You run along."

Run along?

She looked down at the gun now in her hand. She looked back to Evan, a broken man who sat, crying, a wounded soul. She looked at Doc.

Run along?

And leave Doc with a man who could have killed him?

Doc leveled his sight on Faye. His voice seemed steady, but his face was now quite pale. "Faye," he repeated slowly. "You . . . need . . . to . . . leave." He frowned a bit, as if responding to someone, something else that was not in the room.

And then the light in Doc's eyes faded and his body began to sway, and it only took an instant for him to grab his chest and slump against the old oak desk where he'd worked so many years.

"Doc!" Faye screamed and ran to him. She turned to Evan. "Do something, goddamnit! Move your pathetic ass and get some help."

She quickly cradled Doc. "Now!" she shouted back to Evan, who pulled himself together and stumbled out into the hall.

Cardiac infarction. The on-call doctor said it would be hours before they'd know how severe the attack had been.

"But we have him stabilized," the doctor said, then added, "for now."

Faye rested against the chair in the waiting room. She

looked at Evan, who had waited quietly beside her with his guilt, his pain, barely able to breathe.

Evan closed his eyes. "I'm going to find my wife now," he said. "I'll take her home. Then I have to go to rehab."

"I'm sure it will be for the best," Faye replied.

He stood up and did not look at her when he added, "I'm so sorry. God, I am so sorry." Then he headed toward the hall, toward the radiology department where, according to the schedule, Hannah was in X ray. She'd be surprised it would not be Faye who'd come to pick her up.

Rita stared at the tabloid in the wire rack that stood on the sidewalk outside the newsstand. She resisted saying "Oh, shit," not just because of the twins, but because they were standing on the corner of Main and Water Streets in Edgartown and Rita had attracted enough attention over the years.

"Oh, *no*," she said instead, as she pulled the paper from the rack. Apparently *Celebrity* had been Darryl Hogan's employer.

She studied the large grainy picture that showed a girl in a wheelchair, her hand trying unsuccessfully to shield her face before the shutter clicked. Rita didn't need to say, "Look, it's Katie Gillette." She didn't need to say it because the bold headline said it all:

KATIE'S SECRET BABY.

In smaller type the subhead read:

SUPERSTAR HIDES OUT WITH MOM JOLEEN.

Rita's stomach turned. She held the paper up and squinted in the sunlight.

"Does it say anything about the cancer?" Hazel asked.

"I don't know," Rita snapped. "Let me read it."

Rita quickly scanned the article that was low on facts and high on speculation: about Miguel being the father, about Katie's father confronting him, about Katie turning into a recluse like her mother. It heralded this as a tragedy to befall the star so quickly after losing Ina, who'd been "like a real mother to Katie."

The article then went on to wonder how this would affect the concert in Central Park. Park officials had replied, "no comment."

As ugly and as fabricated as the story was, there was, thank God, no mention of the rest: of Miguel's other life or Katie's unwelcome disease.

"No," Rita said, "they didn't find out."

"Not yet."

"Not yet."

"It's a terrible picture. The poor girl looks sick."

"She is sick, Mother."

"Wait a minute. Isn't that your tan windbreaker?" Hazel pointed to a jacket worn by someone in the photo, whose head was cut off by the headline.

"It's me," she said. "I was pushing the wheelchair."

"Imagine that. My Rita Mae on the cover of *Celebrity*."

Faye wanted to go straight home. She wanted to go home and hug her son and sit in an Adirondack chair outside and think happy thoughts of R.J. Browne and count her blessings one by one. But she could not pretend nothing had just happened; and she could not pretend that Rita should not be told.

Rita Blair Rollins. Who'd hardly been the reason for

Faye and Joe's divorce: She'd merely been another brick along the sidewalk leading to the courthouse steps.

Rita would want to know about Doc's heart attack and about the episode with Hannah's husband. And despite the redheaded woman's transgressions, Faye could not deny her that.

Faye did not have to drive all the way to Rita's house. Luckily, or unluckily, when Faye drove into Edgartown, there was Rita, standing on a street corner behind a two-seat stroller that held two redheaded toddlers. Standing next to Rita, peering at a newspaper that Rita held upright, was a white-haired woman in clogs.

Faye illegally parked right there on the corner, got out of her Mercedes, and approached the small group. "Rita," she asked, "can we talk?"

Rita supposed that sooner or later she would meet Faye face-to-face again, though she would have preferred later to sooner. And she would have preferred somewhere more private than the middle of the damn town, in the middle of the damn day.

"Faye," Rita said, "this is my mother, Hazel, and these are my twins, Oliver and Olivia."

Faye politely said hello, but did not stop to ooh and aah over the twins. "It's important, Rita," Faye said. "It's about Doc. And Hannah. We could sit in my car if you'd like."

If they sat in Faye's car, there was no telling what the woman would do. Kidnap her, perhaps? Drive her off the end of the Oak Bluffs' pier?

Sometimes Rita wondered where her imagination came from, why Hazel was so carefree and Rita could be such a doom-and-gloomer.

In the meantime, Faye stood in front of her.

A *woman scorned*. Did it matter that the "scorn" happened years ago? Did it matter that Rita's choice had been Joe or federal prison?

"Why don't we all walk down to the 1802 Tavern?" Hazel suggested. "We can get out of this infernal sun, and the twins and I can have a cold drink."

"My mother knows most everything about the support group," Rita said when Faye came into the tavern after moving her car to a parking lot. "She was a nurse." Rita hoped the added comment gave Hazel the right to have been told.

Then again, she thought, sliding across the bench of the booth so Faye could sit down, why did she care what Faye thought? She'd already blown the chances for the Center, hadn't she?

She gripped the handle of a frosty beer mug that Amy quickly delivered. "So what's going on?" she asked, feigning nonchalance.

Then Faye told them. She told them about Evan and about his accusations. She told them about the gun, that she'd slipped it into her purse.

Was it still there?

Then Faye told them about Doc's heart attack.

The sadness that washed through Rita was not like one she'd known: It was not the kind of deep sadness she'd had when Kyle died, but the edges of it were the same, a woeful ring of grief, an unwanted reminder of life cycles and of uninvited loss.

"How is he?" Rita asked.

"He's stable. But they won't have a prognosis for a while."

Rita looked at Hazel, who stared at Rita with an odd, disconnected stare, as if she'd had a stroke. "Mother?" Rita asked. That's when she noticed the film that had crossed Hazel's eyes, a light, wet film that looked an awful lot like tears.

"Mother?"

Hazel blinked. "Rita Mae," she said with slow deliberateness, "go to him. Please." She closed her tearful eyes.

"Well, of course I will, Mother. I'll go over later." Rita shifted on the bench.

"No," Hazel insisted. Her eyes popped open, her jaw set firm. "You must go now."

"Now?" Rita looked around the room. Was it her imagination once again or had the clatter of pub glasses and the murmurs of the patrons grown a bit more silent in the low-beamed, cozy room? "Now, as in right this minute?"

Hazel leaned across the table and pried Rita's hand from the frosty mug.

"Now," she repeated. "You must be there for Doc in case anything happens. Because, God forgive me, he is your father."

TWENTY·NINE

They went out to the greenhouse because that's what Evan wanted. Hannah paid no attention to the stale scent of pot; she knew by his expression that was what this conversation would be about. She had not expected the rest, how he'd gone to see Doc, how he'd brought a gun, how he'd planned to kill himself.

"I've had the gun forever," Evan said. "I kept it locked up in the shed."

Locked up in a drawer, Hannah thought. *Locked up like his pain.*

"I didn't load it," he added. "I didn't want to die. I just knew I needed help." He put his head in his hands. He'd aged at least ten years.

"You could have told me," Hannah said. "You didn't need to do something so . . . so horrible."

He lifted his head again. "Isn't it ironic?" he asked. "You're the one who's sick, but I'm the one falling apart."

She wanted to hold him close and love him. She wanted to tell him everything would be all right. But suddenly Hannah was tired of taking care of everyone, from Evan to his mother to their three kids as well. For years she'd done nothing but listen to other people's problems, and here she was again, no matter that her mother was out of jail and her daughter had run away and her husband might have killed himself even though he said there were no bullets in the gun. No matter that she was facing a mastectomy.

She patted his knee, because that was the best she could do.

"There's a good rehab facility over on the Cape," Evan continued. "I heard about it at a recovery meeting." He examined leftover soil beneath his fingernails. *Farmer's hands,* he'd once told her, back in happier times. "I stopped going to meetings after you were diagnosed," he said. "I didn't want to talk about it to anyone."

Hannah nodded.

"Anyway, our health insurance will take care of my treatment. And I think Don Bishop can handle the business this season." Don Bishop owned a competitive nursery, but when need arose on the island, friendship came first.

"No matter." Hannah sighed and patted Evan again. "It will work out somehow."

They sat a few more minutes: Evan said he was sorry. He cried, but she did not. She thanked God that Doc had been kind and not had him arrested. Then she wondered if Doc would be okay and how Evan would get down to the pier to catch the next boat to the Cape.

Rita listened to the story in vague disbelief, though she knew it must be true. Hazel was eccentric, but she'd never tell a lie, not about something such as this.

Doc was Rita's father.

Oh.

SHIT.

They'd met in Boston after the war.

He was a young doctor; Hazel was a nurse.

"When the soldiers started going home, I convinced Doc to come to the Vineyard. We needed good doctors. Doc had a degree from Harvard Medical School." Her old eyes brightened. "Imagine, Harvard!"

But Rita had been working to imagine other things, like how it could have happened that she'd never had an inkling.

"Doc should have been a bigwig in Boston. But he came here instead."

The pieces of the puzzle slowly took their shape. And then came the inevitable wrinkle, because Hazel's life, like Rita's life, made a shar-pei's coat seem taut.

"Doc was a married man. He had a little boy. When the war was over, he realized he didn't love his wife. She was from that awful upper class. She said she only married him because he'd gone to Harvard and that meant he could go to her daddy's private club." Hazel grew quiet for a moment, then she added, "Anyway, Doc left his family and came here because he didn't love them, he loved me."

She told Rita that Doc had never known, not for certain, that he was her father. Hazel hadn't told him. "What could he have done?" she asked.

Well, Rita thought, maybe he could have loved me.

Hazel urged Rita to go. "Don't let him die before he knows, Rita Mae." Then she simply added, "Please."

Rita supposed she could have asked why she had to be the one to tell him. But a lifetime lived with Hazel told her there would be no point, because her mother had already issued her instructions. Rita stood up. "Bring the twins home," she told Hazel. Then she excused herself and silently left the tavern.

· · ·

She walked up North Water Street, past Jill and Ben's house. No Jill, no Ben, not even Charlie was around. No one who could help Rita make sense of what she had just learned.

No one was around, so Rita was on her own like she'd so often been before.

But that was then.

And this was now.

And this seemed worse, because she'd adjusted to the old stuff, and this was new. This was raw and achy and confusing all at once.

She walked toward the Edgartown Lighthouse, because at least that hadn't changed.

She sat on the small strip of rocks that crawled up from the water and laced the edges of the beach.

Above her, seagulls soared.

"Shit," she said, picking up a stone and skimming it over a small ripple of water.

When she was a kid, Rita had been told her father was "a man who'd picked up and left the way most men seem to do." Back in the sixties, that explanation made sense because, well, why not? Hazel never pretended their life was traditional, and though Rita longed for a real home filled with family, she took what they had and tried to make do.

But how she'd envied her friend Jill! Jill had a mother and a father and never had to spend the summers in other people's houses so they could rent out theirs.

Now, it turned out, Rita had a father, too.

Doc.

He'd been there all along, but not under their roof.

And now he'd had a heart attack and Hazel thought that Rita should deliver the unexpected news.

What would she say? "Before you die, Doc, there's something you ought to know"? Could she really say that? She closed her eyes. She thought of Kyle.

"Rita? May I join you?"

Rita flinched. A shadow spilled over her and stretched down across the rocks. The voice belonged to Faye, which was just what Rita needed.

"Please," Rita said, closing her eyes, "please leave me alone."

"I can't," Faye said. "We need to talk."

"We talked."

The water rippled and a few more gulls cried, but Faye did not move to go. Rita opened her eyes. "Faye," she repeated, "I've had a little shock, in case you didn't get it."

"Oh, I got it all right," Faye said, and promptly sat down.

Rita wanted to warn Faye that sitting on the rocks would wreck her three hundred dollar pants, but decided what the hell. It was too late for the Women's Wellness Center; it was too late for many things. She wondered if Faye had her purse and if she should ask to borrow Evan's gun.

"I'm sorry you never knew Doc was your father," Faye said, as if she possibly could care. "I'm also sorry that you screwed my husband. But the way I see it, we can't fix either of those things any more than we can pretend that they're not true."

Rita blinked. This day had gone from good to bad and couldn't get much worse.

But the woman kept on speaking. "Whatever you choose to do about Doc certainly is your business. But Hannah and Katie need us. If anything happens to Doc, they'll need us even more."

Rita looked toward her, away from the water.

"Did you know Hannah's mastectomy is scheduled for the week after next? Did you know she didn't tell us because she didn't want to be a bother?"

Rita didn't respond.

"Of course," Faye went on, "there might be a complication if Doc dies before then. Which might or might not be Evan's fault. I wonder how that will make Hannah feel."

Rita winced. She considered that she hated Faye. She tried once again to believe she'd been right when she'd told herself the woman was a cold, uncaring bitch.

"Jesus Christ, Rita," Faye said, "stop feeling sorry for yourself. Because in case you didn't notice, I'm the one who's dying here, not you."

That was enough. Rita stood up. "I'm not convinced you're dying, Faye. I've seen death, and I don't think it's you."

Faye clenched her fists. "Shut up," she said and marched away, up toward the sand path.

The baby kicked. Katie turned onto her left side, one of three positions she could manage, per Doc Hastings' orders: left, right, or on her back. Her left side was her favorite because it enabled her to see the ocean.

Still, she couldn't get used to being in bed in the middle of the day with little to do except make "healing" pillows, write in her journal, or, worst of all, think.

From time to time Katie wondered if she should look over Joleen's new songs, but decided against it. By now, Katie knew her career was over. She did not have to see the inevitable tabloid to imagine what the world thought and knew about her now.

Which was why, this morning, she had made the call. It had been surprisingly easy.

"This is Katie Gillette," she'd said. "I need to speak with the entertainment booking manager." She hadn't been nervous; she hadn't been upset.

"You'll need to sign paperwork," the manager said when he'd come on the line. "Let's see, is there a Cliff Gillette? He booked the date; he should be the one to sign."

For a brief moment Katie clenched her jaw. Then she said, "No, I'll cancel it myself. Mr. Gillette is indisposed." She gave him Joleen's address. "Have the contracts sent here. Will there be a fee?"

"Hmm," the man said. "Nope. You'll lose the up-front costs you've already paid. But you're over thirty days away, so there's no extra cancellation fee."

Surely Cliff had known.

As she lay in bed now, the relief that Katie felt was tempered by the knowledge that her father would be upset. She also knew she did not have the energy to think about a concert now or then or ever.

She was thinking about those things when the telephone rang.

Turning from her left side to her right, Katie was able to reach the phone, thanks to Rita, who'd rigged it with an extra long cord. Katie waited until the answering machine kicked on and she heard the voice before picking up.

"Katie," the voice shouted, and she knew who it was, because what little talking he did, had to be in a shout.

She grabbed the receiver. "Brady," she said. "How are you?" She, too, spoke loudly so that he could hear her.

"Fine, Katie. I'm fine. Are you okay now?"

"Yes. I'm sorry I ran from you at the funeral. I only wanted to get out of there."

"I saw your picture this morning."

So the tabloids had wasted no time. "Was it awful?"

"I've seen you look better."

She laughed.

"Katie," he continued, "I want to come to that island and look after you."

Katie had known Brady long enough to know that, for him, the request did not come because he needed a job. He wanted to be with her because protecting her was what he did.

"Thanks, Brady," she replied, "but I'm fine here with Joleen."

"No," he said. "It will be worse when the baby gets there."

He said it as if the baby would arrive by ferry at the Vineyard Haven docks. He said it as if they'd already talked about the fact that she was pregnant, which they hadn't done, not face-to-face, not one-on-one, though she knew he knew, had most likely known from the beginning.

"Brady," she said, "I appreciate your concern, but you live in New York. You'd be bored to death here."

"I don't like New York anymore. I need somewhere new to live. I can be a carpenter. I did that before I met your father."

The words *your father* squeezed the sides of Katie's stomach.

"I think you should call him," Brady added. "You don't want things to end like this. No matter what, he is your father."

"Right now, that thought does not make me happy."

"So why bring the heavy baggage of bad feelings into your new life? Call him soon, Katie. I think he might be going away for a while. Leaving the country."

Katie closed her eyes. "Oh," she replied.

"What?"

She realized her voice was now too soft for Brady to hear. She cleared her throat. "Where is he going?"

Her bodyguard hesitated, then said, "I think it's best if he tells you himself."

. . .

When Katie said good-bye, she had no intention of calling Cliff. Not then or next year or maybe ever. But Brady's words gnawed at her: *Why bring the heavy baggage of bad feelings into your new life?* Why, indeed, with all she had yet to face?

She cupped her hands around her stomach as she lay there on the bed. She felt the gentle flutter of another gentle baby-kick.

And then she picked up the receiver once again. And without caring that Cliff was the adult and Katie was the child, she dialed the number to the penthouse that overlooked the Great Lawn of Central Park.

"Daddy," she said when he answered the phone. Her voice was just a whisper, a hesitant, small whisper. "I heard that you might go away."

He did not speak for a moment, and then he said, "Katie-Kate. I am so sorry for all of this."

She wound the cord around her fingers. She tried to think about the good times. *He loves you, Kathryn,* Joleen had said. *You are his whole world.* Apparently that had not been completely true.

She gathered a little strength. "I'm sorry, too, Daddy. I'm sorry that all these years you felt you had to lie." It was the closest she could come to accepting his apology.

Silence followed. It was as if there were a time lapse between the Vineyard and New York, as if they were on a transatlantic call, waiting for the sound waves to catch up.

"I would have called before I left," he said at last. "I would not have gone without telling you."

She did not know if that would have been the case; it did not really matter now. "Where are you going?" she asked.

This time he answered quickly, with no pause in between. "Puerto Rico," he said, then added a brisk, half-hearted laugh. "Latino singers are the next great opportunity. Hey, a man's got to make a living."

Her stomach squeezed again. She did not want to ask, but knew she must. *Heavy baggage, bad feelings.* "Is it Miguel? Are you going to make him a star?"

Cliff laughed. "Well, who knows? It's really up to the fans who becomes a star and who doesn't."

Which, of course, Katie knew was not the truth. She knew it was the hype, the clothes, the style that made a star. The kind of spin created by the likes of Cliff Gillette.

Looking out over the lawn, beyond the dunes and out to sea, Katie felt little more than sadness for what had been and what was gone.

"I cancelled Central Park," she said.

"Yes," her father replied. "I supposed you would."

And it was then that she knew she'd heard enough—enough to quell her anger, enough to leave only a residue of pity for her father, She also knew that, no matter what Joleen said, she would make the Vineyard her home. She had her baby to think of, a baby who soon would be a child with a future. She had her baby and her mother and her new, wonderful support-group friends. She had her breast cancer to deal with.

And she would call Brady back, thank him for his advice, and tell him that if he was serious about coming to the island, she would help him find work. Then she would ask him for one favor before he left New York: to please make sure the billboard in Times Square had been taken down.

She wished her father well and hung up the phone.

Then Katie was distracted by movement outside the window. A tall, unfamiliar guy who wore a white shirt and a tan was walking up the back walk. He carried a foil package and a nosegay of beach roses.

"Evan's gone to rehab," Rita explained to Doc when she finally found the courage to go to the hospital. It was nearly dusk: the melon-colored Vineyard sunset crept into the tiny private room. Good news had awaited: Doc's heart attack had been mild, more scary than damaging.

Still, he looked smaller than normal in the narrow hospital bed—smaller and somehow more fragile. Rita wondered if she would have noticed, had it not been for what she'd learned. But despite his reduced stature, his eyes still held their sparkle. She did not realize until that moment that his eyes resembled Kyle's.

She wished Hazel had told him. She wished that Hazel had told her. Still, Rita reminded herself that she hadn't told Charlie that Kyle was his until it was almost too late. The apple, once again, had not fallen far from the stubborn tree.

A supper tray arrived. Doc lifted the dome, revealing pot roast and lima beans. He peeled back the corner of a chocolate-milk container.

Kyle had loved chocolate milk. Was that a coincidence?

"Hannah's surgery is soon," Rita continued. "It's so sad that Evan won't be there." It was small talk, of course, but her other thoughts kept bumping, one against another, and could not make it to the surface.

"I guess I'll go to Hannah's after I leave here," she said.

Doc nodded. "Good idea."

The only other thing she could think of to talk about was whether or not Faye was really going to die. But Rita knew that Doc would never tell her, any more than he would tell her who was dangling the money for the Wellness Center.

She walked to the window and looked out at the streaks of tangerine now etched across the sky. She was afraid to ask him—what if it hurt his heart?

But if he died . . .

. . . like Kyle had died . . .

She closed her eyes as if the darkness might cushion the shock for him, for her. And then she squared her small but sturdy shoulders.

"Doc," she told him quietly, her back still turned from him, "my mother told me something about me and about you."

She heard him set down his fork. She heard him give a small, familiar chuckle. Then he said, "Well for godssake, it's taken Hazel long enough."

THIRTY

He knew she was his daughter; he'd known from day one.

His daughter!

Her father!

Rita sat down on a small chair beside Doc's bed. She folded her hands and tried to decide if she was happy or if she was pissed off. "Why didn't my mother tell us?"

"She didn't have to tell me. You have my mother's big, red hair. There's no doubt about it."

Rita touched the Brillo pad atop her head. She felt an odd feeling—longing?—to know about the woman who now must be dead, the woman whose *big, red hair* Rita seemed to have, the *big, red hair* that Rita suddenly no longer hated so much.

Doc smiled, then lifted his bifocals. He slowly rubbed his eyes. "Don't blame Hazel," he said.

"You were married," she said, and he nodded.

"I told my wife I was in love with someone else, but she wouldn't divorce me. Her family didn't do that sort of thing." He put his glasses back in place. He peered above the rim. "Divorce wasn't so easy fifty years ago. But my wife couldn't stop me from coming to the Vineyard."

To be with my mother, Rita wanted to add, but for once kept her big mouth shut.

His gaze moved to the pot roast that sat idle on his tray table. "They came down every summer to torment me, I guess. And, I suppose, to keep me from living with your mother. Despite what it must look like, I'm a moral man, Rita. My reputation was important to me. It was important to my work. I couldn't commit myself to Hazel. So I committed myself to this hospital. I'll do that until I take my last breath."

Rita lowered her eyes to her hands, to her fingers that were knotted together like a clump of beach plum vines. "What happened to your wife?"

"She died. But by then Hazel was married and living in Coral Gables."

"And your son?" It occurred to her then that Doc's son was her half brother. She wondered if that should matter.

Doc was quiet for another moment: Rita wasn't sure if he'd heard her. Then he lifted his head and scanned the room, as if looking for reassurance, or, perhaps, for ghosts. "David chose to rid himself of me years ago. The last I heard, he was an attorney in the Midwest. He is his mother's child. I would never force myself on him, because it wouldn't work."

It was too much to absorb. So Rita simply sat there, not knowing what to say, not knowing which of them should make the next move, if one needed to be made. And then the words sprang from her: "Kyle was your grandson."

Doc nodded. Well, of course he would have known that. It was Rita who'd not known.

"And the twins," she added.

He brought his eyes to her. "They're wonderful, Rita," he said. "I'm so glad that you have them. And Charlie."

If she didn't know better, Rita would have sworn she'd

eaten one of the lima beans on Doc's tray, which would account for the lump stuck halfway down her throat. "You know, Doc," she said, standing up, "if it's all the same to you, I'm going to go now. I need some time to figure out what's happened."

He nodded, too, then pushed the rolling table from his bed. "Rita," he added, his voice hoarse with age, his eyes softly clouded, "there's another reason I never left the island. It was because of you. Though I couldn't claim my right as your father, I wanted to keep an eye on you, to make sure you grew up into a happy, healthy, well-adjusted woman."

She could have laughed or made a sarcastic Rita-joke. Instead, she just stood there with that phantom bean still in her throat. "So what's the verdict, Doc?"

He sat up a little straighter. His smile widened into the smile of a much younger man. "You will never know, Rita Mae," he said, "just how proud I am of you."

She stood and watched him, too stunned to cry.

"Now, please," he asked with a quick wipe to his eyes, "I know this has been upsetting for you, but please don't forget about the women of the group. They need you more than ever."

Rita paused. "That's why you did it, isn't it, Doc? You wanted me to lead the support group so you could keep your eye on them. Through me."

He smiled. "And because you might look like my mother, but you're a lot like me. You're my daughter, that's for sure."

Just then, Margie poked her head inside Doc's room. "Doc," she said, "the path report is in. The one you were waiting for."

The second that he grimaced only was a second, but Rita recognized it as a grimace. She also knew that, though

Margie hadn't been specific, the pathology report on Katie's lymph nodes was due back anytime. Rita stopped herself from asking.

Doc regained his composure. "Sorry, Rita," he said, "but even cardiac infarction can't stop me from my work."

She nodded understandingly and left without a word.

"My mother made these this morning," the tall, tanned young man said to Katie. She'd slipped out of bed to open the door: It had not occurred to her that the stranger might be a threat, another paparazzo, this time bearing gifts. The foil package looked familiar.

"My mother brought a woman to the hospital for a blood test this morning," he said. "I don't know why it's taking so long, but she'd be upset if her scones dried up and went stale." His eyes were bright blue, his hair shining black.

He handed Katie the flowers. "These," he said, "aren't from her. They're from me. I'm Greg."

He was Faye's son, of course. Katie clasped the front of her pink cotton robe. "Beach roses," she said, "my favorite."

"They were my sister's favorite, too."

She took the flowers and the foil package and asked him to come in. "Your mother is so nice."

His smile was gentle, friendly, kind. "She likes you a lot," he said. "You remind her of my sister."

"Dana," Katie replied.

"She was 'spirited,' my mother always said. She didn't like to follow doctor's orders, either."

"Excuse me?"

He gestured toward the bed. "From what I understand, you're not supposed to move around."

·   ·   ·   ·

They'd known each other forever, hadn't they? Two kids of privilege who spent warm months on the Vineyard, digging for quahogs and searching for wampum, going to the Regatta and Illumination Night and the fireworks in Oak Bluffs at every summer's end.

Katie and Greg drank tea and ravished Faye's scones and laughed about the "olden days." She had not been on the Vineyard that summer when Dana had been killed; but, listening to Greg's story, she could well imagine the hush that draped West Chop like a giant fishing net, a shroud of grief that one so young had been taken by the sea. Their sea.

"So are you a fan?" Katie asked, grateful she knew that he was gay. There was something reassuring that a man was not there for sex, had not come laden with lust as a stepping-stone to his future.

Greg was sitting backward on a cane-back kitchen chair, his legs wrapping it, his arms resting on top, his hands holding the mug. He seemed to blush. "Not really," he said with an embarrassed smile. "I know you're famous," he said quickly. "I mean, I know who you are. But to be honest, I'm a little busy with my restaurants, and when I listen to music I, well, prefer country."

His words were the nicest thing he could have said.

"I'm a fan of your mother's, though," he added. "I think I know all her songs by heart. My sister and I would play your mother's albums over and over on the old turntable."

Just then Joleen walked into the room and Greg stood up, more flustered.

Katie laughed and said, "Mom, I'd like you to meet a fan."

Joleen said hello, then eyed the plates.

"Any more of those scones?" she asked. "I could smell them in my studio."

Greg smiled again and nervously said he'd fix her a plate and would she like tea?

They all laughed because it was Joleen's kitchen and he was the guest and Joleen was not confined to bed, because she was not the one who was pregnant. Katie realized how quickly life could make a U-turn from bad into good when you least expected that it would.

Then the baby kicked again, and the kick was followed by a squeeze and then another pressing cramp. She smiled at Joleen and Greg and turned to him and asked, "If you're finished with your scone, would you mind driving me to the hospital? I know it's a little early, but I think the baby's on the way."

Shortly after Faye went back to Hannah's house, R.J. Browne stood on the doorstep.

"Ladies," he said, "please come with me. I think I have a clue about where Riley has gone." He did not elaborate.

Tired though she was, Hannah left a note for Casey and Denise to go to Donna Langforth's in case they got home from school before she returned. Then she climbed into the backseat of R.J.'s truck and the next thing she knew, they were parked in front of the church where she'd spent so many hours and so many nights back when Mother Jackson's theater was standing-room-only and everything had seemed so right.

It didn't seem right without Evan there. It didn't seem right without Mother Jackson. But Hannah was learning that life truly could—and would—go on.

R.J. turned off the ignition and the three of them got out. R.J. took Hannah's arm. She wanted to protest that she didn't need his help, but then she figured it didn't much matter. Nothing much mattered, or had she forgotten?

He led her to the fellowship hall.

"Go backstage," he instructed, and so Hannah did, leaving R.J. and Faye behind.

She trundled over mounds of pulley ropes, past dusty set designs, through the door on which Mother Jackson had once lettered BACKSTAGE and added an all-encompassing gold star, because to Mother Jackson, every one of her actors was a star.

And there she was.

Riley.

She sat on a heap of old pillows, stage props from another performance, another time. Her knees were pulled to her chest, tears flowed down her face.

"Mommy," she said. "Mommy, I'm so sorry."

On legs that had quickly turned to water, with a heart that swelled so big that it might burst, Hannah made her way to the pillows, made her way to her daughter. She sat down next to Riley, held her close and didn't mention the pierced earring in her eyebrow or the one under her lower lip. She did not mention the stolen biology book or the yearbook on the floor, from which a yellowed newspaper clipping was sticking slightly out. Time would come to talk about those things later; right now, Riley was coming home.

"She left the island, as the police had learned," R.J. told Faye when they went outside the church and waited for Hannah and Riley to emerge. "What bothered me was how a kid who knew squat about the mainland could find her way around. So I did a little digging and realized there was only one thing that could make sense: She'd gone as far as Woods Hole, then turned around and had come back. When I found her, she admitted she'd paid someone to buy her return ticket so it couldn't be traced. She said she had money that she'd taken from an old trunk in the attic."

"But how did you find her at the church?" Faye asked.

"That was the easy part. Her world is small. When I talked to Hannah, she told me about the theater, how much Riley had loved it. I figured she knew she'd be safe and warm here; she knew she could easily find food. But most of all, this was where she'd been happy. If you were in trouble, wouldn't you want to go where you'd been happy? Where you'd once felt secure and loved?"

Faye looped her arm through his. "I did that," she said. "When I came back to the Vineyard, that's exactly what I did."

"It's a girl," Doc said late that night when he shuffled into the waiting room attached to an IV pole, determined to be the one to deliver the news, if not Katie's baby. Rita and Hannah and Faye and Joleen looked from one to another to another. "The doctor said she's small—only five pounds—but they're both doing well."

Joleen cried, excused herself, and left the room.

"Doc?" Rita asked, because she could no longer stand it, because it was just them, support for one another. "Katie's pathology report . . ."

"I don't think my patient would mind me telling you that her lymph nodes are all clear." A collective sigh spilled across the room.

"So," Faye said, "that makes three of us with good news today. After Hannah found Riley, I went back to the hospital to see about having a mammogram." She laughed. "They did it right away, before I could change my mind."

Doc nodded. Rita suspected he'd railroaded that.

And then a tear or two stuck in Faye's words. "It's fine,"

she said. "I'm fine. I'm cancer-free, and I can live my life again."

"And make that huge donation to the Women's Wellness Center?" Rita asked it with a smile, before she thought twice about the asking.

Faye, however, only laughed. "I don't have that kind of money, Rita. It's not like I'm the daughter of aristocrats."

"So it isn't Faye who was putting up the money for the Center," Rita said to Hazel after she got home. "And I don't think she's pissed at me, not that it really matters."

"Of course it matters, Rita Mae. And the Center matters, too. But if Faye's not behind it, what do you think? That singer has money; what about her?"

Rita shook her head. "I don't think so. Who knows, maybe there is no money at all. Maybe Doc was simply trying to get some interest brewing. He's like that, you know. Cagey and all that."

Hazel winked at her. "Or, Doc might know that the benefactor wouldn't want others to know that she was rich, that when her husband up and died, he left a pile of money. Maybe he wouldn't want anyone to know that she now wants the only man she ever truly loved, to make the most of it."

Rita would have thought she'd had enough shocks for one day. Her eyes locked on her mother as the words sunk in. Then she screamed. "Hazel! You? You're the benefactor?" All that time spent being nosy, Rita could have saved her breath?

Hazel winked again. "Don't for one minute think this old lady is a has-been."

"What about me? Am I a has-been?" The screen door

burst open and there stood Charlie, the long-lost husband home from the sea, or at least, Nantucket.

Rita stood up and flew into his arms. The twins came scrambling from the other room. Even Hazel had stood up with a smirky old smile that was plastered from one conniving ear over to the other. And Mindy thundered down the stairs as only a twelve-year-old can thunder.

"Well, I guess I'm not a has-been after all," Charlie said as he regained his balance. "The good news is that Ben and I are finished and I'm home for good. How 'bout you guys? What's been going on these last few weeks?"

Rita looked from Mindy to Hazel, then back to her husband. She shook her head. "Oh, you know," she said at last, "just the same old boring shit."

EPILOGUE

SEPTEMBER

The summer passed as summers do, and Labor Day arrived. The center of Oak Bluffs was more alive than usual on this end-of-summer night: the stage was set, the fans waited on their beach chairs and their blankets, which were crammed throughout the park. The concert was a first, a benefit performance for the Women's Wellness Center: Charlie and Ben had broken ground last week. The Center's spokesperson, Rita Blair Rollins, had announced that a new machine that read mammograms by computer and would make "early detection even earlier," was now on order and someone had to pay for it.

The fans showed up in droves.

Faye was there with Greg and R.J. She had closed up the Vineyard house for another season: She would not sell it; there would be many summers yet to come. For now, she was going back to Boston to work part-time for Gwen, who had happily bought Faye's business. There was no doubt that Faye would see R.J. on a regular basis. There was no doubt she'd see Greg often.

Greg was headed to Arizona after a "perfect, perfect summer." He missed his partner, Mike, however, and, yes, even his dad.

Faye had tried to phone Claire, to see if she'd like to come to the historic concert, but she could not reach her. Claire and Jeffrey had only been out once this season: Other destinations seemed to lure her sister now.

Hannah was there with her three children and her husband, who had returned two weeks earlier from rehab on the Cape. Though Hannah's hair was growing back, she wore her purple hat. "So none of us forgets the importance of a little fun," she said.

She was healthy now, and beneath the hat's wide brim, a pink glow was in her cheeks. Last week she'd had a note from John Arthur asking about her health, but she'd thrown it out before jotting down the return address. There were other things to live for now.

After searching news articles on-line at the library, Hannah had discovered that her mother was working in San Antonio at a home for abused women and children. She planned to visit her at Christmas with Evan and the kids. There would be no more secrets.

She'd tucked away her journal in Mother Jackson's trunk: She was far too busy now for further introspection. In another week she'd be in Boston on her journey back to medical school. Evan had said he could handle things at home; she would commute on weekends.

Doc was happy: The Vineyard, after all, needed all the dedicated doctors it could get.

•   •   •

Rita juggled the stroller with the twins and Mindy followed close behind, while Hazel brought up the rear along with Doc, who was now fully recovered and, according to Hazel, full of vinegar again, which might be why he held her hand.

Charlie had arrived early to help set up the soundstage, because he was a genius and knew how to do everything. He'd cordoned off a corner down in front for the women of the support group and their families.

"Sorry we're late," Rita said as she took a seat on the ground right next to Faye. "Kids," she said, rolling her eyes. "Olivia thought it would be fun to hide the car keys in her diaper. I love that life is always so full of surprises."

Faye smiled and put her arm around Rita's shoulders. "Me, too," she said, and hugged her friend.

Then Rita leaned over to check on the tiny bundle that rested in Faye's other arm. "How's our baby doing?"

"M.J. is just fine." Bright blue eyes sparkled up at Rita, the tiny pink mouth seemed to smile. Katie had named the baby M.J.—Martha Joleen, after her famous mother and the island that she loved so much.

Then the stage lights dimmed, and the crowd hushed itself without being asked. Onto the stage stepped Katie, in jeans and a pink-sequined top. A small band began to play. She picked up her microphone and saw her friends among the crowd. She smiled at Rita and Hannah and Faye and baby M.J. She smiled at Brady, who stood stage left, his loyal eyes surveying the space around her. She looked stage right where Cliff had always stood. But Cliff remained in Puerto Rico, grooming his next star: rumor was, Miguel would have a CD released before the holidays. Apparently, Cliff had forgiven Miguel, and Miguel had forgiven Cliff. It might take longer for Katie to forgive them both, but she was working on it.

And so, stage right had no man in black, just a bud vase Greg had set there, a vase that held a single, small beach rose. The blossom was deep red now, because it was September; it had matured and flourished, and finally it was strong.

"My name is Katie," Katie said into the mike, "and I'm a breast-cancer survivor."

The roar swelled up from the beach chairs and the blankets. It filled the air as if it were a living, vibrant being, a united cheer of love and gratitude and joy.

Katie smiled and held her hand up to hush the crowd. She did not need to be in Central Park to know her father had been right: performing was in her soul.

"This is a very special night," Katie continued. "First of all, it marks the beginning of my comeback tour." She did not mention it would be a small tour that she and Brady had arranged. She did not mention that she'd just completed radiation and, like Faye and Hannah, had been proclaimed cancer-free. She did not say these things because Katie had learned that the journey truly was more important than the destination, that tomorrow might be different from today, but either would be fine.

She hushed the crowd again. "And because we're so thankful that you're helping out the Center, we'd like to open with a very special song."

Then, just as Katie began to sing, Joleen walked onto the stage. The swell of cheers grew louder; even Brady covered his ears. And then, with arms around each other, high above the resounding crowd, the mother and the daughter sang Joleen's "Goin' Home."

And Faye smiled and Hannah nodded and Rita cried for all the good things that had happened in her life.

ABOUT THE AUTHOR

BEACH ROSES is Jean Stone's tenth novel from Bantam Books, and her sixth to take place on the celebrated island of Martha's Vineyard. A native New Englander, she lives in western Massachusetts, close enough to "leave home in the morning and be on the Vineyard in time for lunch." A graduate of Skidmore College in Saratoga Springs, New York, she volunteers for Goodwill Industries' Radio Reading Service, through which she reads books to the visually impaired. For more information on the author and her past and upcoming work, visit her web site at www.jeanstone.net.